NEVER TRUST A RABBIT

NEVER TRUST A RABBIT

Jeremy Dyson

Duck Editions

First published in 2000 by
Duckworth Literary Entertainments, Ltd.
61 Frith Street, London W1V 5TA
Tel: 020 7434 4242
Fax: 020 7434 4420
email: DuckEd@duckworth-publishers.co.uk
www.ducknet.co.uk

A CIP catalogue record for this book is available
from the British Library

ISBN 0 7156 3015 6

Illustrations © copyright James Hood 2000

'All in the telling' first appeared in *The Blue Motel*,
'City deep' first appeared in *Tombs*,
'The maze' first appeared in *Destination: Unknown*.

Typeset by Derek Doyle & Associates, Liverpool
Printed in Great Britain by
Redwood Books Ltd, Trowbridge

Ne bízzál a njúlban. Játékszernek tünik miközben rávár
a termésedre.

*Never trust a rabbit. They may look like a child's toy but
they eat your crops.*

Hungarian Proverb

for Nicky

Contents

James Hood

We who walk through walls

Johnson couldn't say exactly when it had begun but he knew he was being followed. At first there had been nothing but a slight sensation in the centre of his back. Then the sense that his footsteps had acquired an inappropriate echo in an empty street one night as he walked back to the small basement room he rented on Wilberforce Road. Finally it was the sight of the same dark-suited man three times in one day, each time looking shiftier and more furtive than before.

"Excuse me," Johnson said to the old lady who sat opposite him in the workmen's café, "but can you see a man in a dark suit, looking at me through the window?"

She held on to her blue knitted hat and craned her neck over his shoulder. When she spoke it was with a light East European accent.

"Yes!" She grabbed Johnson's wrist with a white-gloved hand. "Yes! He is there. He is there."

"I thought so."

"You poor young man. Who is he?"

Johnson shrugged. "I don't know him."

"Are you in danger?" A look of maternal concern had crossed her heavily made-up face.

"I've no reason to believe that." Johnson smiled. Seeing that he was not frightened, the old lady's face softened.

"I recognise your face. Where is it from?" she asked. Johnson gestured in such a way as to suggest he didn't know. "Your accent? You have a slight accent."

"Czechoslovakia. Going back a long way."

She clicked her fingers triumphantly. "I thought so. I was born in Seberov." Johnson raised his eyebrows. "You know it?" The old lady looked thrilled.

"I know where it is." He smiled again.

"Your family. Would I know your family?" she inquired.

Johnson's smile became apologetic. "They are mostly dead, I'm afraid."

Her expression joined his in sadness. "Mine too," she nodded. Then, after a moment, she smiled again. "Your friend has gone."

"That's good. Will you let me buy another cup of tea?" he asked.

She looked delighted. "You are a *mensch*, Mr ..."

"Johnson." This too made her smile.

By the third day, Johnson had come by a second shadow. This one also wore a dark suit but carried a camera, which he failed to conceal on several occasions. Their pursuit was so overt that Johnson wasn't sure how he should act. At one point they sat opposite him on the Tube, staring. The day after that Johnson took himself to Regent's Park zoo. It was the one tourist attraction that he had promised to himself during his stay. It was a grey, cold January afternoon, so cold that most of the cages he stood before seemed empty – their occupants hiding beneath layers of straw, or in the corner of their interior enclosures. Eventually he found himself at the reptile house. Although clearly it was once grand, there was something faded about the structure now. Inside the dimly lit walls of tanks, a few snakes were coiled uncomfortably against the glass. There were patches of the place that were not lit at all. It inspired nothing but sadness in Johnson. He was standing in front of a large anaconda waiting to see if it moved on the mouse that had been dropped in front of it when he felt the tap on his shoulder.

"Excuse me, sir. Could we talk to you?" Johnson whirled around. There were his two followers. He had not thought that they would be so bold as to simply walk up to him.

"We have a car outside. Naturally we will refund your admission fee. We will take you wherever you wish to go."

"I'm sorry?"

The taller of the two stepped forward. "It is a matter of mutual benefit, sir. I assure you it will be in your interests to accompany us."

Johnson looked at them quizzically. The first one offered him a mobile phone. "I promise you, sir, you are not in any danger." He stabbed at the keypad with a gloved hand. The device bleeped feebly three times. "This is the emergency number for the police in this country." He swung the phone towards Johnson and showed him the display. "I'm going to give this phone to you, sir, and if you feel threatened in any way, you merely have to press this button to obtain assistance." He looked at Johnson appealingly. "But I would be grateful if you would accompany us and hear what we have to say."

They walked silently out of the zoo, past the red Victorian buildings that appeared to Johnson more like libraries or public baths than lion houses or parrot enclosures. His companions were not exactly inconspicuous in their suits and dark glasses. A group of children, their arms held aloft by silver balloons, stared after them as they passed.

A shiny black sedan car was parked on Regent's Park Way. A uniformed chauffeur got out when he saw them approach and he opened the back door for them.

"Is there anywhere in particular you would like to go, sir?" asked the taller man.

Johnson shrugged his shoulders. "You can take me home if you like."

The smaller man leant forward and whispered to the driver. The other reached for an attaché case that lay on the floor of the car. He placed it on his lap and sprang it open. He removed a large manilla envelope and passed it to Johnson. He gestured that Johnson should open it. Inside was a glossy ten-by-eight black and white photograph of a man wearing a large fedora. His face carried an expression that suggested supreme confidence coupled with an insouciant smile. The man looked remarkably similar to Johnson.

"He looks like me."

"Do you know who he is?" The two men were leaning forward, gazing at Johnson expectantly.

"I know it's not me." The men turned to each other. Their expressions suggested mild disapproval.

"Have you never heard of Trapido?" The tall man seemed particularly indignant.

"Trapido who?"

"Just Trapido."

"Should I have done?"

"Trapido is quite simply, sir, the greatest magician the world has ever seen."

Johnson thought for a moment then said: "I'm not a fan of conjurers." Both men looked suddenly piqued, even offended.

"I assure you, sir, Trapido is *not* a conjurer." The taller man sat back in his seat. "Conjurers entertain at the parties of screaming children. Conjurers pull silk handkerchiefs out of wooden cabinets. Trapido is no conjurer." The taller man sat forward again. "He is a magician. He is an enchanter. He is an artist." He reached back into the attaché case and removed a large and glossy perfect-bound brochure, which he handed to Johnson. He then nodded, implying that Johnson should examine its contents.

The brochure was glossy and expensive. It was titled in gold copperplate gothic *The Art of Wonder*. Beneath was a large photograph of Trapido, wearing oriental silk pyjamas. His legs were crossed and he stared intensely at the camera with a commanding expression as if he were saying, "You *will* believe me." Johnson opened the brochure and turned the crisp pages that still smelt of printer's ink. In order to get to the text he had to flick past several more photos of Trapido in various exotic costumes and locations. Here he was in South America atop an Inca pyramid, in head-dress and ceremonial robe, his arms folded defiantly. Now in the Australian outback, naked but for aboriginal loin-cloth and face-paint. Here in a primeval-looking rain forest, squatting before a fire, clothed in animal skins, holding a carved staff aloft. Next to this was a page of beautifully rendered calligraphy. It read:

Obeah. Shamanism. Thaumaturgy. Necromancy. There are as many names for magic as for God. But as with Him this diverse nomenclature has but one referent: the great mysterious source from which all flows. Over the years of man's brief tenancy of this whirling globe there are those who have learnt to tap this current, to conduct it for their own ends, whether fair or foul.
    Come. Meet Trapido. Conduit of the Power.

Johnson flicked past some more extravagantly staged photographs and arrived at a page of biography. Trapido was born in Liverpool, England where from an early age he was fascinated by all aspects of the occult and the macabre. Shunned at school for "being different" he spent many long hours in the public library deep in study. By the time he was fifteen he already had an encyclopedic knowledge of the great sorcerers of the past: Aaron; Nostradamus; John Dee; even Crowley. By the age of eighteen Trapido had developed a life-style of rigorous discipline. According to the brochure he practised Vipanassah Meditation for two hours daily and abstained from all pollutants: masturbation, alcohol, tobacco. He mastered Latin, Greek and Talmudic Hebrew. He then worked in a variety of mundane jobs in order to save the money to travel to India. There he studied in a Tantric monastery for five years, before relocating to America. He had now acquired his mission – to re-enchant the world, to teach it wonder, which had been obliterated by science and industrialisation. His shows began on a small scale in New York for private clients. He quickly acquired an impressive reputation, his performances becoming highly fashionable events in chic loft apartments of SoHo. But soon he found a wider stage and he performed an extended run of shows in Las Vegas, where he accumulated the money to further his vocation. He knew he had to conquer television, because this was the medium through which he could reach the widest audience. His first show had been a disaster. Commissioned by NBC , the ratings had been so unexpectedly low that they had attempted to sue for recovery of most of Trapido's fee. But a Canadian producer had been so impressed by Trapido's abilities that he immediately began developing a second extravaganza. This time the programme exceeded all expectations. It was a sensation around the world and soon Trapido had gone into partnership with his producer, together plotting his meteoric rise to the position he held today – that of one of the world's highest-paid and most powerful entertainers.

Johnson flicked forward and found some reproduced reviews of Trapido's shows that described a number of the dramatic set-pieces for which he had become most famous. One told of a performance recorded inside the great pyramid of Giza. Trapido, dressed in authentic ceremonial robes, was wired up by radio transmitter to a cardiogram. He then lay in a sarcophagus and a team of surgeons entered, proceeding to stop the magician's heart. The golden lid was then slid over, sealing the casket on the now-dead Trapido. All attention was fixed on the cardiogram's screen. Thirty seconds passed. Forty. Forty-five. A minute was marked. Then the white line flickered and the double-beep of a heartbeat echoed around the ancient stone chamber. Immediately the lid of the sarcophagus was slid open, revealing it to be empty. At that point the camera cut to the pyramid's exterior revealing a triumphant Trapido standing at its apex, holding his arms aloft.

"It makes for impressive reading."

"Even more impressive viewing," said the taller man.

The shorter one reached into the attaché case and pulled out another envelope. "Sir. We have a matter we'd like to approach with you. Would you be good enough to hear us out?"

The car slowed as it turned off Brownswood Drive and approached Johnson's flat. It pulled up outside. The two men followed Johnson inside.

The interior of Johnson's flat was very sparse, but beautiful. The walls were painted white and the floorboards were bare, covered in simple grey rugs rather than stripped and polished. His mattress filled one corner and there was a small pine table in another. The only orna-mentation was a tall vase containing two lilies. Their particular, bleachy odour filled the room. Johnson gestured that they should sit at the table. He offered them each a glass of water, which they declined. He filled one for himself. Both his visitors were clearly surprised at the décor.

"How can you live like this?"

"Like what?" Johnson looked querulous.

"Don't you have a television?" The smaller man's face carried an expression of appalled disbelief.

"I like to read," was Johnson's reasonable response. His guests looked at each other incredulously, then turned to face Johnson again.

"Sir," began the taller one, "I am Mr Grimalkin and this is Mr Jackanapes."

"Are they your real names?"

They looked taken aback. Mr Jackanapes shifted uncomfortably in his chair. "They are the names we have taken in service of Trapido."

"I see."

"We, and many of our brethren –"

"Your brethren?" Johnson interrupted.

"Our associates who are also in the service of Trapido." Mr Grimalkin's voice suggested tetchy indignation. "We have been scouring all parts of the earth in search of –"

"I'm sorry, it's just that I thought you might have meant you were part of some religious order or something," interrupted Johnson.

Grimalkin and Jackanapes looked at each other, both clearly irritated by what they considered irreverence. Grimalkin continued: "We've been in search of people who bear a likeness to Trapido. You, if I may say so, bear the most extraordinary similarity to him any of us have yet encountered."

"Why are you in search of such people?" asked Johnson, sipping at his water. The two men looked at each other, as if seeking a mutual permission. They both nodded and Mr Grimalkin reached into the attaché case once again. He produced a fat A4-sized legal-looking document.

"Sir. I have here a contract which has been drawn up by the firm of Sweetman and Sweetman – Trapido's lawyers in California. We have been authorised to offer you employment in the service of Trapido for a period of three months, with an option to extend for a further year."

Johnson laughed and shook his head. "I'm quite happy as I am, thank you, gentlemen. I have no particular desire to serve your Trapido."

Grimalkin looked incredulous. "What is your current employment, sir?"

"I am a student."

At this Grimalkin's eyes brightened. "I think you'll find the fee we are offering will help cover your graduate expenses. How long do you have left before you complete your studies?"

"That's very hard to say exactly, but the answer is, I suppose, however long I have left alive on this earth." Grimalkin's face twisted in exasperation. Seeing this, Johnson softened his response. "All right, all right. I understand you have a job to do. Just out of interest, what am I being offered financially to do this work, whatever it is?"

Jackanapes stretched himself in his pine chair. He had clearly been looking forward to this moment. "One and a quarter million dollars."

There was a long pause. Johnson sipped his water again. Eventually he spoke. "That seems a lot of money. Presumably then there is some danger, or discomfort, or illegality involved."

"No, sir," said Jackanapes proudly. "I can assure you that the work is none of those things. Part of the payment is rather to secure your silence. Your employment will bring you very close to Trapido and he has to be confident that you are trustworthy. Therefore we must pay you well. Also included within the contract is a clause to the effect that if you were to make any unwelcome revelations, you would immediately become liable to have your tongue surgically removed by a physician of his choosing then delivered to Trapido."

"I see."

"Another part of the fee is to cover the fact that we cannot inform you in advance of the nature of your work. It is a goodwill payment. Finally Trapido requests that if you take up his offer, you have your hair cut short, and you grow a substantial beard and moustache."

"Perhaps I could ..." Johnson gestured to be handed the contract. Grimalkin obliged. He flicked to page one and began to read it.

Johnson read very slowly and very carefully. Mr Grimalkin and Mr Jackanapes could barely disguise their growing excitement. It began to get dark in the flat. Johnson paused in his scrutiny and turned on the single white paper lantern that sat on the table. Grimalkin and Jackanapes shifted in their chairs with increasing agitation. Eventually Johnson reached the last page. He closed the pages and put it on the table.

"Well, why not," he said smiling.

A month later Johnson was sitting at the front of flight VS24 Virgin Atlantic to Los Angeles. He was stretched out in a seat that moved like a dentist's chair when he pressed the buttons in its arm. He was offered champagne, and Belgian chocolates and crackers with smoked salmon at fifteen-minute intervals. He was given a device that sat on his lap and allowed him to screen a film of his choosing at any time he wished. All these things were very pleasant, he thought to himself, but the most marvellous thing was when the plane flew over the edge of Greenland. Johnson had never seen such a landscape, at once so barren and so beautiful. Viewed from thirty-eight thousand feet a desolate freezing wilderness of stone and ice was transformed into a stupendous fractal mural inspiring within him a feeling of infinite wonder.

Johnson had never been to Los Angeles. It was hard to get a sense of it from the air. It was flat and even and draped in haze. Once in the absurd stretch limousine that Trapido had provided, it was easier to get a better idea of the place. It did not strike him as one of the world's more beautiful cities. Or even as being a city at all. There seemed to be not quite enough buildings spread over too large an area – a thin layer of jam scraped over a dry dusty slice of toast.

It hadn't taken long to settle his affairs in London. He'd packed his possessions into one small suitcase, and treated himself to a book for the flight – a new translation of Julian of Norwich's *Revelations of Divine Love*. (Whilst reading it he had come across one phrase in particular that he liked very much indeed: "All will be well, and all will be well, and all manner of things will be well." He repeated it to himself several times when the plane hit a nasty spot of turbulence over the Atlantic.)

Trapido had installed him in a huge hotel in Pasadena that resembled an Italian castle. Folded on the bed in his opulent room was a copy of *Variety International*. A letter poked out from amongst the pages. Johnson opened the magazine and withdrew the letter. There was a news item announcing Trapido's latest extravaganza. Johnson unfolded the creamy vellum paper. It was from Trapido.

September 18th

My dear Mr Johnson,
  I am very much looking forward to meeting you. I have a table

*reserved for us tonight at The Sky Bar at 8.30 p.m. We will talk
and generally get to know each other.*

God bless you.

                                                                    T

Johnson put the letter down and picked up the article. It was
written by someone called Alan W. Mozart and was entitled "Trapido
To Win World With Wonder Show." It read:

*The world's most famous magician Trapido has secured an
historic deal with his just-announced extravaganza "Walking
Through Walls". Described as "a revolutionary new concept in the
presentation of magic on television" Trapido will broadcast live
around the globe through deals signed with several leading digital
and satellite broadcasters. The show will be available to a potential audience of three quarters of a billion viewers. It will feature
a "feat of genuine sorcery the like of which has never been seen
on television". This climax will take place in the Old Jewish
Cemetery in Prague.*

*Trapido has a record of staging previous extravaganzas which
have included stunts as varied as the swallowing and excreting of
a live cobra – a feat recorded in the Brazilian rain forest – and
apparent immolation at the stake in the center of Barcelona. This
is the first time he has ever planned a live broadcast. The event
will be produced by Trapido's own company, Hegemony.*

Johnson took the magazine with him while he went to run a bath.
On the lavatory he flicked through the rest of it and concluded this
was a strange country indeed.

"Mr Johnson, Mr Johnson. What an absolute, unqualified pleasure."
Trapido grasped his hand far too firmly. "Come, join me, join me."

Unlike his pictures the man appeared relatively small in the flesh – the same height as Johnson in fact. He sported a beige-coloured tailored suit, and his hair – which was much longer now than in his photographs – was swept back, slick with pomade. He nodded to the assistant who had brought Johnson through the crowded bar towards him. The man nodded back, turned and left. Trapido slipped his arm through Johnson's as if he were his lover and led him towards their dinner table.

The tables were lined up in long parallel rows across a veranda, which overlooked the rest of Los Angeles – a huge and distant circuit board that flickered in the evening haze. Johnson thought it looked much better in the dark. Trapido sat him down with a certain amount of force, as if fearful that left to make his own mind up Johnson might have scarpered out of the restaurant and off down Sunset Boulevard.

"And what would you like to drink?"

"Just water, thank you."

"Still, sparkling, a twist of lime?"

"However it comes." Trapido was studying Johnson's face as he spoke. The waiter came over and took his order. Johnson was surprised to discover that his host was imbibing vodka and cranberry juice.

"I don't mean to be rude, Mr Trapido –"

"Trapido's fine."

"I don't mean to be rude, but when I read your mini-biography it said that you had given up all 'pollutants' – alcohol included."

Trapido smiled, revealing a striking set of teeth. "Indeed, when I was a younger man, taking my first faltering steps on this path, it eased the way to cultivate such discipline. I've found since that a more relaxed approach is beneficial. To paraphrase Trotsky – speaking in a different context I admit – 'whilst we struggle to change life, let us not forget the reasons for living.' " Johnson nodded and smiled but said nothing further. He was intrigued by Trapido's voice, which was a disconcerting mix of Liverpudlian twang and LA drawl. "It *is* remarkable." Trapido was still lost in wonder, studying Johnson's face. "They say that every man has his double somewhere on this planet. I've truly located mine."

Johnson said to himself: This man is clearly better acquainted with his reflection than I, but he refrained from expressing the thought.

Trapido's reverie was broken by the arrival of their drinks. He held his vodka and cranberry juice aloft. "If you resemble me in spirit as much as you do in looks, sir, you will be itching to know what the nature of your engagement is. But before we get to that, I propose a toast – to a long and fruitful collaboration." Before Johnson had a chance to raise the glass of elaborately prepared water he held in his hand, Trapido had clinked his drink against it.

Whilst they were eating Trapido explained how he had set up the search for his double, nearly a year ago, and how he had nearly abandoned it several times. "I've acquired far too many advisers, Mr Johnson. They mistake the fact that something is very difficult for it being impossible. I have discovered over the years that everything is possible, in one way or another." Johnson opened his mouth to respond but Trapido got in first. "I know what you're going to say. Why now? Why the obsession to find me now?" Actually Johnson had been about to ask Trapido to pass the olive oil, but he didn't bother to correct him. "The answer is timing. Timing is all. The idea for this performance came to me fully formed. It was the right time. I am on the cusp of reaching an audience five times the size of any other entertainer in my field. Imagine being able to convince that many people about the existence of magic – to bring wonder into that many lives. The feat I intend to perform for them has been approximated before, but I will show them the actuality. And you, my friend," he clasped Johnson's bread-filled hand, "you will help me achieve this."

"I'm not sure how."

"All will be explained, all will be explained. Patience is everything. Something else I have learned at cost. Does your beard itch?"

"I'm not quite used to it yet."

"A necessary evil. We could not be seen together in public without it." Trapido stuffed a final forkful of sea-bass into his mouth and then rose unexpectedly from his seat. "I will see you tomorrow morning, my friend. Until then, sweet dreams. Mr Thumbpricks here will take you back to your hotel. Feel free to have dessert." And with a flourish of napkin Trapido was gone, abruptly replaced by another dark-suited familiar who had appeared out of the night and now occupied the seat opposite Johnson. The man stared at him stony-faced as Johnson finished eating his meal.

The following morning Johnson was chauffeured to an anonymous-looking studio building somewhere in Burbank. Waiting for him inside were Trapido – now dressed in black sweatpants and T-shirt, augmented with a white silk scarf – and a gaggle of yet more suited men. This group looked different to the others – they carried a sense of authority and grave purpose. In the centre of the room, quite absurdly, was an enormous section of a stone wall. It was standing on a large raised platform. Laid on either side of the wall were pieces of turf covering the platform.

"Mr Johnson. Good morning, good morning. These gentlemen are my representatives from the firm of Sweetman and Sweetman. They were very keen to meet you." Trapido exhibited the same mixture of effervescence and stand-offishness as he had done the previous night. "I believe they wanted to judge your soundness before authorising the first payment."

"I must confess, sir, we haven't been able to find out much about you," said the sternest-looking of the three men. "Hence we wanted to meet you and glean a sense of your character."

"Do you have any strong religious beliefs, sir?" inquired another.

"Have you ever had any homosexual experiences?" asked the third.

"Gentlemen, gentlemen," Trapido laughed. "You will have plenty of time to question Mr Johnson on these matters this afternoon. If you don't mind I would like to be alone with him while I explain the details of our impending performance." The men nodded and quietly withdrew.

"Honestly, Mr Johnson. They're so fussy. Even though I've explained to them I'm quite wealthy enough to have you disappear if I had the slightest suspicion you might open your mouth to anyone you shouldn't."

"And if I did I would have to forfeit my tongue."

"Quite. Although the damage would be done by then." For a moment Trapido's lightness evaporated. He became somebody quite different – perhaps closer to who he actually was. "Make no mistake, I would have you killed well before that time if I sensed you were going to betray me. And I have a very good instinct for these things." He reacquired his original persona. "But we have no need to talk of such matters. You are a man of honour, Mr Johnson. I can sense that. And a man who delights in wonder, if I'm not mistaken."

"I find it everywhere."

"I knew it, I knew it." Trapido reached for a nearby chair and sat on it the wrong way round. "What do you know of the Kabbalah, Mr J?" Johnson cocked his head and frowned uncertainly. "The Jewish mystical tradition. An ancient and arcane system of natural philosophy. A source of genuine power. Of all esoteric systems it is perhaps the most covert, the most inscrutable." Johnson nodded to suggest he understood. "Let me tell you a story," Trapido continued. He was clearly a man who enjoyed the sound of his own voice. "I want you to imagine yourself in Prague. In the sixteenth century. In the old Jewish Town." His words coincided with exaggerated hand movements, as if he were telling the tale to a group of primary school children. "At one edge was a quarter with a bad reputation. Houses of ill-fame stood there. One street in particular, named Hampejzka, which literally translated meant 'brothel'. Paradoxically here also stood the old Jewish cemetery, which had been there longer than the city. At this time there was a rabbi – Rabbi Eliazer Ben Ruben – who was very learned in the ways of the Kabbalah. He had acquired a certain reputation for being a man of great power, having eschewed a more conventional worldly life and devoted himself to study. There were several occasions on which he had invoked mysterious and mighty forces to protect his beleaguered community. There were those who said he had even fashioned a *golem* from the clay of the Vltava, and that it stalked the edges of the old town every night, watching over its inhabitants. The rabbi had made many personal sacrifices in order to become a protector. But amongst the Gentiles his reputation was misunderstood. Fearful of what they heard a large group of Gentiles had organised themselves in order to find the rabbi and end his threat to their dominance."

Trapido paused slightly. The way he was telling his story suggested that its delivery had been rehearsed many times. "One terrible thunderous night a mob formed and tracked the rabbi to the Old Synagogue on Reznicka. He was deep in prayer. Upon seeing them he darted out of a back entrance, but they chased him down Brehova and in the end they cornered him against the wall of the cemetery. The crowd gathered in a circle around the fearful rabbi, pausing to catch their breath before they enacted their punishment – whatever it might be. In this unexpected moment of quiet the rabbi turned his back on the horde and faced the stone. The moment of quiet was extended. Those gathered were surprised by this simple action. But not as surprised as they were by the one that followed. Quite casually the rabbi walked forward and into the stone wall. He passed through it as if it were made of cloud. The crowd gasped in amazement, then roared in anger. They pelted around the wall of the old cemetery, but the nearest entrance was over forty yards away. Once amongst the gravestones there was no trace of Rabbi Eliazer Ben Ruben. In fact he was never seen again." Trapido concluded his story with a little flourish of his hands that Johnson felt it hardly needed. After a moment Trapido continued. "They examined the part of the wall where the rabbi had disappeared very thoroughly. They brought out measures in order to determine its height and thickness. (It was over nine feet high and four feet thick.) They searched every inch of the ground, but there was no clue as to how he had achieved his miracle." He paused again, then said: "We are going to re-enact that miracle, Mr Johnson. We are going to show them that magic is alive."

The next few weeks passed in a blur for Johnson. He spent several intensive sessions with a physiotherapist and a choreographer who taught him with surprising thoroughness how to move like Trapido. By the end of the sessions he knew how to adopt his gait, how to swing his hands, even how to slightly tilt his head as he began any new action. He was then introduced to Wardrobe who measured him for a set of suits and costumes that matched his employer's in every way. Next came the hairdresser, who meticulously reproduced the magician's colouring and then his coiffure. Finally Johnson was introduced to Ness, a tall English lady who supervised Trapido's make-up as well as looking after his general skin-care. She shaved Johnson's moustache and beard and organised several sessions on the sunbed – until his formerly pale complexion came to resemble the magician's Californian tan. The transformation was now complete. Johnson was taken to see Trapido for the first time since he had told his story.

They were back in the room with the segment of stone wall on the platform. Trapido sat on the turf holding a bound black and white document.

"The time has come, Mr Johnson, to take you through what is required of you." Trapido took a step towards him. "It would be wrong to continue, however, without acknowledging the transformation that has been effected. Remarkable. Quite remarkable."

"It's still me underneath." There was a hint of protest in Johnson's voice, as if he were resisting being consumed by the Trapido mask he had been obliged to don.

"Oh of course, absolutely. But let's not forget you have been employed to do a job and there is no reason not to take pride in your work." Trapido handed him the bound document. It was entitled somewhat grandly "Walking Through Walls – a methodology". "Now this volume details the whys and wherefores and mechanics of the piece we are going to be performing. But I think it may be quicker if I explain it to you." Trapido leapt off the platform and sprang towards Johnson, filled with a sudden and apparent enthusiasm. "I am sure that since the first moment my organisation made contact you have been wondering, Why? Why does Trapido want a double so badly? The truth is, Mr Johnson, I didn't just require a double, I needed a simulacrum, someone to all intents and purposes who *was* me. I was beginning to think I would have to resort to plastic surgery, until I received the call from England to say that you had been found. And with you working for me, miracles are possible. I can literally be in two places at once."

Trapido's brown skin was beginning to redden with excitement. "Imagine it, sir. Imagine it. The camera can be on you – the lens pressed against your face – and it is me. In seven days' time we will be broadcasting live to the world from Prague. You will stand on one side of that four foot thick wall. You will pass briefly through the small tent that has been erected and I will emerge from the other side. How will we do this? The ground on either side has been prepared. On each side there is a capsule just large enough to contain a single person. The entrance of each is covered with the turf and has been arranged in such a way that the edge of the trapdoor is undetectable. You will enter your tent, and throw yourself into the capsule, closing the trapdoor behind you. I will by then have emerged from mine and be ready to leave the tent on the other side of the wall. Assistants will pull away each tent on cue. The viewer will have not a shred of doubt that *I* have walked through the wall. The action will be covered simultaneously from three angles. Timed correctly – which is what we are going to rehearse and rehearse and rehearse – the switch will be undetectable. To all intents and purposes I *will* have walked through the wall," he reiterated. "Now, you will have to stay still in your capsule for ninety minutes. By then the area will be sealed and the de-rig will take place in secure conditions. I'm afraid that the capsule will have to be sealed by remote control to prevent a premature exit by yourself. There is enough oxygen for four hours however. This is the most discomfort you will have to endure."

Johnson looked uncertain. "How do I know you *will* release me at all?"

Trapido laughed loudly. "Mr Johnson. What do you take me for? Besides, having discovered an asset such as yourself do you really think I wouldn't go out of my way to protect it? Think what miracles are possible if we continue to collaborate."

There was a pause whilst Johnson took in what had been described to him. He flicked through the printed manual thoughtfully, then gathering himself he began to speak.

"I hope you'll forgive me for sounding naïve, but doesn't all this amount to deceit?"

"I'm sorry?" Trapido looked at him nonplussed.

"Well. All this talk of wonder, and teaching the world magic?"

"We are teaching the world magic. We're firing the imagination. Empowering a sense of miraculous possibility."

"By means of a conjuring trick."

Trapido laughed again, but his laughter had taken on a less pleasant tone. "I don't think that word is accurately applied to a performance on this scale."

"It's just a trick," Johnson repeated.

"It's an illusion brought about by mechanical means."

"You're lying to people."

"I am enlightening people. I am opening their eyes to the fluidity of things."

"You're passing yourself off as having powers that you don't possess –"

"*Mr Johnson!*" Trapido barked. "What on earth did you expect?"

"Your biography said you'd studied, meditated, mastered every aspect of yourself."

"Fifteen years ago I was conjuring at children's parties and working for the Liverpool public library. I can assure you that the position I hold today has not just landed in my lap."

"But you don't possess these abilities you profess."

"Are you insane?" Trapido's face was redder in anger than it was in excitement. "Nobody does."

Johnson looked at him curiously then began to move towards the door. "I'm sorry. I don't know if I can co-operate with this."

Trapido was virtually dancing up and down with rage. "What are you *talking* about? What did you think I wanted with you?"

"I'm not sure I can violate my principles –"

"Violate your principles? *Violate your principles?* You have signed a contract so fucking watertight that for the next three months you cannot take a shit without my say-so. You are going nowhere, sir, except to Prague, where you will perform this *trick* and then you will keep silent about its method until the end of your days or I will have you killed, sir. Do you hear me?"

Johnson paused by the door and hung his head. After some time he looked up. "I will complete this assignment and no more. I will not be interested in working again with you after that. You can be sure I will speak of this to no one, but you can be also sure that from this time on I hold you in very low esteem. I will do as you say from now on, but I will not converse with you – unless you are prepared to call off this deception." Trapido glared at him with murderous eyes. After an unpleasant pause, Johnson added: "However I'm aware of my obligations. I have no choice but to co-operate in every other way."

Johnson remained true to his word. He diligently rehearsed every move dictated to him, memorised each gesture and in general did everything in order to be seen to be fulfilling the obligations he had signed up to. He did not however utter another word to Trapido, at least not until they were in Prague.

The build-up to the broadcast of *Walking Through Walls* was considerable. Trapido's PR machine was powerful and effective. There were several international magazine features about his relationship with Chocolate Marlowe – a beautiful mixed-race fashion model and singer – and a live television interview with Larry King which was later syndicated around the world, in which Trapido argued how his performance proved magic was a living force for those, such as him, who were prepared to cultivate it. Meanwhile in Prague, all the apparatus required for the broadcast was being put in place, surrounded by much security. Johnson was lost somewhere in the middle of all this activity, shunted from hotel room to hotel room, quietly waiting to fulfil his role. Although technically he was supposed to be rehearsing his moves, he felt confident of his responsibilities and that he would be able to perform them correctly.

The walk through the wall was, of course, the dramatic climax to a show that featured other many smaller, if no-less-perplexing acts from Trapido. There was a segment where he donned *tefillin* – the phylacteries worn by orthodox Jews when at prayer – and invited a member of the public to describe a dream he had had the previous night. From this Trapido divined the most extraordinarily accurate information about every aspect of the volunteer's life. Later he unpinned a large dead bumble-bee mounted like a butterfly on a wooden board, and placed it in a small glass vial together with a scrap of paper with one of the secret names of God inscribed upon it. Whilst the camera was trained closely on it the insect's motionless wings began to twitch and then strobe as life was bestowed once more upon a thing that had clearly been without it – or so it appeared. Finally the moment came when in close-up, covered live with five cameras, Trapido was going to walk through the stone wall of the old cemetery. An hour earlier Johnson had been brought out from his Winnibago into the performance area, which had now been emptied of all but essential personnel. In the few brief moments he had to gaze upon it Johnson had marvelled at how beautiful the place looked, lit so brightly in the dark of the night. The chaotic clumps of memorial stones stretched away from him, jagged shards of white and grey at crazy angles, time and weather having made an expressionistic sculpture of them.

What was to be shown on-screen had been given much thought. There were to be five separate camera viewpoints on screen simultaneously, one of them large, the other four thumbnailed across the bottom. Those viewing with the latest digital technology would be able to switch at will between the five images.

A recording had been made of Trapido telling the story of Rabbi Eliazer standing against the exterior wall of the cemetery. In the wide shot Johnson walked on and adopted the same position. Viewers at home then saw a cut into the recorded sequence. When it ended, perfectly on cue, Johnson walked over to the area of the wall where the magic was to be performed, just as the cameras cut back to a much closer shot of him. The illusion that it was Trapido was seamless and perfect. Johnson, a hand-held camera right over his shoulder, pulled across the thin screen being used to cover the designated segment. He stepped behind it.

Trapido meanwhile, who had been concealed in his buried capsule on the far side of the wall, received his cue and emerged silently from the ground. He then hit the mark required for him to walk out from behind the screen. As he prepared himself to emerge with the casual flourish he had been practising for several weeks he was disturbed by a sudden movement behind him. A pair of hands were poking out from the stone of the wall, white against the mossy black. They stretched out and became a pair of arms, then, very gradually, they were followed by a chest, swelling out of the limestone like bread rising in an oven. Then a cloud of white breath followed by a head. Johnson's head. It seemed that Johnson had done in actuality that which Trapido was attempting to simulate. He had quite simply walked through the wall.

Johnson inhaled deeply, then said: "Forgive me for having taken a form so similar to yours, but we felt it the surest way to get to you." He smiled broadly before adding: "Incidentally, I can do this as well!" He plunged his hand into Trapido's chest. It passed through the skin, muscle and bone as if they were soft cheese. Trapido looked down, finally speechless. He felt Johnson tickle his heart. Johnson shook his head, then withdrew his hand. There was no wound. The white satin of Trapido's shirt was unblemished. "Not that way, don't worry," said Johnson, who then took the shivering conjurer in his arms. "But I'm afraid I have to show you what it is like, to do what you wanted to pretend to do. I fear you will not like it." He held Trapido tightly then turned at speed and moved the man towards the dark, solid wall. Trapido began to scream but before any sound had a chance to emerge his mouth and teeth and tongue had met the cold, wet stone. Their atoms began to pass between one another. Whilst Trapido's ears remained in the open air Johnson bent towards them and whispered with force: "You left us no choice. You cheapen wonder, you defame it by using it for your own ends, you don't add it to this earth, you remove it, you divert attention from it. Magic is all, magic is this world, it does not lie in your tatty mummery but in every flower, every stone, every sod of earth if you would only stop and think. However, I'm afraid that time has passed." Before the conjurer's ear finally melted into the rock Johnson added softly: "All will be well, and all will be well and all manner of things will be well," then pulled Trapido all the way into the wall.

At this point those watching the broadcast became aware of some consternation. They had seen what they had taken for Trapido walk behind the curtain, but a noticeable amount of time had passed and nothing seemed to have happened. A perturbed-looking assistant pulled the other tent aside to reveal only bare stone and empty ground. The first tent was removed a moment after Trapido had emerged from the wall, now quite dead. He had landed in a broken heap on the damp grass.

And that is what the cameras found and what was broadcast live to the world. It appeared that the magician had stepped behind his screen and died of heart failure before he could perform his greatest feat. And as the technicians and assistants buzzed around the conjurer's corpse not one of them saw the figure that had been Johnson descending into the ground in a dark corner of the cemetery – fusing with the earth like Adam in reverse. In silence he disappeared, until he should be called upon again to police this imperfect realm of mountebanks and scoundrels. Nobody noticed; they were too busy examining Trapido's corpse, puzzled by the greatest piece of magic of all – that same black trick that squats at the end of all our lives. One minute you're here. The next you're gone. And where you go to nobody knows.

A slate roof in the rain

If there was one thing Dicky-Bow Dyall thought his fellow teachers would agree upon it was surely this: that there was nothing extraordinary about Bernard Sunset, other than his name.

The boy's school career, all must concede, was marked by mediocrity and low achievement. To Dyall he appeared a creature of little imagination and basic ability, one of those boys teachers despaired of.

What concerned Dyall now was the typed sheet in front of him. It detailed the requests for admission to his A-level art class. There was Marlowe – a good draughtsman and neat dresser who'd excelled in his GCSE with a fine and detailed drawing of a floor polisher. Then David Hall. Well, that made sense. Hall was a brilliant musician and almost as accomplished a painter – particularly of natural scenes. Dyall remembered the watercolour of a kingfisher Hall had completed when he was twelve. And Hindmarsh. Yes, Hindmarsh was good. His fondness for reproducing album covers in art classes was offset by a genuine graphical ability as well as an infectious enthusiasm. But Sunset. Bernard Sunset in the Dicky-Bow room. The boy had done poorly at his GCSE. He had no skill, no talent and worst of all no imagination. Dyall thought about Sunset's round plate of a face and his ill-defined mess of fair hair. The thought of him sitting in his room staring blankly up as Dyall talked about Titian or Cézanne was almost too much.

He filled his pipe and sucked on it to ignite the bowl. He puffed out a cloud and watched it roll against the glass of the annexe window. The A-level classes were special to him. Real work. The boys were

James Hood

nearly adults. Some of them became friends. Only two years before, his class had helped Dyall complete a kit-car and then take it out to Pickering to race it on the airfield. Sometimes they went up to the Playhouse when they screened films. Dyall tried to imagine Sunset watching *The Third Man*. He saw him slumped in his seat slack-jawed as if it was *The Bill*. He drew a staccato of small puffs on the pipe to secure its ignition. It was decided. He would speak to Masher, the deputy head, in the morning. Reason enough could be found to prevent Bernard Sunset's artistic aspirations.

Like many other teachers at St Luke's, Dicky-Bow Dyall was a bachelor. Since it was a boys' grammar school it was assumed by some that bachelorhood was interchangeable with homosexuality. In fact this was not the case. True there were a number of queens to be found skulking in the classrooms but Dyall was not among them. (When he had first joined the staff one colleague – a predatory music master who had since departed – mistook Dyall's eponymous habit of wearing a different bow-tie each day as a signifier of something other than flamboyance. Dyall took advantage of the opportunity this presented to express his heterosexuality to all in an aggressive and public staff-room rebuttal.)

Although he had no wife or girlfriend (he hated the word "partner" – it was for tennis and bridge, not love) he did engage in regular sexual activity. The fact that he paid for it did not lessen his enjoyment or the sense of subtle superiority he savoured on the Monday morning after one of his encounters. He looked at his married colleagues with their conventional lives and humdrum habits and was grateful for the freedom he allowed himself.

Conventionality was what he sensed in Bernard Sunset. A deep and stifling ordinariness. There was no place for it in his A-level class and so he felt quite justified as he sat in Masher Grange's office and explained why the boy's request was wholly inappropriate.

"It's pointless, Maurice. The board's tough as it is. Where's the sense in letting him waste two years of my time – not to mention his."

Masher tilted his head to one side. "I hear what you're saying, DB, I hear what you're saying. I'll speak to Blanchflower. See if we can't talk the lad into a more suitable choice."

And that, thought Dyall, would be the end of it. So he was surprised to see Mr Blanchflower gesturing timidly through the glass doors at the back of the art room, as he demonstrated the best technique with a diffuser to 8JK.

"Fill your jampots with water now. Start mixing your paints. I'll be back in a minute." He strode to the back of the class and carried on talking in teacher mode.

"Yes, Mr Blanchflower. Can we help you?" Some of the class turned round to watch, as Dyall had intended.

"Can I have a word, Mr Dyall?"

"Of course you may. Though it's a bit difficult through half an inch of toughened fire glass."

"I mean, can I come in and have a word?"

"There's no need to ask." Dyall turned round and pulled a face. Some of the class laughed. "It is rare indeed, 8JK, for Mr Blanchflower to find his way to the art room. The language laboratories are his natural home." Blanchflower twitched nervously as he entered. "To what do we owe this pleasure?" Dyall added.

"Perhaps we could go into the back."

"But I have a class to teach, Mr Blanchflower. Are they to remain unsupervised while we are engaged in our dialogue?"

"It's about Bernard Sunset. Your refusal of his admission to your A-level group." Blanchflower spoke in a low whisper, keen to give the impression of two teachers talking like adults about a professional matter. Dicky-Bow Dyall refused to co-operate, continuing to bark out his speech at a tutorial level.

"A decision was reached about his suitability."

"But Bernard's shown a real interest in this. I think it would be a great shame if he couldn't follow it up."

Dyall inhaled fully and pulled himself erect. He began walking to the front of the class. "Art is not just a matter of interest, Mr Blanchflower." 8JK had gone quiet. They sensed that one of Dicky-Bow's scenes was taking place. "There are many other pre-conditions if one is to take it up at Advanced Level. Skill, aptitude, personality, and not least flair." With very precise movements Dyall pulled himself on to an empty desk at the front and then folded his legs beneath himself. "Despite what you may think, my subject is not some kind of arty-farty hobbycraft – something you might do to fill a rainy afternoon." Dyall allowed his Northumbrian accent to become more pronounced, clipping the Ts out of his invective. "It is a subject every bit as serious as yours. It has a history. Its practice requires discipline and application." Blanchflower's twitching had become more pronounced. His lips tightened over his teeth. "Therefore we must be selective about who we allow through those doors." Dyall gestured to the Dicky-Bow room behind him. "If a child came to you who couldn't read, wishing to study A-level German – what would you do?"

Blanchflower looked at him, his lips even tighter. Then he spoke: "I would teach him *how* to read, Mr Dyall." Blanchflower surprised Dyall by holding his gaze then turning and leaving the room.

"I'm sorry, DB." Masher was adjusting his gown. "But it's the Head's decision. It seems Blanchflower felt very strongly about it and since he's made a big success of the chess team this year he's to have his way."

"I see."

"Anyway, who knows." Masher shook his arms out at the side. He looked like a smug owl. "Bernard Sunset may surprise us all."

And so, on the first Monday morning of the new term, Bernard Sunset arrived in the Dicky-Bow room. He shuffled in with his ordinary sports bag hooked over his slumped shoulders, rumpling the back of his ordinary jacket from which poked his ordinary light brown shirt. And whereas Hindmarsh, Hall and Marlowe were filled with a vibrancy and vitality and potential which lifted Dyall, Sunset seemed governed by fear and embarrassment. As he peeked through the glass of the annexe doors Dyall could see the other boys sitting on the grey plastic chairs talking animatedly while Sunset skulked at the back of the room, his eyes fixed on the parquet floor. He almost fell backwards as Dyall burst into the room playing the Northumbrian pipes – his usual opening technique for a new A-level group. He squeezed his own arrangement of "I am the Walrus" from the antique instrument. Hindmarsh's face shone with awe and amusement. Hall laughed out loud. Marlowe smiled and nodded as if he'd been expecting it. Bernard Sunset looked absolutely terrified.

"What has the twentieth century taught us?" Dyall raised his eyebrows and cocked his head as he pulled the pipe from his mouth. "To expect anything and be shocked by nothing? Some might say that. Others might say, myself included, that it has demonstrated clearly that there is a canon that stretches back hundreds of years. And that the wilder excesses of many so-called twentieth-century artists illuminate that canon even more clearly. Bernard Sunset. What is your favourite piece of art?"

Sunset looked up at him blankly. The second button of his shirt was undone, revealing a white vest beneath. "Sir?"

"Do you have a piece of art that you like, Mr Sunset? That is a particular favourite of yours?"

Sunset thought for a minute. Then he nodded.

"And what is this painting or sculpture or installation?"

"It's a picture, sir."

Dyall took a number of long strides towards him. "And what is it a picture of?"

"An owl."

"I see. And who painted or drew it?"

Sunset looked worried. "I'm not sure, sir." He paused for a moment before adding, "It's in a book."

"It's in a book." Dyall nodded and then walked backwards to his original position. "Mr Marlowe. Do you have a favourite painting, sculpture, installation or indeed picture in a book?" He raised the pitch of his voice for the last three words.

Marlowe smiled. "It's a sculpture, sir."

"Ah, a sculpture. What is it a sculpture of?"

"It's *The Kiss*."

"And who is it by?"

"Rodin."

"Indeed yes. Monsieur Rodin's sculpture of two lovers kissing. To be found in the Musée Rodin in Paris. I have been privileged to stand before it and have myself marvelled at its clarity." Dyall wheeled back to face Bernard Sunset again. "Detail, Mr Sunset. Detail is all. You must remember details. Like who painted what picture. Or drew what drawing." He placed the pipes down on his desk. "We will begin with an exercise …"

As the weeks passed, his students' conduct only served to confirm Dyall's initial judgements. Sunset's capability proved as limited as he had suspected. The boy was virtually ostracised within the class. He had no interest in his fellow pupils and seemed to spend his time there as if it was a kind of punishment to be endured. One day however he did something that surprised Dyall.

Dyall was sitting in the annexe on a mid-week lunchtime looking out through the smeared window at the wet playing field. It stretched away from the New Building where the art room was housed to the edge of the old gymnasium on the far side of the grounds. Dyall filled the bowl of his pipe with Auburn Leaf and watched Mr Slack the groundsman repairing a wall near his outhouse. The rain drummed on the glass and Dyall allowed himself a moment to enjoy being indoors in his own space, warm and safe. He drifted off into the memory of an encounter with Eva at the First Class Sauna in Bolton the previous weekend. He was surprised to have his reverie broken by a tap on the window of the fire door behind him. His heart sank at the sight of the dusty-blazered, fearful-faced Sunset.

"Yes, Mr Sunset. You may enter."

Sunset shuffled in, looking at the floor. He was carrying an old brown book. "Sir? That picture, sir."

How was it, thought Dyall, that boys of the same age numerically could be so different in maturity; Marlowe and friends could have been first-year undergraduates. Sunset was still a child.

"Which picture is that, Mr Sunset?"

"My favourite picture, sir. I brought it to show you." Without warning the boy spread the book he held before Dyall. The aged pages brought a peppery smell to his nostrils. Dyall looked down.

There was something bad about the picture. Not badly drawn or badly composed. It was neither of these. It was mostly black – or very dark brown. The left third was dominated by a huge brooding owl, naturalistically rendered in coloured ink. It gazed out at Dyall and looked him in the eye. It was perched on a winter-stripped branch that spread out like crabs' legs across the rest of the image. Behind the bird, some distance away in silhouette against a storm-soaked sky, was a dark, sprawling castle. The castle was surrounded by impenetrable woods filling the space around it like thick, old cobwebs. The strangest thought occurred to Dyall as he stared at the image: if someone were to say "You have to go to this place" he would fight and kick and scream and cry to avoid it.

Dyall had to puff sharply on his pipe such was the picture's effect. He flipped to the cover to find out the book's name. The dust jacket was long gone, but the brown cloth-covered spine was embossed with the title *Twenty Fairy Tales with Illustrations*. "A striking image to be sure, Mr Sunset. But who is the artist, eh?" Dyall flicked to the front of the book. There was no title page. He flicked to the back. No one was credited with responsibility for the illustrations. He closed the book quickly and handed it back to Sunset as if it were diseased and might infect him with something. "There is a difference – which I hope you will learn over the course of the next two years – between liking an illustration in a children's book and the appreciation of a work of art that has been so defined by the gaze of many generations."

Sunset stood for a moment then turned to go. As he did so he said, "It was my Nan's book. She gave it to me." There was a pause, then he left.

There had been somebody once. A tall girl at St Martin's where Dicky-Bow Dyall had done his post-grad (when he was called Des). She had dark, dark eyes and a curtain of black hair. Her name was Francesca. On first meeting her he'd been very surprised. He hadn't expected to find anyone who shared his enthusiasms so completely. She was quite mannish. Not butch exactly, but authoritative, confident and assertive. She even smoked little cigarillos. Unclothed, her androgyny vanished and Dyall had found himself scared of her elegant beauty. He hadn't thought about her in years.

It was time to move the A-level group on from drawing exercises to the rudiments of painting. He showed them slides of Cézanne to demonstrate the depiction of form and Monet and Turner to illustrate light. Marlowe asked him a question about Rothko and abstract expressionism. "Detail, rigour and transparency," he declaimed scornfully. "These are the elements that define great art. A great painting should be capable of being grasped and understood, even by Mr Sunset here." The boys laughed.

As it so turned out, Bernard Sunset was to surprise Dyall a second time. Dyall had set a small still life which the four boys sat around: a tall green bottle that had contained olive oil placed in front of a red and black beer tray. The boys had palettes and oil paints. The air was filled with the bite of white spirit. The only sound was the light tapping of their brushes on their boards and the distant reverberation of Mr Cooke's choir rehearsing the St Matthew Passion in the music room. Every fifteen minutes or so Dyall would get up from his desk and circle around his students. On the third occasion he passed Sunset, then found himself shuffling backwards to take another look at the boy's work. Marlowe, noticing this, laughed, assuming the movement to be comical in intention – a parodic version of Michael Jackson's moonwalk. In fact the action had been spontaneous, so taken aback had Dyall been by what he had witnessed on Sunset's easel.

Although the composition was crude and the proportions of the bottle and tray were inaccurate the colours shimmered and glowed. The shades Sunset had chosen performed magic in their juxtaposition. They illustrated a casual beauty one would never have expected to find in such a mundane subject or to find coming from such a mundane hand.

Dyall bent down to examine the painting more closely. Sunset turned his head, his round face fearful of ridicule or rebuke.

"I was observing your use of colour, Mr Sunset. Carry on, carry on." The fact Sunset looked so surprised showed Dyall that the boy was quite unaware of what he had done. He resumed his circling of the students, pausing before Hindmarsh's predictably clear rendition of the arrangement. "Very good, very good. Mr Hindmarsh's precision is to be admired."

The date was fast approaching for the group's first major test. As a prelude Dyall had arranged a trip to Leeds Art Gallery to observe the variety of paintings to be found there. Although not a renowned collection, there were many items of interest including several works by Stanley Spencer and some unusual Victorian portraiture.

They passed through the new entrance hall, its sterile glass and steel giving way to the more solid and impressive polished granite within. A resonant monument to nineteenth-century civic pride and responsibility. Dyall enjoyed the echo of their feet as they made their way into the first hall. He gathered the boys in front of an absurdly large canvas depicting a stormy sea. The ocean looked as solid as the wood in the frame surrounding it.

"Now, we are here not to seek inspiration but to observe. I want you to note the variety of subject matter." Sunset was looking around, his mouth slightly open, his dull eyes wide. "Mr Sunset. I suggest you pay attention."

Sunset looked at him ashamed. "Sir, I didn't know paintings could be so big."

"Have you never walked these rooms before?" Sunset looked to the floor in answer. "Astounding though this revelation is, it somehow doesn't surprise me. You must listen now, for what it's worth." Dyall turned so he was addressing the whole group once again. "Your first major project is a painting that you will complete over the Easter break. Now this is not to be a subject taken from life, but rather from your own imagination. I want you to go deep within and find an unusual or dynamic subject to base a composition around. The elements that make it up should of course be observed from life but the image itself must well from your unconscious. Understood?" The boys nodded. Sunset's face wore an expression of such seriousness and attention that Dyall had to stifle a laugh. "Now we can take some time to explore on our own." Dyall calculated that he just had time to make it down the newsagents near the old Queen's Hall which stocked a spectacular range of pornography – including many Continental titles. "We will meet back here in an hour and then I want each of you to take me to see a picture you have selected as significant."

The boys' choices weren't really that surprising: Hindmarsh singled out the Gilbert and George which dominated the Modern room of the upstairs gallery; Marlowe was impressed by the dynamism of Epstein's

Maternity and Hall liked the luminescence of the gallery's single Seurat. Predictably only Sunset confounded in his selection. The other boys giggled when he stood them in front of the reclining nude he had found. A rather ordinary late nineteenth-century reworking of Manet's *Olympia* by a since-forgotten artist. The major difference was the composition. This artist had placed his nude much further back in the frame. In all other respects it seemed unremarkable.

"I trust what makes your peers giggle is not the reason you singled out this – what I must confess at first sight seems – quite dull figure study, Mr Sunset." Sunset blushed. Dyall gestured that he should elucidate.

"It was how it made me feel." The other boys laughed again. He blushed more if that was possible.

"I think you'd better clarify."

"I liked the way it makes you feel really sad, even though there's nothing in her face that says she's sad." It suddenly seemed very quiet in the gallery. Dyall looked at the picture more closely. He'd walked past it fifty times or more barely registering anything about it at all. Could Sunset be right? He looked from the picture to Sunset's face.

"Hmm. A very generous interpretation, I feel." He looked back at the painting once more before moving the boys on.

Dyall was surprised enough to find he had returned to the gallery after school. Maybe it was the fact he himself hadn't visited the place for over a year. If he was honest with himself he might admit that he'd never been truly comfortable in art galleries. He'd always found them slightly perplexing. He was never quite sure how one should behave. He wandered round aimlessly for a little – pausing in front of the circle of stone by Richard Long, and the Union Jack made up of pieces of rubbish. Not art to him but still interesting items. He even found himself in front of Sunset's reclining nude, whose distant, complex expression reminded him of Francesca's, the last time he saw her twenty-two years earlier. He thought of that final afternoon. Telling him she couldn't see him any more. The gas fire hissing. The shock. Something ceasing inside. Could twenty-two years pass so quickly? The answer was that they had. How little there seemed to be filling the intervening time between then and now. She was seeing a painter called Brett who was exhibiting in Paris. Des felt stupid and naïve and young and ordinary. He knew he could never really have had someone like her. He'd left London and taken up teaching. It was only a relationship. Only a woman. He'd shrugged it off. Funny how he'd never met anyone else. He thought that he wouldn't but at the same time beneath that resignation somewhere deeper he felt that he would. Tired of waiting, he'd visited this girl someone had spoken about at the Car Club. It was only supposed to be a stop-gap, a treat for himself, something to ease the stubborn ache of Francesca's absence. He'd enjoyed it very much – the thrill of climbing the girl's stairs, watching her undress in her darkened bedsit, lit only by a street-lamp outside. He knew he'd do it again. It wasn't like sex with a girlfriend. It was easier. It was predictable. It was about him, not two people.

The Easter holiday passed with unwelcome speed and Dyall found he was back at school for the summer term. The first session with his first-year A-level group. They had brought in their paintings. Hindmarsh was there with a graphical study of a marathon runner completing a race. He had attempted to create a suggestion of motion by painting the runner's arms in a number of consecutive positions – doubtless inspired by Duchamp's *Nude Descending a Staircase*. David Hall arrived and unveiled a small canvas. It contained an immaculately rendered riverside scene of a cormorant spearing a fish. Marlowe appeared not long after with an A2-sized piece of board. His picture depicted a row of tins in a supermarket with a hand reaching for them. The scene was presented from the point of view of the tin cans.

Dyall walked among the pictures drawing on his pipe and noting details of their making. It was some time before he noticed Sunset's absence. He registered it about the same time he heard the stumbling clatter of a chair being knocked down outside in the main art room. Sunset was, of course, the cause of the commotion. He was struggling with a very large flat shape covered with a pink blanket. The shape was square and a few inches taller than the boy himself. Dyall motioned for Marlowe and Hindmarsh to go and help.

"I thought perhaps Laurel and Hardy were out there moving a piano but I should have realised it was only our very own Mr Sunset," Dyall declared as they entered. "Have you brought us an advertising hoarding, I wonder?" The boys laid the giant pink oblong against their teacher's desk.

"It's my picture, sir."

"Is it indeed? And I wonder if you can explain why it is the size of a small cow?"

Sunset looked even more uncomfortable than usual. The other boys smiled.

"You said to imagine ... to go into your subconscious." Sunset stuttered slightly, uncomfortable with the terms he remembered his teacher using.

"Indeed I did. You must have painted the entire contents of yours. Let's have a look then." Dyall positioned his pipe firmly between his teeth and used both hands to remove the fluffy pink blanket from the board.

He had to drop the blanket and grab his pipe to stop it falling to the floor. His jaw had unclenched involuntarily. The picture was one of the most arresting things he had ever seen. The words "remarkable" and "unsettling" swapped places several times in his head. It seemed to be done entirely in shades of grey although when he bent close to examine the surface, Dyall could see there were many other colours including blues, greens and even yellows combining to create that impression. He had to stand back to get a full impression of the image.

What Sunset had painted was the view through a large, unclean window of a huge slate-covered roof in a rainstorm. There were no other features of note – no distant people or roosting birds – just the struts of the neglected window and the unforgiving expanse of slate tiles glistening in the downpour. The atmosphere of gloomy mystery this panorama conveyed was quite unspeakable. Above and below the window was the hint of dark wall giving the impression to the viewer that he was within an unlit room. Although the detailing was crude, the quality of Sunset's use of colour so exactly caught the feel of a wintry rainstorm that Dyall shivered as if he was cold. He had to look away out of the real window in order to catch a glimpse of the sun and remind himself he was not cold at all.

The other boys looked from the painting to their teacher, waiting for his judgement to be passed. Dyall could not understand why he was speechless. He looked at the painting again and its wide, forbidding vista. His heart was beating far too fast.

"And what do you think the A-level board might make of this? Hmm?" He was trying not to see anything of merit in those extraordinary shimmering colours. "Is it something you imagine they would grade highly?" He felt dizzy for a moment as if he had stared into an emptiness of a scale he would not have thought possible. He turned his back on the picture.

"Don't know, sir."

"No, I bet you don't." Dyall held up David Hall's riverside tableau. It felt small and insignificant in his hands. "This is the kind of work examiners expect to see. Careful, detailed, skilled." He placed the image down again and crossed to Marlowe's supermarket shelves. "Or this. Something that demonstrates imagination. A picture should be about something, Mr Sunset. A picture tells us what it means." He paused to pull on his pipe but the flame had died. "Now please. Take that away. I want to forget I ever saw it."

*

Bernard Sunset was never again to produce anything that anyone would describe as being extraordinary. He remained in Dicky-Bow's art class for the next fourteen months, settling even more into the shadows than before. The work he produced took the form of less competent imitations of his classmates and his particular use of colour faded with each painting as he strove to assume the conventions of his colleagues. He received a D grade for his final exam and what happened to him after that this story does not tell.

Dicky-Bow Dyall continued to teach and took up a new sideline alongside racing his kit-cars (the building of which none of Sunset's year ever chose to get involved in) – painting portraits. Beginning with a commission from the then-headmaster Mr Richardson, several other members of staff asked if he would "do" them. The paintings were straightforward – vanity items mostly, his subjects desiring not much more than painted photographs. Dyall found them easy to do – the only one he abandoned was a self-portrait begun on a whim. The money he collected from them over the months and years enabled him not only to pay more visits to his favourite women but also to begin to save for a special holiday he'd been planning.

Dyall concluded the internet was a marvellous thing. He'd only been on-line for a short time but already had found much to amuse him. It was a haven for working girls too. And what a marvellous thing to be able to see pictures of a woman before you visited her. Even better were the review sites he'd found. Modelled after consumer magazines they reviewed girls as if they were cars, giving unified details of their physical characteristics down to the style of their pubic hair. Their performance was rated too, along with a list of the services they would or wouldn't carry out. It was through such a site that he'd discovered *www.euro-angels.com*. This organisation arranged visits to European cities (mostly in Eastern Europe) and paired you off with a girl of your choice. Their web-site contained details of over sixty young girls – all of them thumbnailed, many of them beautiful. The visits could range from one night to two weeks. It was up to you (and your wallet). Dyall had scrolled up and down the pages in a state of excitement, not knowing where to begin. Eventually he settled on a girl called Daria. She was studying Economics and was fluent in English, French and German. She had dark hair and looked very young. He clicked on the booking icon and withdrew the Mastercard from his wallet, pleased that something so simple could still make his heart beat faster.

Dyall had settled on a three-night mini-break. The package was all-inclusive – return air-fare to Bucharest, hotel and the girl. He would certainly come back refreshed after half-term.

Dyall was not that well travelled. But he'd been in enough airports to note that they all seemed very similar regardless of their location – he'd observed the same of dentists' waiting rooms. He was expecting Daria to meet him at the airport but instead he was greeted by a man in jeans and a check shirt. The man was holding a piece of card upon which was written "Diall" in black marker pen. He was about the same age as Dyall. He wasn't particularly friendly.

Once in the car Dyall attempted conversation. The man didn't seem very interested so he turned his attention to the motorway. Shades of grey flicked past at high speed broken by the occasional unreadable sign.

The city itself was a strange mixture of slab-like tower blocks and more ornate, decaying architecture from an earlier time. The glass of the new buildings reflected a sky that blended with their concrete. A number of the shops they passed carried the names of familiar chains but there was little comfort in them. They didn't help alter Dyall's upsetting sense of not knowing where he was.

Eventually the car turned down a small street and pulled up at what looked like a bar. There was a sign hanging outside with an illustration of a red beer mug. Dyall could see a door opening on to steps that led down into a dark room. The man opened the car door for him and retrieved his small case from the boot. Dyall had been advised in the e-mail he received confirming the details to tip the people in US dollars. He reached in his pocket for the small roll he had ready. He handed over the money as he took his case. The man looked begrudgingly down at the notes in his hand. He looked at Dyall with distaste and got back in his car.

Dyall descended the stairs into the darkened bar room. The place was relatively empty. He ordered a beer. There was no sign of Daria. He was upset that he wasn't more excited. Somewhere down the street someone was arguing violently. A dog began barking.

Daria arrived about forty-five minutes later. She smiled at him. She looked a lot younger than her picture on the web, if indeed it was the same girl.

"You are Mr Dyall?" He could see that she had acne beneath her make-up. The rims of her eyes were red.

"Would you like a drink?" He ordered some red wine. "Here. Sit down."

They talked for a while – about his flight, his job. But he soon realised that Daria's English wasn't that good and the conversation dried. They sat drinking in silence, looking at each other every so often and smiling foolishly. Dyall had hardly thought about having sex with her at all. Eventually she suggested they walk to the hotel.

It was quite a distance from the bar. Dyall wished that they had got a cab. But the girl was enjoying pointing out buildings and being a guide and he didn't want to interrupt her. They seemed to have left the main part of the town centre and had crossed over into a more industrial sector. It must only have been about three o'clock in the afternoon but the sky was heavy and dark. After some time they turned down a street running between two huge buildings whose walls were covered with corrugated iron. Dyall was surprised when they arrived at a door with a hotel sign hanging over it.

Daria already had a key and led him up a narrow staircase. "The lift is not work." She smiled.

The room wasn't so bad. Daria went in ahead of him and he heard her draw the curtains. She turned on a bedside light and sat on one of the twin beds. One was covered with an orange bedspread, the other was beige. She smiled again.

"Would you like me undress?" Dyall smiled back but it had nothing to do with how he felt. As she pulled off her black jumper he caught a sharp hint of sweat beneath her rather heavy perfume. It reminded him of another afternoon, over two decades earlier.

After they had finished she asked if he would like a cigarette. He declined but she searched in her bag anyway. Failing to find one she explained she would go downstairs where she thought there was a machine. She quickly pulled on her clothes and padded out. After she had gone Dyall turned out the bedside light and lay in the dimness. Even with the heavy curtains drawn he could tell it was still only late afternoon. He shivered, realising he was quite cold. He thought about putting his clothes on but was interrupted by Daria's sudden and anxious return. She was in a state of some consternation.

"Mr Dyall, you must leave. You must go now. Get clothed. Please."

He sat up, alarmed. "What is it? What's up?"

"He is here, my … my …."

"Who is here? Your boyfriend? Who?" Dyall cried.

She pulled at his wrists. "My mother's … boyfriend." She stumbled over the word. "Only he make me his boyfriend too. He not let me do this. He says I am for him only. You must leave. He is drink."

Dyall scrambled out of the bed, reaching for his clothes. He could not remember where they were. There was a terrible shouting from the hall. A furious voice calling Daria's name. Dyall found his shoes and the door exploded.

The man was huge. A large pig-headed red face beneath a blond crew cut. Dyall could smell the alcohol mingled with the stench of his sweat. The man tried the light switch but it didn't work. He stumbled to the curtains and tore them down. The room was illuminated with a gloomy grey light. Shadow rain slid down the walls. The pig man screamed at Daria who stood in front of Dyall. She screamed back and he reached for a glass vase of dead flowers which stood on the window ledge. He smashed the vase against the wall, releasing a small amount of black water. A rotten odour filled the room. The rain was thudding against the window. The man moved toward Daria with the broken vase. Dyall stood up. The fear was so intense it felt like pain. He shouted at the man to stop, wishing he didn't have to do anything that drew attention to him. But the man was about to cut the girl. Dyall shouted again. Abruptly the man pushed Daria out of the way and lunged at him.

It was as if he'd been punched in the neck and couldn't get any air. But as he fell back on to the bed Dyall put his hand to his throat and felt it was hot and wet. He couldn't scream. Nothing happened. No noise came out.

The girl's cries were very distant now. Dyall looked up at the window for the first time. With the curtains pulled down he could see the view. If only he'd looked earlier.

The slates glistened dully, the rain hissing white stars on to their grey, repeating flatness. Above the roof spread the terrible sky – an impossible dark whose colour had no word.

It was the same smeared glass, the same arrangement of bars making up the window frame, the same unforgiving tiled expanse beyond. He knew it instantly. He couldn't move now. Sunset's vision filled his own. And as the blood and the breath and the piss flowed out of him the same five words ran on a loop in his head.

If only he'd looked earlier. If only he'd looked earlier ...

At last

It's late.

It must be about three in the morning, although I'm past looking at my watch. If I do so it'll only make the chance of sleep recede. The less time available the more frustrated I become.

So I get up, throwing the duvet off, and wander over to the record player. I've been staying here for three or four weeks now. Mum and Dad are away. My brother arrived two days ago. He's asleep but fuck him, I need to hear something loud and raucous.

Just as I was going to dig out Dinosaur Jr the thought "Put on some Dylan" flashes in my head, so I slide across the floor to the next pile of records where I have a hunch some Dylan may be found.

Although I've been here some time I've made no attempt to unpack anything. Everything totters in unsteady mounds around the perimeter of the bedroom, where I imagine it will be for some time to come.

It's been six or seven years since I last lived here. Tell you the truth I don't want to remember exactly because I'm less than proud of myself for getting in a situation where I'm forced to move back.

The room hasn't changed. There are bits of old NMEs still stuck around the walls. Why on earth they didn't get around to redecorating I don't know. I suppose I was happy here before. But I was a kid then.

The pile of records I'm levering up threatens to collapse completely. Somehow I manage to steady it and locate *Highway 61 Revisited* at the same time. It's a slight concession to noise because the drums on "Like a Rolling Stone" thunder and crash in a pleasing way. I slide the album from its tatty sleeve and place it on the turntable.

James Hood

Before I set it spinning I get the urge for a cigarette. Actually I get the urge for some of Toby's devilish skunk but what remained of it was smoked last night, so a cigarette will have to do, although technically I don't smoke. There's a packet of Superkings somewhere that somebody left in the car. Reaching inside assorted jacket pockets I successfully locate them. I get that I'm-being-bad feeling as I put one in my mouth.

My hand hovers over the fat volume knob on the amp. I light the cigarette, inhale deeply, get a hit from the nicotine, but feel too guilty to enjoy it.

I open the window to let the smoke escape – I wouldn't want Mum to know I'd been smoking in here – and it occurs to me that the music's loud enough to be heard in the street. Oh it doesn't matter. Bob Dylan's Jewish, I think to myself. Mind you, this being a posh Jewish area the residents aren't too accustomed to loud music in the small hours, or at any time, even by artists born into our own faith.

"What are you doing ...?" My brother has appeared indignant at the door.

"Oh, thanks for knocking, Dan," I snap.

"It's twenty past three."

"I can't sleep."

"Well, that's not going to help." I detect a disparaging tone in his voice. Bob's not really his cup of tea. Or anything I like. More Mozart and Bach, Queen and Elton John.

"I'll turn it down a bit, Dan. Just chill out, man." This is guaranteed to incense him.

"You're smoking!" He points at me in disbelief.

"No I'm not," I say, taking a big drag on the cigarette.

"Mum'll kill you," Dan says with glee.

"Who's going to tell her?"

"I will."

"Oh yeah?"

"Yeah."

"Yeah?" I knock off the glowing end of the cigarette on the corner of the saucer I've been using as an ashtray. I stand slowly upright and then pounce across the room, leaping on Dan. He tries to defend himself spastically, his arms flailing around. I'm pinning him securely enough to wrest one of my hands free and ease it down the back of my pants.

"That was a foolish thing to threaten me with," I suggest.

"Fuck off!" he manages. I'm sitting on him now. My finger's in between my arse cheeks.

"Because you know what's going to happen now, don't you."

"Don't … don't you dare." My finger's in my arsehole. I'm twisting it around to ensure an even coating.

"And I think you'll be truly sorry." I pull my hand out, forefinger extended.

"No …" I slowly move it towards his Fagin-shaped nose. Dan squirms beneath me, desperate to escape. "You … dirty … bastard." With superhuman effort he is somehow freeing himself …

The doorbell rings.

We both freeze. It rings again.

"It's half-past three. Who the fuck could that be?" I ask, as if Dan would know. He's on his feet by now, face pressed against the window. The bell rings once more. A long incessant ring. Whoever it is isn't going to go away.

"Turn the light off," he whispers, somewhat absurdly beneath the music. I stand up and reach for the switch. "Oh shit!"

"What is it?" I hiss, a little concerned.

"You're in trouble." The gleeful tone has returned to his voice.

"Why?" I've joined him at the window by now. "Oh shit!" It doesn't take me long to recognise the agitated figure caught in the porch-light beneath, finger pressed unrelentingly on the bell.

"She's come to complain about the music. Mum's going to kill you." Mrs Zermansky, my parents' next-door neighbour, is not noted for her tolerance. A tough, no-nonsense woman in her late fifties, with an invalid husband to care for. It hadn't occurred to me that my stereo was loud enough to wake her up.

The ringing ceases. Mrs Zermansky steps back and looks up.

"Mrs Franklin!" she calls. There is desperation in her voice. Fear. The wind blows her nightgown about her. Her hair is a messy grey cloud around her head. Wide-eyed and pale-skinned, she looks like something from a Hungarian ghost story. "Mrs Franklin! Please come down!"

"Shit. We'll have to go and speak to her, Dan." I'm beginning to think it's nothing to do with the music at all. She looks terrified, not angry. Perhaps something's happened to Mr Zermansky. Perhaps they need help. Taking on the unfamiliar role of responsible older brother I head downstairs.

I'm shocked to hear her hammering on the door. My heart's racing now and there's a dry metal taste in my mouth. I struggle with the lock and unfamiliar keys.

"Mrs Franklin! Mrs Franklin! Can't you hear?" Even in the dim light of the porch I can see tears rolling down Mrs Zermansky's face.

"Mum's away, Mrs Zermansky. What's the matter? Can we help?" I feel awkward now, as well as frightened, embarrassed at observing the distress of someone I hardly know.

"Can't you hear?" she repeats. She's not talking about the music. Dan's turned it off. I look out into the night. It's black, moonless and the air is dry. A faint wind picks at the leaves which rustle out of sight in the darkness. And there is a sound. I can hear. It's a big sound. A throbbing roar that is both loud and distant but carries a huge sense of scale. It is the sound of a crowd. A giant, roaring crowd. And I understand Mrs Zermansky's fear.

The sound would not have been out of place if you were walking past Elland Road on a Saturday afternoon, or a concert at Roundhay

Park. But this was Alwoodley, at three in the morning in the middle of the week. This isn't the sound of a few stragglers, late back from a club. This is a vast, organised noise. And it's getting louder.

Dan has appeared behind me. He too has heard the unseen rout. The three of us stand there silently registering the noise. Perhaps if we say no more about it it will go away. Perhaps it's nothing to do with us. The chaos at its heart seems to be coming into some kind of focus. The multitude of voices even out in tone. They begin to unify. They begin to sing.

At first I think I recognise the tune, although I can't place it, nor am I able to distinguish any words, but I stand there staggered by the sheer power being carried towards us, a magnified wave of choral might. They sing a marching song, a rallying song, a song that carries them inexorably closer, a human glacier sliding unchallenged through the otherwise silent night.

"They've come for us," whispers Mrs Zermansky staring behind herself. She turns to look at me and Dan. "They've come for the Jews again." She seems to speak with absolute certainty. I say nothing. At this moment I am incapable of speech. I am struck dumb. I feel like I've slipped into an altered state. I am silenced by awe. I feel dwarfed by this vocal power rolling towards me and I'm thinking of watching *The Ten Commandments* as a child and imagining myself wandering between those two towering walls of water in the "Red Sea" sequence: an immense, unthinkably giant force, capable of crushing me out of existence at any moment. Mingling with this sense of wonder is a feeling of profound fear. I have no reason to, but I think that Mrs Zermansky may be right.

Other people have emerged from their houses. Powerful lights have come on, pushing back some of the darkness. A sense of crisis infects the air.

"Run inside. Lock your doors," shouts Mrs Zermansky. Others start calling out to one another, their attempts at calmness betraying a sense

of panic. It's as if everyone knows what to do, as if they've been anticipating this, as if all their lives there has been this unspoken
expectation, shared by every single one of us, so that now it's actually
happening no one is caught by surprise.

I turn around and leave them to it, taking Dan with me. We double
lock the door and I go upstairs in search of another cigarette.

"What's going on? What's going to happen? asks Dan, forcing me
back into that older brother mode.

"I'm going to have a cigarette." I want to avoid acknowledging the
situation we are in.

I can't decide whether to turn the bedroom light on or keep it off.
Is it going to be better if they think the house is empty, and risk them
breaking in and looting? What if they are here to drag us from our
bedrooms into the streets?

All these thoughts. Subtle reminiscences that I've pushed to one side
for the whole of my life suddenly come rushing into my mind. A play-
time at primary school: an older boy accosting me and saying "Jew,
Jew, Jew." Recalling it now the memory seems to be accompanied by
a feeling of jaded familiarity as if this – my first experience of anti-
Semitism – was greeted with a weary "Here we go, then" by my
five-year-old self. Learning to stand in public urinals holding my cock
in such a way as to disguise its circumcised state. Nobody had told me
to do this. I just felt the need to. I must have been about seven or eight.
I remember school assemblies, shoved into a corridor, standing in rest-
less silence while the rest of the school prayed. Then we were ushered
in, a small uncomfortable crowd, who took their seat on the floor
while the Gentile mass looked on, tolerating us. The racism in class
from the first year up. The jolly bigotry of Simon Walker and Nick
Thomas, telling me that Hitler wasn't such a bad bloke, and how he'd
made sure there was a car and a washing machine for every person,
and I was supposed to smile when direct relations, only two generations behind me, had been slaughtered, doubtless by German Simon

Walkers and Nick Thomases. A group of skinheads stopping me and my friends one Saturday evening on Street Lane and asking us if we were Jewish. The terrible moment while we decided whether to answer honestly. In fact, I can't remember what we said but I can remember being head-butted and I think I can remember smiling at my assailant as if the violence was supposed to be a joke I could share.

Why did I never get angry? Was I too frightened? Did I think that if I smiled and laughed, even when I was being kicked, the threat might somehow be nullified? Or was there something else? Something I felt just now when Mrs Zermansky cried out, "They're coming for us!" A belief that somehow we deserved what we got. Wasn't there the flicker of something going through my mind that hinted at a willingness to suffer at their hands, an emotion somewhere between self-martyrdom and self-loathing? Didn't I catch myself responding to her cry of "They're coming!" with my own "At last!"?

"Turn it off," says Dan. I can hear a tremor in his voice which I find terrible because it makes me all the more aware and ashamed of my own fear. There's nothing worse than seeing your family terrified. I remember having a party that was gate-crashed by a load of motorcycle boys. Mum and Dad had refused to go out, instead spending the early part of the evening under siege in the front room before deciding to let us get on with it. But the motorcycles roared and honked outside, and the bikers wouldn't go away. They banged and kicked at the door and my father came down in his dressing gown to threaten them from the corridor. I stood watching blankly as through a pane of glass two worlds confronted one another. The formerly rigid and absolute safety of my family and the violent and unreasoning adolescent realm of my classmates and their unsavoury acquaintances. I realised my dad was no more able to deal with them than I was, it was just that normally he did everything he could to avoid them. Eventually the bikes roared off after the threat of the police was invoked, but I saw the fear in my dad's face and wished that I hadn't.

So I wonder. I wonder what it must have been like for other people. People who were after all probably very similar to me. Pulled from their beds. Kids watching their parents beaten and shoved and kicked. Kids having the safety of their world irreparably shattered. Brutally learning that it was just an illusion, these notions of safety and protection that we connect with our families. Seeing the horror bleach their parents' faces. Knowing they would come to harm while their parents were there with them, as helpless as children themselves.

I just thank God (thank God, that's a laugh) that my mother and father aren't here now.

What's going to happen? What the fuck is going to happen?

The chanting and singing swells through the open window. The wave's going to break any minute now. Dan stands next to me. He holds my arm. I can feel his fingers gripping my skin for fuck's sake. My little brother. I reach out for him.

We both kneel down, trying to obscure ourselves, but desperate to see what's happening at the same time. I realise that when you talk about loving your family, your brother, that it's true. It's not just something you say. I want to kiss him, to hold him, to tell him it's going to be all right.

The noise of the crowd is very loud, like the crash of the sea sampled and played on an endless loop.

They begin to appear. The mass reveals itself as people.

They flood from the ginnel opposite our house, pouring into the street in great numbers, streaming out into the road, around the BMWs, Rovers and Volvos.

I try to see what they look like, these thugs, these bastards, and am surprised to see that they look utterly normal. Nor are they just men. There are women, there are children. They wear normal clothes: suits, jumpers, trainers, skirts, no uniforms, no jackboots. Some of the men are carrying mobile phones.

The phone rings.

Dan looks at me.

"Shall I answer it?" he asks, waiting for a lead. He wants me to tell him what to do. He wants to think that I know how to make everything all right.

"Leave it for a bit," I suggest without knowing why. I'm observing the crowd, scanning them for clues to their behaviour. I can't get over their mundanity. Most of the men with mobiles are holding them to their ears. The others flow out on to the pavements and up the drives. Security lights flick on automatically, stretching the crowd's shadows across the tarmac.

The phone still rings. Impulsively I reach for it. Dan's head flicks nervously from the window to me. I don't say anything. I wait for speech.

"Hello. Mr Franklin?" The voice isn't English. It has a hint of European. The voice knows who we are. Dan stares at me, wide-eyed with fear.

"No. Well yes. Sort of. It's his son."

"Is your father there?" It's not European. More like … Middle Eastern.

"No … who is this?" For some reason I return my attention to the street, to the men with mobile phones.

"Look out of the window."

"I am doing." I can see a figure on the grass verge opposite. He looks tallish, dark, youngish. Plainly dressed in a grey jumper and black trousers. Mobile receiver pressed to his head, which is inclined slightly upwards, in our direction. He could be a dentist on his day off, about to go to the golf club.

"Perhaps I can talk with you?" I don't respond. "Do you know who we are?"

"No." Dan still looks at me, wide-eyed. I squeeze his arm and mouth, "It's OK."

"Can I ask you what you felt, when you heard our approach." Although his turn of phrase is odd, it sounds measured and confident, as if he has said what he is saying many times before. People are still running out of the ginnel entrance into the road. Others are leaving their houses and locking their doors. I don't think the Nazis let anyone lock their doors when they came in the night.

"I ..." I try to speak, but it's not easy to talk about such things, particularly with a plainly dressed Israeli on a mobile phone at half-past three in the morning.

"Can I perhaps make a guess as to what you were feeling?" I get the impression that he is about to launch into a much-repeated spiel, doubtless concerning fear and anger and all those other things I was feeling. I sense this because his tone of voice reminds me of a Lubavitch rabbi. For the first time I begin to get a glimmer of what might be going on. This makes me angry enough to speak.

"How dare you? How dare you? No, you cannot perhaps make a guess as to what I was feeling. Who the fuck do you think you are?" Dan is looking at me quizzically now. He wants to know what's going on, naturally enough.

"Now, Mr Franklin –"

"What is this? Some kind of fucking shock tactic to scare us out of complacency?"

"Yes, Mr Franklin, that is exactly what it is –"

"Well, I think it fucking stinks, you stupid fucking bastards. How dare you? How fucking dare you?"

I'm crying now, tears streaming down my face, oiling the sobs of my anger and fear. I'm surprised at how much I need to weep. Dan puts his arm around me, although he still looks bemused.

"You're not the first person to cry tonight, Mr Franklin. There is a lot of crying to do. I hope you might forgive us when you see that this 'tactic' is, to say the least, effective." I wipe my eyes with the back of my hand and look out of the window. I try to find his eyes, but he's too far away to be able to do that.

"But why? Why do it this way?"

"Because you can't ignore it. And everyone wants to. Isn't that right?" I breathe deeply. Yes, I think, trying to circumnavigate my anger, they do. "But do you see," he continues, "it cannot be ignored this time. We would truly deserve it if we keep our heads buried at the end of this, of all centuries."

Dan still wants to know what's going on.

"It's all right. It really is all right," I tell him. For some reason I'm smiling.

"Who is that with you?" asks the voice.

"My brother."

"Will you join us? Will you both join us?"

"Where are you going?"

"We're collecting. Everyone here, in this city. We're showing ourselves."

"And then where?"

"We'll meet up. With other groups. Will you come?"

Yes, I think. "Yes. Yes!"

And so, with the minimum of preparation, we both leave the house to join the mass that still streams through our formerly quiet street.

Having been away for some time I'm out of touch with a lot of those people around us, but I still recognise faces from my youth. People who I once might have looked away from in the street because I was ashamed to acknowledge my own connection to them. Mrs Tobias, whose youngest daughter I used to fancy something rotten. Mr Delvin, who I remember had the seat in front of my father at shul. Simon Newman, a boy I wanted to look like in adolescence, who I now note has lost most of his hair.

It's not as if I suddenly feel like they are all my family again, or anything corny like that. It's more as if a weight's been lifted from me that someone placed round my shoulders when I was a small child, whenever it was that I first realised I was different from the mass and I interpreted that difference as a lack.

Dan walks next to me. He keeps looking at me with this bemused expression on his face although I can tell that he's enjoying himself. Others around us seem similarly happy, particularly the older people. It feels like a festival, one of the happy ones. There's a man in front of me with a cap and a stick. He keeps laughing out loud and talking to himself and wiping tears away from his eyes.

The men with phones (and there are a lot of them, more than I realised) fall out of the crowd every so often, pausing for conversations on grass verges, persuading others from their homes.

As we walk I hear a voice call my name through the crowd. I turn round to see Marcus Frieze, who was my best friend and next-door neighbour when I was seven years old. I haven't seen him since I was thirteen.

"Marcus!" is all I can manage. Dan says hello too, obviously forgiving us both for the time we tied him to the climbing frame and weed in his hair. "Will you walk with us?"

"Sure," Marcus says.

We talk for a bit, filling each other in on the events of the past fifteen years without referring to what's going on around us. Then people begin to sing. I recognise the tune. "Mo Atz Tzur" it's called, or something like that. You sing it at Chanukah when you light the lights. Marcus looks at me, waiting for me to join in.

"I don't know the words," I admit a little sheepishly.

"Neither do I," he says, "but I can remember the tune." He starts to follow it in "la's", looking at me and Dan and nodding, indicating that we should join in. I only have to think for a second and I realise that I can remember the melody too. I begin to sing quite softly, then as my confidence grows my singing becomes louder. So does Marcus's and so does Dan's. Our voices join the others pouring out into the dark night air and I smile to myself, wishing that Mum and Dad were here to see this fucking incredible sight.

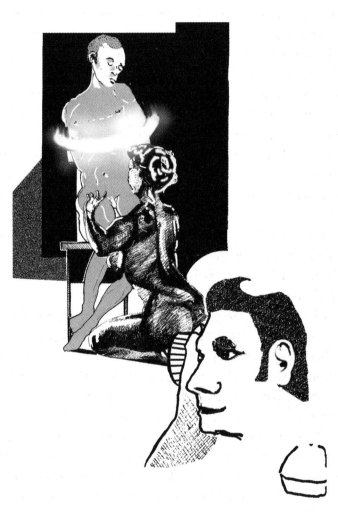

James Hood

Love in the time of Molyneux

Molyneux was Berry's best friend. Berry hated Molyneux. There. It was as simple as that.

They'd known each other for some time, since school in fact. There had been a period where they had drifted apart – or at least not spoken for two or three years. But then Molyneux had got back in touch again when he heard that Berry had been ill. It was Molyneux who resolved that they shouldn't let things drift so easily.

Molyneux was a doctor. His path to medicine had been unconventional. Unlike many medical students he had a genuine vocation. There was no parental pressure influencing his choice of career. Molyneux's family were not wealthy. His father had abandoned them when Molyneux had been a child. His mother had worked hard to raise them well, doing a variety of menial jobs often two at a time, though while Molyneux had flourished, his younger brother had fallen in with a bad crowd and was now addicted to cocaine.

Berry worked in a bookshop called StarGate that sold science fiction and fantasy stuff as well as comics and American magazines. He was not a fan of such material but the work was undemanding and he was very much king of his own castle. He had been employed in the housing benefit office for a time but it was depressing, the sense that you couldn't do anything to change those people's lives. There had also been an abortive relationship with a girl called Anne Louise who later became his supervisor. These factors combined had pushed him into the world of print retail.

Molyneux was not conventionally handsome but he was remarkably attractive. He had thick black hair and dark brown eyes – and although he had been the victim of virulent acne in his teenage years, his skin was now smooth and honey-coloured. He knew how to dress well too – even when he was living on virtually no money. He had an eye for bargains and could throw together marvellous outfits from charity shops and markets. He also had an instinct for good music. Berry remembered how he had bought the *Stone Roses* album three months before anyone else and had dragged him along to see Oasis when they played the Duchess of York, just before *Supersonic* came out. Molyneux was also possessed of disarming sincerity and a sharp sense of humour which made him extremely likeable. Consequently he had never wanted for friends although he was remarkably selective about whom he spent his time with. Long ago, when their association had first begun, Berry had been extremely flattered when Molyneux chose him as a friend. They came into one another's orbit at school in the sixth form although they had been aware of each other's existence prior to that. At first Berry was suspicious. They both liked music and Berry was uncomfortable with the fact that Molyneux might know more about the subject than him. Molyneux, too, had been wary, but a night out dancing in Manchester, followed by an extended smoking and drinking session at Molyneux's mother's house, had sealed their friendship. They had laughed a lot about stupid things, their friendship was secured by an equivalent desire to talk about the problems of the world until the sun came up accompanied by the sounds of Bowie, the Velvet Underground, the Clash and Motown.

While Berry secured temporary employment at the café in the art gallery, having no ambition to pursue his education any further, Molyneux flourished at medical school. This was the first time that Berry had a sense of darker feelings towards his friend. He was surprised by Molyneux's burgeoning ability. At first Berry wasn't sure how he should be about it. He experimented with being proud and boasting about it to other people, but he realised there was something wrong with that. In the end Berry decided he was jealous although he spoke of it to no one.

The first time Molyneux saved him it was to do with money. Berry had got into a bit of trouble. He'd borrowed some money from someone called Chris Woodhall. Berry should have known better for Chris Woodhall was an unsavoury individual, but Woodhall was the only person he knew who always had cash. It was only for paying rent, but he'd missed two months already and if he didn't manage this time he'd lose the bedsit. Berry knew the reason Woodhall had cash was because he was a dealer, but he put the fact to the back of his mind and borrowed the money anyway. It should hardly have been a surprise then, when Woodhall got a bit nasty about being repaid. There was no actual mention of violence but the implication was there. Berry could have gone to his brother, but he couldn't bring himself to admit to his family that he was in a mess. He sat up all night on the edge of tears. He didn't know what to do. In the end he went to the payphone by the front door and called Molyneux in his hall of residence. Two days later Molyneux was there with the cash. He'd spoken to his bank manager and pretended it was for a car. Berry promised to pay him back. (He did – eighteen months later when he got his first Christmas bonus at the benefit office. In fact the whole incident – and Molyneux's rescue – had inspired Berry to find a proper job so he could at least support himself.)

Molyneux's second major intervention had been an emotional one. It was the girl, Anne Louise, Berry had been seeing at work. She'd finished with him. She'd claimed it was because they weren't suited for one another. She wouldn't give much more of an explanation. He then found out she'd been seeing someone else for two of the three months that they'd been together. He was distraught. He was surprised at how upset he was. He couldn't sleep. He couldn't eat. He felt as if he were in pain. The thing was, Anne Louise was the first proper girlfriend he'd ever had. The only girlfriend. Although he was twenty-seven he always found it difficult to be with women. And yes, it was for the obvious reason that he only had one arm.

Berry only had one arm. He hadn't been born that way but he might as well have been because he couldn't remember having two. There had been an accident when he was three years old. A freak thing with a sudden gust of wind blowing a branch down in the garden where he'd been playing. The branch hadn't actually taken the arm off but it had shattered it so badly that the doctors had no choice but to amputate it. He only knew this because his mother had told him many times. He'd been pretty tough when he was growing up. The prosthetics he wore through school were not the most attractive of things. (Even today – regardless of all the advances technology had made elsewhere – they were fairly repellent.) But he'd got through the shouts and the taunts and muttered comments and the people drawing away from him as if he might infect them with a disease of arm-drop-offness. He knew it helped that he had a strong physique and that he wasn't inclined towards self-pity. But – and it was a big but – he couldn't extend the fuck-you attitude he had carefully nurtured through childhood and adolescence to how women were with him. He'd had friendships with them, but somehow they always shied away if he hinted he wanted something more.

From the very beginning of their association Molyneux had been comfortable about Berry's single arm status. Or maybe comfortable was the wrong word. He had always been sympathetic, always considerate. To Berry, who had understandably developed a sensitivity about these things, these qualities were not the same as being comfortable.

"Look at her!" Berry was sitting by the window, staring out into the street. He sat just behind the curtain so whoever was walking past was unable to see him directly.

"You have no shame, do you?" laughed Molyneux.

"What do you mean?"

"You look like my Great Aunty Annie sat there, staring into the road."

"No one can see," said Berry. "Come on. She's going."

Despite himself Molyneux went over to the window and joined his flatmate. "I can't see anyone."

"Well, she's gone now," Berry complained.

"Who was she?" asked Molyneux.

"A gorgeous girl. She had long black hair."

"Go out and find her if you fancied her so much," Molyneux suggested.

"Don't be stupid."

"I'm serious," said Molyneux, looking his flatmate in the eye.

Berry shuffled his chair back so he was even further behind the curtains. "You know I couldn't do anything like that," he bleated.

Molyneux shrugged his shoulders. "I don't see why not. I've got to go to the hospital. I'll see you tonight." Molyneux wrapped his scarf around his neck and was out of the front door.

Berry and Molyneux had been living together for just over a year. After Berry became ill (he'd somehow picked up hepatitis A – not the one that killed you, but pretty nasty all the same) and fully recovered, Molyneux – whom he had not seen for a while – had suggested that they share a house. Berry had been very aware of being alone of late and jumped at the chance. It was Molyneux who located the property on Royal Park Avenue. It was in the middle of student-land but the house was more comfortable than most – with a little fitted kitchen and new gas central heating. Berry liked his bedroom – it had a blue roller-blind and plain carpet and it was close enough to town for him to be able to walk to work. The only problem was Molyneux. It had been fine at first. It was good to have someone to talk to at the end of the day. But after a couple of months Berry realised that it was not like before, not like when they had been eighteen. The thing was, Molyneux was irritating. Not in himself – his behaviour was impeccable and he was consistently amusing and entertaining. It was these very plus points that began to grind on Berry from day to day. His friend's good humour rarely dropped. There was never a time when he wouldn't look for the positive. Or even worse, find it. Molyneux was annoyingly humble too. There was never any sense that he considered himself superior in any way. Rather Molyneux was just comfortable with who he was, at ease in his own skin. Berry longed for something to undermine this infuriating perfection. He found that he would search Molyneux's room in his absence looking for evidence of a dark concealed underbelly. Perhaps a secret cache of vile pornography that would indicate cravings and tendencies other than the wholesome ones suggested by Molyneux's earnest and sincere serial monogamy. (He'd had three relationships in the time that Berry had known him – each of them had ended for seemingly positive reasons, always without rancour. For example he and Jill, his first girlfriend, had made a decision to separate when she had begun university. They both recognised they were still exploring themselves and it would be wrong to make an inappropriate commitment at this time in their lives.) But there was never anything to be found – unlike in Berry's own bedroom, a cursory examination of which would yield up enough distressing material to condemn him even in his own mother's eyes. Molyneux remained pure and that merely added another layer of salt to Berry's slowly growing bitterness.

Later that night – after his return from the geriatric ward – Molyneux was preparing the dinner. It smelt delicious as usual. He seemed uncertain, as if there was something he wanted to say. He stood in the doorway sipping a glass of wine.

"Are you going out tonight?" he said. Berry shook his head. Molyneux stood there for a little longer as if he was going to say something more, then disappeared back into the kitchen.

After a while he came out again and said: "Can we have a talk?"

Berry was surprised and his first thought was that he had done something wrong. He didn't like the serious tone that Molyneux had adopted. Maybe Berry had snooped in his room one too many times, or maybe Molyneux had simply tired of living with him.

"Yeah," was all he managed to get out. Molyneux disappeared back into the kitchen. Berry heard him fiddling with the pans and the cooker. "I was going to do the hoovering later. I know I said I was going to do it this morning but I'd thought I'd wait till after we'd eaten, that's all."

Molyneux emerged once again, smiling. "It's not the hoovering." He perched on the edge of the sofa, resting himself close to Berry's armless side. "It's a bit difficult, that's all. Maybe you should have a drink."

Berry immediately perked up. Perhaps Molyneux was going to tell him he was gay. Maybe he was going to confess to ten years of furtive and sordid encounters as he struggled to repress his true self. And how he had finally lost the battle. There was going to be no nuclear family for Molyneux. It might be even better. Maybe there was kinky stuff. S&M. Humiliation. Coprophilia.

"I'm not quite sure how to say this ..." he began again. "So I think it's best I just come out with it. The thing is, Mike, I'm the Messiah."

Berry looked at him blankly. That wasn't what he'd expected. Had Molyneux gone mad? Berry found himself edging towards the centre of the sofa.

"I know what you're probably thinking," Molyneux continued as he rose and returned to the kitchen. Berry heard him rustling in the fridge. "But it's all true. All that stuff. I am what the Jews call 'Meshiach', others, the Christ. And your flatmate's not going mad. It's been revealed to me."

Finally Berry spoke. "I see."

"Yes. Pretty recently actually," Molyneux continued. He handed Berry the bottle of Becks he'd opened. "And now I've got to save the world."

"Hmm ..." There was a pause. Berry sipped his beer. "How was this revealed to you?"

"It's a bit difficult to explain actually. And anticipating this moment I've got special dispensation to show you something that will help you go along with all this."

"Go along with it?" asked Berry.

"Yes. Because it's important that I have someone to help me bear it," said Molyneux.

"Is ... that me?" Berry inquired nervously.

"Well, you know how it is. Normally I think it would be my mum or my brother but, given how things are, I thought it would be best if it was you." Berry felt like he was being asked to be best man at Molyneux's wedding. He began to run through in his head what his options might be. He could call the police. Was that the correct proce- dure or was it to call the GP? "Anyway ..." Molyneux said.

He did something with his hands, bringing them close to his face. Suddenly the living room was filled with the most enormous and unbearable bright white light and what could have been the ecstatic cries of a thousand angels. Berry simultaneously dropped his bottle of Becks and wet himself. After what seemed an eternity of eternities the noise of all creation ceased.

"Sorry," said Molyneux, "but you understand?" Berry nodded his head slowly. Molyneux approached him and put his arm around his shoulders, shaking him slightly. "You're a good mate."

Berry cleaned himself up and they ate their dinner in silence (mush- room risotto – delicious) then Molyneux said: "I'm going to my room. There's still an awful lot to get my head round. We can talk more tomorrow."

Later Berry lay in the bath trying to make sense of what he had been told. He wasn't religious. He didn't really know what it meant for Molyneux to say he was the Messiah, but, rather disturbingly, now he found he instinctively knew that it was the truth – as if the fact had been burned into his consciousness by the white heat of the "demonstration". As he got out of the bath he heard voices coming from Molyneux's room. Was he talking to God? It was even more distressing – God sounded like Ned Sherrin. Berry stood on the little landing holding his breath. It was only when the pips sounded announcing ten o'clock that he realised Molyneux was listening to Radio 4.

It wasn't easy to get to sleep. There were so many ramifications. If Molyneux was the Messiah, that surely brought a whole lot of other stuff with it. Like the Bible being true – or at least parts of it. And heaven. And sin. And hell. And what about the powers that Molyneux might now possess, now he had come into full being? Powers of healing. Surely it wouldn't be possib … It might be possible that … No. Might it be possible …? He lay there thinking about what Molyneux might be able to do for him. Strangely it brought to mind a memory from when he was six years old. The whole of his year at primary school were being taught their steps for the maypole dance. He was in amongst them, the only one allowed to hold his ribbon in his right hand. However, since this was the wrong hand for the dance he kept forgetting when he should be moving in, and when he should be moving out. He ended up making a mess of the whole thing. Mrs Morris shouted at him and he cried.

Berry would have to talk to Molyneux. He would have to be brave enough to ask him.

"It's not as precisely prescribed as you might think …" Molyneux was explaining the details of his "position", as he kept referring to it, over morning coffee in the Clock Café. "There's no heavenly script with it all written down somewhere about what's going to happen." Berry toyed with a Danish and listened acutely. "Nor is there anybody giving me instructions, or who I have to report to. It's not like Mork and Mindy."

"But how do you know you are … what you say you are?"

"Messiah. It's all right to say it."

The word did not come easily to Berry's lips. Nevertheless he tried. He thought it politic in the circumstances. "Messiah. How do you know?"

Molyneux thought for a moment. "It's a subtle thing, but it's a *definite* thing. Somehow it's more certain and more definite than anything else. Even the chairs we're sitting on or those students over there." Molyneux pointed to a pair of crop-haired young men sharing a large bowl of warm chicken salad. "And what's equally definite is my task. Which is to lead and to inspire through action. And by so doing to perfect the world."

"Is that all?" said Berry sceptically.

Molyneux smiled. "Mike. I can understand how you feel. But it's the way things are. We'll just have to see how it happens."

Berry saw an opening. His heart-rate seemed to have doubled. He took a sip of lukewarm coffee to wet his dry mouth.

"So how will you inspire people? Will you perform miracles and heal the sick, you know, that kind of thing?" Berry asked, hoping Molyneux would infer his subtext.

"Possibly – it depends."

"So that kind of thing is ... do-able?"

"It depends what you mean by 'do-able'," said Molyneux. He wasn't being very helpful here.

"Well," *say it – just say it* "if something had happened to someone close to you, something bad, could you ... reverse it?"

"Mike –"

"Is that something ... something that would be ..."

"Mike, it's –"

"I mean, if somebody got sick or something ..."

"Mike, don't –"

"Or me, for instance, you know, with the accident, I mean my ..." Oh, it was so hard to actually say the word. "... arm. Could you undo that ... for instance –"

"It doesn't work like that," Molyneux interrupted him, with a firmness Berry was unaccustomed to hearing. "It doesn't work like that," he said again, but softer. "I can't intervene so directly ... as I would wish." He took Berry's hand and looked into his eyes. "As I would wish," he said again. The two men looked at each other for some time. After some silence Molyneux continued: "I'm only just beginning to get it, but I know this. It's not a chess game. It's not like Jason and the Argonauts with some all-powerful figure above moving pieces around, making things happen. The only beings with the power to make it better are us – human beings. I think I'm here to bring that about. To make that one point clear." There was another pause. "We'll talk more. I've got to go to work." The Messiah stood up and pulled his anorak on. "I'll see you tonight."

Berry left the café slightly dazed. He very much needed something to remind himself he was an inhabitant of Planet Earth and that he hadn't slipped into something on the shelves at StarGate. Since he was on a late shift he thought he might attend to the washing that had been piling up in the corner of his room.

He could never understand why the launderette didn't have proper seats in it. There was a wooden bench that ran the length of the driers that was a little too wide to sit upon comfortably and a table with a wobbly leg. His prosthesis weighed heavy against his side. He was even more aware of it than usual – the laundry being one of those tasks which having one arm made more difficult, particularly when it was conducted publicly. Thankfully this morning the place was empty and Berry's addled head could be soothed by the mechanical, sloshing roll of his washing. As he shut the machine door he became aware of a subtle but powerful smell – a musky, heady but delightfully feminine perfume. He turned his head and saw the beautiful girl from Royal Park Avenue. She approached an empty washer with a small sports bag. She must have been about nineteen or twenty. She wore light grey trousers and a short camel coat over a clingy brown polo neck. Her hair was dead straight and raven black in the harsh launderette strip-light. Her skin was pale but her lips were full and ruby red. As she loaded the machine Berry caught a glimpse of delicate and lacy black panties and bras. She slammed the door and seeing that he was looking at her she smiled almost to herself. Berry turned away quickly and went to sit on the wobbly table. He had a hard-on.

"Excuse me." Berry turned sharply. She was talking to him. Her eyes were deep green, so unusual it was almost a joke. He felt the colour and the brightness tugging in his lower belly. "Do you have any fifties?"

He searched in his pockets hoping his erection was not visible. "Er, I think so." Actually he didn't think he had any change at all but when he looked in his pocket he discovered six pounds in fifty pence pieces. He handed two over in exchange for her pound. Her hands were smooth, her fingers long and delicate, nails unpainted but neat. He was ashamed of the carnality of his thoughts, even about her fingers. He had a sudden and vivid memory of something a friend had told him once: about being able to tell the nature of a woman's vagina from her fingers; if they were fat and round it would be big and loose; if they were thin and narrow it would be small and tight.

"Thanks." She went to put them in the machine. As the coins dropped in she turned back to Berry. "I'm sorry, but don't I know you?"

"Er ..." He felt hot. He hoped he wasn't blushing.

"Do you live on Royal Park Avenue?" He tried to place her accent. It suggested intelligence without refinement – power and independence.

"Yes." He nodded at the same time as he spoke, like an idiot.

"That'll be it then. So do I. Number 25."

"Are you at the university?" He'd noticed her eyebrows now. They were black and neat and slightly arched. They reminded him of another sexual apocrypha – about being able to tell the colour and style of a woman's pubic hair from her eyebrows.

"My housemate is. I'm just here for a bit." Now Berry found he had an image in his mind of a beautifully neat black pubic mound cupped in a tiny pair of lacy black panties. "Do you want to go for a coffee? I hate waiting in launderettes."

"Yes." His voice was high and cracked. He spoke again, deliberately lowering it. "Yes."

"Come on then." She laughed and touched him on his armless shoulder.

"When did you lose it?"

"I'm sorry?" Berry had to keep making an effort to bring his mind back to her conversation. He was flying too high to think or follow another's thoughts.

"Your arm. When did you lose it? You don't mind me asking, do you?"

"Oh no, erm, when I was three … an accident in the garden."

"How terrible."

"I can't really remember anything about it."

"But it must have been hell growing up."

"Sometimes. Not all the time."

"Michael, I'm going to suggest something now and I don't want you to take it the wrong way – or take me the wrong way, I'm not what you think – but would you like to spend the morning in bed with me?"

There was a pause whilst he looked at her quizzically. After a moment he spoke.

"What about the washing?"

As they walked back to her house, it was only natural that Berry found himself wondering why this was happening. It was also only natural that he thought it unwise to inquire, in case this would jeopardise the proceeding. He did, however, think it sensible to ask the girl's name. She said it was Mary.

Her bedroom was neat and ordered although – in contrast to the rest of the house, which was more conventionally Ikea in style – it was surprisingly theatrical in its décor. There was a lot of black and red and the bed, which was low and large, was placed in the centre of the room.

"Would you like to sit down?" There were no chairs so Berry took his place on the edge of the bed. She removed her camel coat and hung it on her door. She adopted an idiosyncratic pose almost like a dancer, with one foot lifted off the ground. Berry thought it was perhaps the most arousing thing he'd ever seen. "I know this must seem a little strange for you, Michael, but my advice is just to go along with it. You might as well enjoy yourself – and I can guarantee that you will." Berry nodded meekly. If it was a dream there would be no sense in waking up at this point. "But before we continue I have to ask something of you." She grasped the bottom of her jumper and pulled it over her neck. Beneath she was wearing a tight V-neck T-shirt which displayed a spectacular cleavage – whose curves were delineated with such grace and beauty that they resembled a piece of fine graphic art. He found his head was filled with the sensation of inserting his fingers between the two breasts and feeling himself held by their tightness. If just *imagining* felt that good what would it be like to actually do it? "I need you to do one thing for me, a very simple thing." She took a pace towards him, but no more.

"Yes," Berry heard himself saying, or moaning.

"I need you to introduce me to your friend. The one you share a flat with. Molyneux, isn't that his name?" Her fingers worked with the fly button of her trousers.

"Yeeeeessss!"

"You don't really need to know the ins and outs of it, but I need an introduction – if I'm going to get to him – from somebody he trusts."

She began to inch the trousers down. The top of her panties was exposed, dark and shiny – like unwrapped chocolate of the finest quality. "I don't want to be a pain about it, but if we're to continue I need you to agree." He nodded in clarification. She smiled. "It will be worth it." She stepped out of her trousers with uncanny grace, then knelt down before him. One of her thighs was covered with an extraordinary red birthmark. It spread across her pale skin like a map of some imaginary country. Somehow it only added to her beauty. "We won't go all the way today, but if things go well – with your friend, I mean – we will another time." She reached for his trousers and released his iron penis, moving towards it. "Let's make a start then," she said. Berry closed his eyes and thanked God that he was alive for this moment.

When they were lying on the bed later, Berry broke the silence. He thought for some time about what he was going to say and settled on a simple question:

"What's going on?"

The girl smiled. There was another lengthy pause before she responded. "The thing is, Michael, your friend … he's got it all wrong."

"Got all what wrong?"

"All. Everything. His … people are acting on behalf of perfection. It's unnatural. We're only interested in preserving a delicate balance."

"Who's we? Who're his people? Who …"

She put a fragranced finger to his lips. "I can't really explain so you'd understand." She sprang upright. He noticed for the first time that there were delicate black hairs surrounding one of her nipples, like lashes around an eye. She sat herself astride him. "Let's try something very few other people could." She reached behind his back and levered him from the bed. Her hands worked with the straps of his prosthesis. It came away with ease and Berry found himself more naked than he had ever been in the presence of a woman.

"Please ..." he began but she silenced him again. Her hands began to stroke his chest.

"It's all right. It's OK ..." Her voice was like song. Slowly she moved her hands along his side and delicately brought them up to the skin beneath his shoulder blade where his arm once hung. Her touch was divine. Berry found he was hard again. "There's nothing wrong here, nothing ..." She lowered her head and began kissing his neck, working her lips slowly down. Soon they found the mound of skin that Berry himself avoided touching, never mind anyone else. "You are as you are, Michael," she said in between kisses. Soon his eyes were closed and he felt her pressing other parts of herself against him. Slowly, very slowly, he received a sense of her whole body through that part of himself that he had made taboo. Her hardness, her softness, her wetness. Somehow through her skill and sensitivity he became more excited than he had when she had worked directly on his cock. He felt the beginnings of an orgasm's approach except it was larger, huger, more profound than any climax he had experienced before. He was floating in a dark place now, but there were warm waves pulling at him from a great distance. "Let go," he heard her say, "it's OK. Just let go." And, although he was frightened, something did let go and he was pulled, almost through a tunnel, with no sense of being a person any more until he returned in an incredible release, reunited with his voice which was calling out at great volume, filling the emptiness of the room.

The concept of time returned to him and he became aware of his breath. The girl sat upright on the bed next to him. She held him and he began to cry.

Later she explained that there was no need for anything complicated. All he had to do was invite her round one night when he was sure Molyneux was going to be in and to be very casual about the circumstances in which they met. On no account was he to mention that there had been anything sexual between them. It would be useful too if he could deny any physical attraction to her. Then, later in the evening, if he could go to his room, she would do the rest. She had no worries about pulling off a successful temptation. It seemed that was what she did best.

"And how will this stop ... his Messiahship?"

"Let's just say that energy will be neutralised."

"But won't he ... burn in hell or something for all eternity?" asked Berry.

She laughed her throaty laugh in reply. "Oh, you can't believe all that rubbish. No. He'll be eaten up with guilt for a time, I'm sure, but he'll just become a man again, that's all. Like you."

There was an uncomfortable pause. Berry was mustering courage.

"And what about us ...?" he faltered.

She smiled at him. "I'll have to be on my way again, I'm afraid, but I can pay you one more visit if you like – and we can spend an evening together, the memory of which will bring a smile to your lips for the rest of your life. How does that sound?" Berry put his arm behind his head and lay back on the bed.

"Pretty good."

Molyneux returned home that night in a very happy mood. It seemed his speedy intervention had saved the life of a newborn child, whose brief span the maternity ward staff had decided was already over. The baby's mother was a local newsreader of some popularity and the story was covered on that night's *Look North*.

"There was nothing premeditated about it," said Molyneux as Berry stared at the television with an expression of mild distaste. "The opportunity presented itself, that's all. I was only doing what I'd do anyway." Berry thought the action seemed a little cheap and obvious but he refrained from saying so. "Do you want some dinner?"

As Molyneux pottered in the kitchen, Berry started to mull over the implications of everything that had happened. Might he be about to make a terrible mistake? The cooling memory of the girl's lips at his shoulder extinguished the question in his mind before it could be kindled into fuller debate.

"Mate," he called into the kitchen, "are you going to be in tomorrow night?"

Berry explained that he wanted to cook for a change, without mentioning the girl. He considered it prudent to have her arrival seem a surprise – as if the invitation had been a matter of such little consequence to him that he hadn't thought it worth referring to. Although he had never regarded himself as an actor he found he relished playing his part with some subtlety. In order not to arouse suspicion Berry would behave in such a way as to imply that he hadn't mentioned anything because he wanted to impress his flatmate with his casualness. The hope was that Molyneux would, in his usual way, think he had Berry sussed, and choose to go along with things as a knowing parent might indulge a six-year-old child.

Indeed this was how it happened. The girl arrived about nine thirty. She was dressed completely differently, almost chastely, although still with allure. She wore a long grey woollen dress with a black long-sleeved T-shirt beneath. It suggested intelligence and cultivation rather that predatory sexuality, although there was something about the way the dress hung around her curves that hinted at an explosive sexuality beneath. Berry explained that he "forgot to mention" he'd invited her around to dinner. Molyneux smiled his indulgent smile. Soon the three of them were getting on like old friends, laughing about embarrassing incidents from their school days and adolescence.

Berry knew it was important that he signal an authentic lack of interest in the girl to Molyneux, in such a way that he communicated he wasn't being shy. Once again he was surprised to find he had been endowed with the acting skill of Kevin Spacey. The girl had nipped upstairs to the bathroom, and Molyneux began an elaborate dumb-show, winking and pulling a face that suggested something like "Good on you, son." Berry responded with a shrug of the shoulders and a slight grimace, implying "I dunno, I don't really fancy her." This was followed with an incredulous raising of the eyebrows from Molyneux that said "Come on!", capped with a convincing brow furrow from Berry adamantly stating "No, I mean it" just as the girl returned. Her performance was even more exceptional – not even a conspiratorial glance when Molyneux was out of the room. So when the moment came for Berry to retire, it seemed to have sprung so naturally from the turn of the conversation that even a paranoid schizophrenic would have been comfortable with the motivation.

As Berry mounted the stairs he heard Molyneux laughing, lewdly and loudly as if at an off-colour joke. He smiled to himself and entered his room.

He undressed and took off his false arm, laying it with surprising care on the chair near the window. He sat for some time with the curtains open, staring at the receding pools of orange streetlights that ran down Royal Park Avenue. Then he got into bed, lying in his usual position. After a time he turned over, resting on his armless side. He drifted off to sleep. He dreamt about the maypole dance. He was back there with the six-year-olds, tripping in and out of their bare-legged revelry with a random choreography all of his own. Mrs Morris was calling to him to stop but he didn't care. He savoured the thrill of his own wild jig. He looked up at the maypole. There was no order to the interlacing pattern of red, white and blue traced by the tapes but it was beautiful all the same. He laughed and danced until he was woken by two sets of footsteps climbing the stairs below, trying to be silent.

Sometime later there might have been a sound, subtle, huge and low. It could have been the earth sighing, although it was impossible to say whether with regret or relief. Whatever, he thought. The main thing was Molyneux had finally fucked it up and that night Berry slept better than he had done for twenty-seven years.

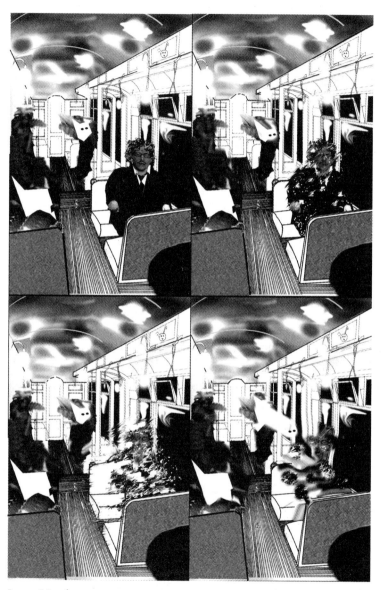

James Hood

City deep

Foster hated the Tube. He hated it because he feared it. His fears were grounded in a combination of claustrophobia and pessimism. The intolerant crushing crowd, the confined carriages, the tight tunnels that pressed in around the trains, the sense of weight above: concrete, basements, roads. All these factors were at the front of Foster's mind when he reluctantly rode the lines that wormed their way through London's depths.

Perhaps his fears might have been reined in if he had more faith in the management and working procedures of the London Underground – but the constant "fire scares" and the stifling delays merely fed his phobias and made them more real. At any time it seemed the train he was riding might collide with another. Some terrible bomb left by a vengeful terrorist might explode, bringing London crashing down to crush his carriage. Perhaps a fireball belched from the Victorian bowels of the archaic system might roar down the tunnel, engulfing the coaches, baking their screaming occupants alive. These terrors, while Foster acknowledged their improbability, were all plausible enough to keep him from using the Tube whenever he could.

His work, thank God, did not necessitate much travel. His position as a sales co-ordinator for a small building publication kept him safely within an office off Tottenham Court Road. His flat in Hammersmith could be reached as easily, if not as quickly, by the Number 9 bus as by the Piccadilly Line. And so, over the years, he had reached a tolerable enough compromise. He had to leave half an hour earlier in the morning and accept less time at home in the evenings, but it was a small price to pay for his peace of mind. Without even noticing it, his life had been shaped by his fears. Friends who did not live on the bus routes were neglected, venues not easily visited overground remained unvisited, and large areas of the capital city had become, albeit subconsciously, out of bounds. Perhaps if Foster had bought a car – for he could drive – his social life would have been more eventful, but it was an action that had been postponed once too often for it to become a reality.

If Foster had voiced his dread more frequently, maybe it would have become manageable, but fear of ridicule had kept it internalised so that it had become ingrained within his psyche and remained there like a dark stain. On the few occasions he had been forced to venture underground (an appointment at St Bartholomew's Hospital, a nightmarish trip to Heathrow), he had spent each journey in a state of abject terror, perched on the edge of his seat, reacting frantically to every tortured scream of the rolling stock as if it hailed an imminent destruction.

And yet, despite all this antipathy, Foster now seriously considered descending the steps at Piccadilly Circus. It was pouring with rain. Worse than pouring. Great sheets of water tumbled from above, dispersing in the freezing wind. It was six thirty. Every other bus but his had been past five times. He was becoming increasingly annoyed as Number 14s paraded round the corner of Haymarket in groups of two or sometimes three, even though nobody wanted to board them. Similarly, clutches of 19s made their way empty to Battersea Bridge, as did every other bus apart from his that stopped at the top of Piccadilly. What looked teasingly like a figure 9 as it trundled through the downpour would become a 21 as the vehicle drew closer.

Foster was cold enough and wet enough to think about entering the warmer and considerably drier environment of the Tube. After all, it was only ten or fifteen minutes at the most. He had the *Standard* to read and then he would be home. The rush hour was in its closing minutes, the weather having discouraged people from lingering in the

West End. He could at least be sure of getting a seat. It was decided. Purposefully he looked at his watch, tutted loudly so that observers might understand his behaviour, and marched toward the pelican crossing.

The rain became noticeably heavier, balls of water falling from the skies, bouncing off the flooded pavements. Eros cursed the heavens with his bow as Foster entered the station.

People stood dripping in the golden glow of the renovated concourse. Most seemed to be sheltering from the rain. Suddenly Foster was seized with an urge to join them, to wait for the storm to pass and return to the bus stop. However, with a great effort of will, he walked resolutely toward the ticket machine and paid for his journey. This would do him good. It would prove that he was still able to overcome his fear in the face of necessity and therefore that it was founded in common sense, not neurosis.

The entrance gate swallowed his ticket, ejecting it as he passed through. The escalators yawned ahead of him, waiting to take him to the station's belly. He stepped on and looked down at his distant destination. Strange to experience vertigo underground. Hamburgers and pizzas slipped slowly past, marking his descent. Once the length of these moving staircases had filled him with awe. They were monuments to their creators' ingenuity, carrying endless lines of passengers elegantly up and down. Now their extension was daunting, merely reminding Foster how far he was actually slipping beneath the surface of the city. And their age made him nervous, bringing to mind the decrepitude of the whole system.

He watched the faces rising toward him, all of them raised in anticipation of surfacing, or so it seemed. Did they share his fears? Were they relieved to reach fresh air? Or was he alone in his anxiety?

The tinny sound of a busker drifted closer as the steps flattened out, depositing Foster on the walkway. An impatient businessman pushed past him, rushing hopelessly toward a distantly departing train. Foster mentally congratulated himself on his calmness and strode casually around the corner to the second escalator, the one that would carry him to the Piccadilly Line platform.

The light seemed brighter down here, the air drier, removed as he was from the stormy conditions of the streets. In fact, it occurred to him that this was one of the advantages of an underground transportation system: the consistency of the atmosphere. Passengers could wait for trains without being frozen or soaked. There was a certain sense of shelter in depth. Which was why Foster found it strange to see puddles on the floor when he reached the bottom.

"It's been dripping all day," the morose-looking busker informed him, putting down his guitar. "Whole bloody place is falling to pieces." Foster tried to smile in agreement, as if the decayed state of the station was something that amused him. He threw a couple of coins into the busker's empty cap and passed through the arch down the tunnel towards the trains.

How appropriate a vernacular "the Tube" was, thought Foster, on this last leg of his voyage to the Piccadilly Line platform, for it referred not just to the tunnels through which the trains passed, but to the shape of the pedestrian passages as well.

A rush of air met his face, heralding the imminent arrival of his train. He ran the last few yards, panting as he reached the platform – which seemed astonishingly empty. The grey carriages poured screaming out of the black mouth of the tunnel, and as they came to a halt, the doors snapped open. Foster jumped on board, wiping away the water that had dripped on to him from the roof above.

The doors slid shut as he found a seat in the sparsely populated carriage. Its few occupants were hidden behind newspapers. He waited for the train to move. The platform remained immobile. He read an advertisement for Kelly Girls written in the style of a diary entry. Whatever a Kelly Girl was, she led a very drab life. The outside world juddered once and became still again. Foster suppressed a flash of panic.

He had been doing well, but this pause in his motion had allowed his usual fears to begin their slow ascent. What if the train remains stuck here? What if the doors won't open? What if there's a fire? What if there's a bomb? What if? What if? What if? These negative hypotheses spiralled upward together, taking his heartbeat with them.

"Stop it," he said firmly to himself, trying to regain reality before it slipped away altogether.

"It's the rain," said the man opposite, which didn't help matters. Unless things had changed since he'd last journeyed on the Tube, it was not the done thing to converse with one's fellow passengers. "I said, it's the rain." It was no good. Foster had been singled out to join this unusually talkative commuter in conversation, whether he liked it or not. "It does things to the rails when it gets in. Shorts them out." Foster wasn't sure he wanted to hear any of this. He had enough difficulty dealing with his own imaginary fears; he did not wish to share anybody else's. "I used to work the tunnels, see."

"Really?" Foster responded dutifully. However, he found his curiosity was sparked, despite himself, as people are often intrigued by things which they morbidly fear.

"Yeah. Before I was a driver. Started just after they opened Leicester Square station." Foster looked incredulous. The few strands of his fellow traveller's grey hair suggested age, but his soft pink skin made him look no older than sixty. "1935. I can remember it like it were yesterday. Fifteen I was." A few *Standards* rustled further down the carriage, wielded defensively against this all-too-public autobiography. He continued unabated. "There was a flood in one of the Northern Line tunnels then, even though it was May. They had to divert some steam engines from up the line to keep it going."

"They had steam engines ... down here?" Foster had assumed the Tube had always been electric.

"Oh yeah, right up until the sixties." Quite suddenly, the train shuddered into life and swept off toward Green Park.

"I thought we were never going to leave. You sometimes think the whole place is going to fall down on your head."

"Oh, there's no danger of that, mate. They knew how to build things in those days. The electrics might go occasionally, but these tunnels are built to last. Even the ones they don't use any more are still in good nick."

"What do you mean, 'the ones they don't use any more'?"

"There's a load, extra lines built at the start of the war. Bet you didn't know about the one between Whitehall and the Palace."

"No, I didn't."

"Then of course there's the Coronation Line." There was a hint of conspiratorial pride in the man's voice, as if he was imparting some treasured secret.

"The Coronation Line? Which one's that?"

"It was an extension of the old Metropolitan Line which used to run between Paddington and Farringdon at the end of the last century. It went right through Shepherd's Bush, Kensington, Hyde Park Corner, up through the West End and back to Farringdon via Holborn. In fact, we're in a bit of it now."

"Really?" Foster was genuinely intrigued.

"Yeah. This stretch of the Piccadilly Line between Holborn and Green Park was part of it. 'Course it had a load of stations of its own which they don't use any more: Sussex Square, Craven Hill, Moscow Road. They built over 'em but they're still there."

"Why don't they use it any more? London could do with another line, I would have thought."

"They couldn't use it now, not without knocking down half the new office blocks in London to reopen the stations." He stared out of the window into the strobing blackness beyond. "Anyway they're still probably 'prohibited'." Green Park arrived to halt the man's discourse. Foster was too fascinated to tolerate a pause.

"What do you mean, 'prohibited'?"

The man looked at him as if he was weighing Foster up, deciding whether or not he was a worthy recipient of this information. He must have reached a positive conclusion, for he leaned forward and lowered his voice:

"Well, it hadn't been in use as a line since the turn of the century. The company that owned it went bust. The Piccadilly Line was opened in 1906, and the Coronation had been closed at least a couple of years before that. But in '37, just after I started working, they were getting ready for the war – that's how I knew there was going to be a war – and they were talking of using the Underground for air-raid shelters. Well, they was going to reopen the whole of the Coronation Line and put beds down there, a sort of massive dormitory. Some of my mates started on the cleaning-up, but then the army took over. They must have changed their minds 'cos they never used it for civilians."

"You mean the army used it for themselves?"

"That's what we reckoned. You see, the Coronation Line ran deeper than just about anything else in London. The army decided it was perfect for testing – there was s'posed to be all sorts of secret weapons on the go – and the whole thing remained off-limits right through the war." Green Park slipped backward, replaced once more by the conspiratorial blackness of the tunnel. "They kept it sealed off, though. All sorts of rumours went flying. We 'eard that they'd found things." He paused slightly. Foster couldn't resist the urge for clarification.

"What do you mean, 'found things'? What sort of 'things'?"

His companion leaned even closer, lowering his voice yet again.

"Strange things," he whispered. "Tunnels that weren't man-made and that went down." He made an appropriate gesture with his finger. "Old things like you get in a museum: pots, flints, spears."

"Spears!"

"Bones, skulls, all sorts."

"Are you suggesting there was a prehistoric community *down here*?"

"I ain't suggesting anything. I'm telling you what I heard. Anyway, it wasn't just what they found. We heard some soldiers had disappeared. Went investigating one of the tunnels and never came back."

"I don't understand. Where could they have possibly gone to?"

The man shrugged his shoulders theatrically. "Who knows? I will say this though: it never surprised me. Every driver's got his own story. Things he's seen on the late runs. There was even a story about how they lost a train once, complete with all its passengers."

"I don't believe it."

"Oh, I do. There's old things down here. Things best left undisturbed. I can remember when I was cleaning tunnels – we had to defluff them every night, the tracks get clogged up with hair. I used to hear things, chitterings and scratchings, like monkeys at the zoo."

Suddenly the train shuddered to a halt, although Hyde Park Corner was still some distance away. Foster tensed in his seat, gripping the upholstery with fear-stiffened fingers. This was what he hated the most; when the motion ceased in between stations, he suddenly became aware of his location, hundreds of feet beneath the city, frozen in concrete. His alarm must have been noticeable, for his companion tried to comfort him.

"'Ere, there's nothing to worry about. It's just a logjam. One train gets delayed at a station, the one behind has to stay where it is. You're a nervy devil, aren't you?" Foster started playing with his hair and pulling at the skin of his neck as he always did when agitated. The other passengers still steadfastly shielded themselves with their evening papers, some of which were being shaken with more than usual vigour as the pages were turned.

"I ... I get claustrophobic sometimes," he proffered, aware how foolish his fear must seem to this hardened subterranean.

"Just relax. We won't stop for long. No matter what the problem is, the priority's always to keep things moving." The lights dimmed and flickered, and for one terrible moment Foster thought that they would be abandoned to the darkness altogether, but they soon returned to their usual intensity. There was an enormous creaking and screeching of metal as movement was resumed. " Told you!" the man declared triumphantly. Foster relaxed a little. He tried to remember what it was he was going to ask, but the sharp fear had driven the questions from his mind. "You see, we're quite safe down here," his companion continued. "Quite safe. I've spent me whole life down 'ere, and no 'arm's ever come to me."

The train began to slow in anticipation of the next station. Foster had to admit he was tempted to get out. The rain must have eased off a little by now, and he could catch a Number 10 as well as a Number 9 from Hyde Park Corner. He could have a cigarette while he waited. Reaching for his briefcase, he eased himself out of the seat, ready to get out when the doors opened.

"You getting off 'ere, then?" the man smiled at him.

"Yes, yes. Thank you for the history lesson. It was most interesting."

The train slowed to a stop. Foster peered through the glass, waiting for the doors to open. The sign on the wall read "Cumberland Gate", clearly illuminated by the gas lights above it. The doors slid open, revealing the silent platform beyond. There were no people, although Foster noticed that green filing cabinets somewhat absurdly lined one of the walls, partly obscuring a large Ovaltine poster.

"I must have lost track of the stations," he said to the man, who was still smiling. Before he could decide whether to step down to the concrete, the doors had closed once again and the train had resumed its journey. Unsure quite what to do, Foster returned to his seat. None of the other passengers seemed concerned about the disappearance of Hyde Park Corner. They remained resolutely hidden behind their papers. Only their hands were visible, fat and pink, all without fingernails.

"When they retired me, I couldn't cope with life up there. After all, I wasn't used to it." The man had resumed his autobiography, somewhat inappropriately Foster thought, feeling the embers of his panic rekindling themselves. "I kept coming back down 'ere, on me own. Did a bit of exploring. Couldn't believe what I found. I was made welcome, so I decided to stay. It's much safer down here."

As if on cue, the papers were lowered. Strangely, it was only then that Foster noticed that they all carried different headlines, all referring to long-gone events.

"We do like to get dressed up and go for a ride every so often, though. See what we can find."

Foster was reminded of fairground chimps wearing human clothes. Except these mockeries of mankind were completely hairless, their eyes huge and white, their lips slack and wet. The lights went out before he could study them more closely.

"And they've taught me so many things." Even in the darkness, Foster could sense they were travelling downward at an alarming rate, and he would have screamed were it not for the soft fingers that filled his mouth. "You won't believe what's down 'ere!" the man reiterated gleefully as the train shrieked onward through London's ancient bowels.

A last look at the sea

"Look, here's the windmill. I didn't think we were that close." This had always been one of George's favourite sights. Partly because it was the first "sign" that Long Cross was getting near and partly because of how it looked. There was something magical about the way the white arm swooped out of the horizon, disappearing into the turf of the moor before reappearing a few moments later. Then as you came over the brow of the hill the whole structure was revealed – a huge, slightly conical post, five storeys high, with the great arm turning unstoppably, its weight somehow apparent in the speed of its motion.

"Can we stop?"

"I knew you were going to ask that."

"No, you didn't."

"You always ask." Tessa smiled as she slowed the car. "But I don't mind."

She pulled up on one of the grassy banks, not bothering to make a good job of it since there wasn't much traffic. She shivered a little as they got out. A brisk wind blew off the still-distant sea. It brought a hint of salt to the empty moor. George had run up to the base of the windmill, or as close as the barbed wire would allow him.

"You can hear it. That's what I like most." The swoosh of displaced air was surprisingly loud.

"Why don't you go and stand right under it?"

"You're not allowed."

"No one's going to see."

"You know I can't."

James Hood

"Just climb over the wire." George shook his head. Tessa smiled. There was a little pause before she added: "You like it because it's big too, don't you?" He nodded like a child who was being indulged. Another pause, then: "That's your trouble. You're too easily impressed."

"You don't think that's big?" He gestured to the windmill.

"Not by my standards."

"You've got me worried now." He looked her in the eye, the corners of his mouth turning slightly, no longer a child.

"You've nothing to worry about." She moved behind him, put a hand on his bottom and pushed him towards the car.

If any place could still truly be described as being in the middle of nowhere, then it was Long Cross. Half-way along the north coast of Cornwall, four miles from the nearest village, which wasn't even really a village, perching defiantly on the side of a cliff – a strange monument to Victorian stubbornness. George and Tessa had found it in an old book when they were staying in another, more ordinary B&B in Brighton the previous year – just after they'd started seeing each other.

"*Off the Beaten Track.*"

"Hmm?"

"*Off the Beaten Track.*" Tessa read from the back of the battered paperback she'd pulled from the shelf. "A guide for the traveller who likes to escape." George had lifted her T-shirt and was kissing her tummy. She carried on reading, deliberately ignoring what he was doing to her. "Do you yearn for a place a million miles from anywhere, where you can put life's difficulties on one side and forget about everything? Then this is the book for you. Listed within are over 300 separate establishments – all of them truly 'off the beaten track'." He had unpopped the fly button of her jeans and begun to lower her zip. She dropped the book on the bed.

Back at the flat in Finsbury Park George had been surprised to see the book poking boldly out of her travel bag.

"You can't just take things," he protested.

"Yes, you can."

"What if someone sees?"

"Oh, George. What do you think's going to happen?"

The objection to her spontaneity didn't prevent him from browsing in the book. In fact it became quite a favourite of his – mainly because its age led him to assume the contents were long out of date and that therefore he was gazing through a window into a dreamy, unvisitable past.

"I bet you'll find they're all still there," Tessa had said one evening as he flicked through its yellowing pages.

"Tessa. It cost 99p. Look." He showed her the back cover – and then the flyleaf that stated the book's date of publication as 1971.

"I'll prove it to you. Go on. Pick one." He searched for the most antiquated photograph he could find. A few moments flicking led him to an engraving of a stern-looking Victorian residence with a florid description beneath: "*Long Cross Victorian Country House and Gardens. Maxwell and Jennifer Fenton invite you to join them at their distinctive cliff-top retreat. Once famous for its Victorian maze garden (now unfortunately in a state of disrepair), Long Cross still offers unparalleled views over the Atlantic and is ideally situated for those who enjoy walks along Cornwall's splendid coastal paths. March–October. Bed and Breakfast £5.50. Evening Meal Supplement £2.00. No Dogs.*" Beneath was another engraving, presumably of the dilapidated maze garden. It showed a Venus-like sculpture, tightly cloaked in ivy, making it appear as if she were growing from the ground, like a tree.

"Ooh, let's go there." Tessa bounced up and down on her knees demonstrating excitement.

"I think you'll find, my dear, that Long Cross has probably long since vanished into the sea."

"I bet you it hasn't." She snatched the book off him. "It doesn't look like the kind of place that would just crumble away."

"Give me it back. It's mine."

"I stole it. Anyway, if you moved in with me, it could be ours." Tessa got down off the bed. She put the book in her bag.

Three days later she announced that she had telephoned Long Cross and booked them in for a long weekend. Maxwell and Jennifer Fenton were long dead, but the place was still open for business, now run by another couple – the Freans, who had renovated the garden and installed central heating. George could imagine the conversation. Tessa would talk to anybody at great length without fear. But then she did most things without fear.

"Let's really explore this time." She had wound down the window even though it was far too cold.

"The maze garden?"

"No. Cornwall."

"But you've got to be back on Wednesday."

"Well, around Long Cross. We've never done the cliff walk."

"It's dangerous."

"It's not dangerous." Tessa laughed. "It's a wonder you get out of bed in the mornings." They had been to Long Cross twice before. The first time had been a shared adventure – discovering the house and its forbidding beauty. The extraordinary garden with its absurd profusion of details. The colour of the sea – a vivid, tropical blue seemingly at odds with the Atlantic wind that rolled off it. It was the first time either of them had been to Cornwall and it took them both by surprise. It was like another country. The second visit had coincided with their six-month anniversary. Tessa had wanted to go abroad – Amsterdam or Barcelona – but George claimed it would be difficult to get the time off work: couldn't they go somewhere in this country? Normally Tessa hated to do the same thing twice, whereas George liked it. Tessa took some persuading but George knew she had enjoyed Long Cross as much as he had – albeit for different reasons. George had accepted she would never have agreed to a third visit were it not for the fact she was going away.

The first hint of the night had begun to spread across the sky. Late September, but still summer in spirit, there were no clouds. A nearly full moon was visible in the upper left corner of the windscreen.

"There, there." George pointed with extravagant mock-anger at the tiny road they had just driven past. "The signpost to Trelights."

"All right," Tessa protested. "It's not as if we do this journey every day." She backed up far too fast and turned the steering wheel sharply. Overhanging branches brushed noisily against the side of the car. Within five minutes they saw Long Cross up ahead, the only geometry visible, against a horizon broken with the crinkle of hawthorn hedges.

"This is the point I expect some dark figure to step out into the middle of the road."

Tessa raised her eyebrows: "Can't you ever imagine anything good?"

They rounded the corner into the car-park, past the sign advertising cream teas, and the barn with its renovated weathercock. Tessa pulled up in front of the glass-fronted porch.

"Let's put our things inside and go and walk round the garden, before it gets dark."

"I knew you'd want to do that too."

"Don't you?"

"It'd be nice to see it again."

They went through the usual procedure for checking in: standing in the oak-panelled entrance hall that smelt like an antiques shop, waiting for one of the Freans to emerge from the door marked "Private" carrying the leather-bound guest book. Signing in. Small talk on the walk up to the room. Hoping for a sea-view. They dumped their bags then hurried outside again, down to the garden.

You rounded a corner into a children's play area. Chickens strutted around a see-saw. At the bottom, at one end of a long, brick-built cloche, was a wall of heavy green hedge. In its centre was a low wrought-iron gate, at one side of a small wooden honesty box on a post. You were supposed to leave 50p if you went in – although guests had free access. The wind was stronger here than on the moors. Its bite was keen. The sky was a dark blue now. It was hard to see colours.

"It's freezing." George put his arm around Tessa. She responded with hers. They pressed themselves together. George turned to kiss her. She kissed him back.

"Come on then." Still holding him tightly she ran them both to the entrance.

The gate squeaked open and they passed within. Immediately they were surrounded by walls of spruce, higher than both of them. The wind all but disappeared.

"I didn't use to feel this cold," said George.

"You're getting old, aren't you."

"In eight and a half years you'll be just as old as me, so there's no point in being smug about it."

"I'll never be as old as you." She let go of him and ran off down the path, before disappearing around a corner. He chased after her.

The maze garden wasn't really a maze. It wasn't a puzzle to be solved. Rather it was an example of dogged Victorian ingenuity. The patch of cliff-side that had been chosen was particularly exposed and vulnerable to the force of the adjacent ocean. Virtually anything that had been planted there would not have survived a season. But Long Cross's architect was not about to deprive his clients of their garden pleasures. By constructing a series of high and sturdy hedges, it was possible to create patches of peace and serenity untouched by whatever gale roared beyond. Hence the garden was able to contain hydrangeas and even peonies which flourished, for the general climate was temperate, it was only the sea which brought the extremes. There were so many corners that the design had made a feature of them by making it a surprise what lay around each one. A pool with giant water lilies floating around a reproduction of Michelangelo's *David*. An oak gazebo with wicker benches. A small enclosure containing well-fed-looking goats. It was intriguing in itself that so much variety had been packed into such a small space.

George proceeded stealthily. There was no sign of Tessa. He headed for the bottom end of the garden which backed on to the cliff's edge. There was a little turret in one corner with a spiral staircase. You could climb it and look out over the ocean. He always felt deliciously safe leaning out over the sea but with the thick stone wall pressed against his chest, holding him up against the wind.

"You're dead!" Tessa shouted. George nearly fell to the ground as she leapt on his back from behind. "You weren't being very careful, were you," she giggled.

"I didn't care." George shrugged his shoulders.

"As if," said Tessa, putting her arms around him.

"Look at that." George gestured with a nod of his head. They stood together in the turret looking out over the choppy ocean. It was black now, broken with thin white waves, like creases in crumpled origami paper. "You won't have that in America."

"Actually, I think you'll find that New York is by the sea."

"I know, but it's not the same, is it? There're no cliffs, or windswept Victorian gardens to look out from." She didn't say anything for a minute. He took the opportunity to add: "Or me to look at it with."

"And whose fault is that? It's not as if you're not invited."

"Oh. And what am I supposed to do? Pack in my job and come and live in Manhattan?" grumbled George.

"Yes!" She turned from the sea to look at him. He carried on staring at the turbulent water.

"Well, I'll be visiting, won't I? And it's only a year."

Tessa faced the sea again. "Only a year," she nodded.

They left the turret and walked slowly in silence round the rest of the garden's perimeter, finally exiting through the gate at the top where the spruce branches almost met overhead, making a tunnel. It was dark now and hard to see anything. They hurried towards the lights and warmth of the hotel.

"It's hard to believe that my name is Steve, and yours is Matilda so – clear are the signs that you're made of wine and I'm made of diddly doe." The old man at the table behind them broke down laughing as he finished his incomprehensible sea shanty. George assumed it was a sea shanty, although it verged on nonsense. It was quite possible he was making the lyrics up as he went along. They were sitting in the basement bar and restaurant – a solid-looking but knocked-together construction, fitting into what looked like half of Long Cross's cellar, with a portion resembling a conservatory built on at the back. It appeared from the room's box-like nature that the Freans had fabricated it themselves. It was hard to imagine a professional choosing to partition the space so eccentrically, or selecting such materials to build it from. Small dividing walls of chunky pine stood between tables in the restaurant section, while the counter of the bar seemed to have been put together out of a pair of old sideboards with their backs to the customers. There were large blackboards screwed to the wall above, displaying the restaurant menu – a small selection of conventional pub food and a large selection of peculiar-sounding home-made curries, each one titled with a comical but charmless name hinting at its strength, such as Gandhi's Revenge, or The DynoRod.

"Do you want to eat?" asked George. But Tessa was turned away, her attention caught by the old man's dog – a large, shambling, shaggy crossbreed somewhere between an Alsatian and a spaniel. She was looking at the collar round its neck, doubtless for a name. George looked at her face. Sometimes he wasn't sure he fancied her at all. When she tied her hair back, her head was shaped like a rugby ball and

her ears stuck out. But other times, like now, when her hair hung
down in straight black ropes and she was smiling, lost in thought, he
felt like he never wanted to be with anyone else. She was only twenty-
two. He knew how much she wanted to go to America. He wasn't
looking forward to being apart from her for a year. He kept thinking
about one thing, one night, when they'd gone to the pictures in
Bradford, to the film museum. It was Polanski's version of *Death and
the Maiden*. It wasn't something he'd particularly wanted to see but
there was nothing else on and they both fancied a movie. One of the
things he loved about being with her was the ease with which they
found things to entertain them. He'd ended up really enjoying the
film, absorbed in the intensity of its drama, but even more because he
was aware of Tessa at his side equally captivated. It was the first time
he had been with a girl and not felt simultaneously alone. Still, she'd
be back in a year. There would be many more such nights.

George went to the bar and when he returned Tessa was chatting
happily to the old man about his dog and its genealogy. The dog had
its black paws on her lap and was licking her face.

"Oh, he like you, missee, very keen on you he is." The old man
laughed and rolled himself another cigarette. Mr Frean had come over
to stand behind them. He was smiling his usual, distinctive smile – as
if he were a beneficent and indulgent god and his clientele were his
child-like mortal subjects. "He's like that though, you wanna watch
'im. That's how he started with me and now we's stuck with one
another."

"But you were made for one another, Kenny." Mr Frean looked
down at him, still smiling.

"How so?"

"You both have a fondness for Pedigree Chum." A couple of the
other customers who were looking on laughed. The old man did too,
clearly not taking offence.

"Anyways, we be celebrating our anniversary."

"Anniversary?" George somewhat self-consciously joined the conversation. He felt he had to if he were to take his place back at the table.

"Oh aye." He pulled on his cigarette. His fingers were brown like cigars. "I'm never likely to forget. September is the time of the Wash. That's where we found each other. In the Wash."

"The wash?" The old man didn't look like he was acquainted with the launderette.

"What's the wash?" Tessa asked, impatient as always to have her questions answered. The old man laughed. Mr Frean maintained his superior smile.

"The Wash. You not heard of the Wash?" He carried on chuckling.

"The Wash is a tidal phenomenon, peculiar to this part of Cornwall, in the early autumn," Mr Frean explained. "The sea goes out much further than is usual."

"And stays out longer than is usual too. Then it comes rushing back. All in one go."

"I've never heard of that," said George, incredulously.

"Well, that's no surprise." The men laughed again.

"I meant I don't remember it from geography lessons." This seemed to amuse the old man even more. He slapped his legs hard and his dog let out an excited bark.

"I don't s'pose you would have, young sir. I don't think there's much science in the Wash."

"What do you mean?" Tessa was intrigued.

"Wash is more about magic than science."

"Don't pay too much heed to what he says. He likes to think he's a sailor, but there's more salt in that cruet-set." Mr Frean gestured to the table with his pint glass.

"I knows what I knows. And you ain't been lost in the Wash, Mr Frean." The landlord's smile slipped a bit. He took a sip from his beer. "Wash isn't just about the sea hiding. It's the fog as well. That fog ain't a natural fog. It's all that's left of the sea when it goes. It comes down and if you get caught in it, you're well and truly lost."

"What were you doing walking in it if it's so easy to get lost?" asked Tessa, never shy about getting straight to the point. The old man shifted in his chair and turned slightly towards her.

"Well, missee. I tell myself it was 'cos I was looking for oysters. They're easy to find, sticking out of the sand like wafers in ice cream." He placed both his elbows on the table, interlocked his fingers and rested his head on his hands. "But I'll tell 'ee the real reason. If you walk long enough you come out the other side of that fog bank. And the other side of it is the most beautiful thing I ever seen. If I was a painter, I wouldn't bother with no landscapes or nudey woman. I'd set my easel right up there in the middle of the sand and I'd spend every minute I could painting that scene, until the water came galloping back."

"What was so beautiful?" Tessa asked. The old man chuckled again, but there was a different quality to his laughter this time.

"You'd have to see it for yourself to know that." He sat back in his seat, his wrinkled face suddenly unreadable. Then Mr Frean interjected a little too quickly:

"Don't take old Kenny too seriously. You don't want to go wandering off on a wild-goose chase, only to come back with wet feet and crabs in your socks."

"Anyway this old dog here. He must've run through and got himself lost too. We found each other, then made our way back through the fog to the land." The old man put his hand underneath the dog's chin and pulled at the loose skin that hung down. "We's been together ever since. Don't know where he came from, but he's stuck on me now."

One of the things that George and Tessa both loved about Long Cross was the size of the beds. That night they went to bed early to get themselves lost amongst the soft white blankets and countless pillows.

George was sometimes surprised to find that he still had a facility for getting lost in Tessa too. The buttery expanse of her skin, the frenzy of her response, hugging her afterwards. It was a surprise to him because one of his assumptions about relationships was that a couple had a finite reservoir of passion which was slowly drained over weeks and months and years. Therefore it didn't make sense to him when he found – as he often did – that the reservoir was suddenly full again.

Later, sometime in the night, George awoke. It was very dark in the big room. He could hear the slow in and out of the sea, but it seemed a long way away. He could just discern the pale oval of Tessa's face. Asleep she looked even younger. Gazing at her a sharp feeling arose in his belly and powered up to his head. It was so strong it was like a flare going off, a bright white light, fizzing upwards, that if it were material would have illuminated the room. The feeling nearly became an action. He almost grabbed hold of her shoulders and woke her and asked her to marry him. His mouth had begun to prepare itself to say the words, but he told himself not to be stupid, that he was just being sentimental, that it was just because he thought she wanted him to, because she was going away. The light faded, the flare went out, and he lay in the darkness for a while before sleep found him again.

"Well, what would you like to do today?" asked Tessa brightly.

"I thought we could go to Land's End."

"Oh, not again."

"You know I liked the look of that stupid funfair thing. It was closed last time."

"Come on. We're going to do the cliff walk to Port Quinn. I'm the one that's going away, so I should be the one to decide."

And so they put on their thermals, and their walking boots – which George had reluctantly been persuaded to buy in a sale, "just in case" – and they made their way out of Long Cross across the gravel driveway, and on to the tiny road that followed the cliff-edge down the coastline.

"I'm tired now, can't we take the car?" whined George.

"I'm not even going to answer that."

They walked on in silence. Before they set off George had thought to himself they might talk about Tessa's impending departure, if only about the practical aspects of when he might first go and visit her. Somehow the subject didn't come up.

The wind was lighter than the previous night, the air less salty. The hedgerows were high, broken occasionally by a gate. For some reason George found himself nervously looking over his shoulder. He was searching for Long Cross, silhouetted against the smudgy clouds. Each time he turned his head it had shrunk a little more. Eventually the house disappeared behind the horizon as the road began a steep descent. The feeling of being away from anywhere and anybody was very uncomfortable. He thought, It's all right – a car will pass sooner or later, but none did. After about ten minutes' more silent walking a sign appeared, jutting out of the hedge as if it had grown there. "Coastal Path 2/3 mile", it read. It was hand-painted in black and white, rather than the more comforting brown and cream favoured by the National Trust. The thought flashed through his mind that someone might have placed it there for a joke. Tessa obviously had no such suspicions – she was already obeying the sign's instructions.

"Are you sure that's the right way?" George asked suspiciously.

"Where do you think it's pointing to?"

"It just doesn't look very official, that's all." But she was already disappearing through a ragged tear in the side of wild foliage. George looked over his shoulder one last time, then pushed his way after her.

The pathway, if indeed there was one, was even more overgrown. George followed the flattened stalks of grass until he caught up with Tessa. She was scrambling down the hillside, along a course that seemed far too steep. The air was very still, unbroken by gulls' cries.

Even the ocean seemed silenced. George had to look at his feet all the time, just to negotiate the rocky decline without tumbling out of control.

"Tessa – slow down." But she just laughed and continued her mad descent.

It was only when he reached the bottom that George was able to look up for the first time and register the absence of the ocean. The beach was there, curving around the steep grassy bank, a wet, camel-coloured boomerang clinging to the hillside. But, where the sea should have begun, the sand faded out. The sky seemed to have come down to meet it. Tessa was standing, staring into the off-white cyclorama as if she saw something other than cloud. She turned her head when she heard George approach.

"Come on then."

"Come on then what?"

"Let's go and explore."

"You're joking, aren't you?"

"Well, we're not going to get this opportunity again, are we?"

"Opportunity for what? To get lost, or drowned in quicksand?"

"It's beautiful."

"Tessa! There's a James-Herbert fog bank stretching as far as the eye can see. We can't just walk into it."

"Oh come on. It's not as if we can get lost. We can just follow our footprints back if we want to."

"Tessa!" He wanted to stamp his foot and shout at her – not so much out of anger, more from the desperate fear that sat beneath it. "Tessa. Let's go back and do something else. This is just silly. We could drive down to Heligan, or do St Ives again." But she was already moving, dissolving into the mist. "Tessa!" he called, a final time before she vanished altogether. He stood there for a moment alone on the sand. He looked over his shoulder again in both directions. He couldn't even see the path they had taken down the hillside. The air was still but it was damp and cold. He didn't want to wait there alone, until she returned. He searched the vista for any signs of other people, but nothing moved in any direction. "Tessa!" he called one more time. She didn't reply. There was another moment's silence, then, because he didn't know what else to do, George found Tessa's footsteps in the wet sand and began to follow them, his boots replacing her imprint one pace at a time.

What was strange about the fog was how abruptly it began, as if it was a wall or a hedge. Once within it there was nothing to see. Just a blurry, vaporous brightness the colour of a dead light bulb. George kept his eyes on the ground, and also on Tessa's footprints which were mercifully clear. He kept calling her name but there was no response. He worked to blot out the rising panic. Nothing was going to happen, he told himself. He could turn back at any time and find his way to the road, even back to Long Cross. Tessa was nearby. There was nothing dangerous about walking along a beach, even if it was foggy. All these statements were just words now, however, and words were irrelevant in the realm of fear that George had passed into. He must catch up with her. How far away could she be?

Something about the light had changed. George looked up from the shell-strewn sand at his feet. He found it hard to believe what he saw. He could feel his heart thumping, hear it even, a rapid pulse fired by the terror he felt at what lay ahead of him. He had never seen such a space in his life. His first thought was, No man is supposed to see such a thing – however bizarre that was. It was as if the sea was gone – as if someone had taken it, some celestial hand had swept down and scooped it into the heavens. There was nothing but the beach – or rather the exposed ocean floor yawning ahead of him in every direction. It was nothing like the tide being out. That was a recognisable natural phenomenon, something familiar and understandable, something which one held a model of in one's head, like rain, or a thunderstorm or a frozen lake. It didn't perturb the senses in the way that George's were now disrupted, confronted as he was by this vast and inexplicable area. It wasn't just the absence of the water either. The light was different here. On the other side of the fog bank the sky was more like a roof, impossibly high above him. The place he was in now felt boundless, but somehow contained, as if he were inside a hollow space, the size of the world.

It would have been too much for him to keep looking were it not for one tiny feature a long, long way away in front of him. It was Tessa, who had carried on walking and walking and was now a distant point. She was not so far away from him however that he couldn't make out her movements. She seemed to be scraping something in the sand with a stick. She looked up and acted as if she had spotted him. Now she gestured to him, waving that he should run out to join her. But George knew that was an impossibility. For George suffered from a terror of large open spaces. He found it hard to walk across a playing field, never mind the indescribable expanse that he was now faced with. She waved again, her arms flailing wildly. To step forward would have been inconceivable. The idea of walking out into that immense flatness evoked a vulnerability within George so intense as to be physically excruciating. For him the feeling was an acute vertigo, a dizzying yawning sensation within – as if he had been dropped into the hugest, deepest ocean and had suddenly forgotten how to swim. He thought Tessa was aware of this phobia. Maybe she had forgotten. She waved at him again. He stood there frozen, caught between wanting to go and see what she had scratched in the sand and needing to run in the opposite direction. He wanted to go, because she was going away from him soon and he feared she would take his refusal to join her as a sign that he didn't love her, a sign which she would carry with her to America. He did love her. He couldn't bear the idea that she would think that he di 'n't. He contemplated stepping out but he knew it wasn't possible. He was frightened that if he went he would never get back.

He turned around to face the fog and retraced his steps, letting the blankness engulf him.

Somehow he found himself back at Long Cross, within the tight green walls of the garden. The air was filled with a light drizzle. He zipped up his hood and walked around for a bit, staring out of the restricting oval that circled his face. He knelt down in front of the goats then walked around the narrow hedge-lined tunnels and passages. After some time he came to rest at the bottom corner by the turret that overlooked the sea. He realised as he climbed the stairs that he was still trembling. He looked out over the thick cold wall that came up to the centre of his chest. The heavy fog had begun to disperse; it was now a lighter mist that spread everywhere, drifting inland. The stillness was suddenly broken by the cry of a gull and beyond it, another, subtler sound: a rushing, rolling, whooshing flush that gradually grew and grew until it became a magnificent tumbling roar. The ocean – now released from whatever unseen force had restrained it – came hurtling back, pushing the mist away, once again concealing the naked ground as it powered towards the shore.

"Tessa!" He shouted her name against the roar, then turned and ran down the stone steps, out into the corridor of green that led around the perimeter of the garden. Before he reached the exit, a cowled shape emerged through the mist from around the corner. It reached for its hood and pulled it back. It was her, not dead, not crushed beneath the waves. She must have walked a little further then followed him back to the shore.

"Tessa?" She smiled slightly and he ran up to her and held her tightly, feeling the tears pressing their way out of his screwed-shut eyes.

She didn't talk about what had happened, or what she had seen, out there in that great uncovered space. Nor did she refer to what she had written in the sand with the stick. George assumed it was "I love you" but he could never be sure.

Tessa went to America and never came back. Nor did George ever visit her there. Rather there were increasingly difficult phone calls and eventually a muddled, agonising letter from her that struggled to say what he already knew. In some ways George felt that she had never returned, that distant day in late September, that he had left her, or she had left him, off the coast of Long Cross, and that somehow she was still there, a tiny dot beneath an infinite sky.

For many years he was haunted by the sense that he had brought about this end himself, through his own inability to stand up to his fear. It was only later in life that the truth occurred to him, when he found someone who saw the fear on his face and recognised it. It was she who gently took his hand and said: "Come with me, I'll show you how to do this." And she led him easily into the wide, open space.

James Hood

A visit from Val Koran

Feddy, not for the first time, was thinking about the star in Miranda's bedroom. They had both noticed it in the morning, quite early, high up on the whitewashed wall behind her bed, almost touching the ceiling. A strange, luminous star, looking as if it had been stencilled on to the woodchip. It seemed at first to be caused by a shaft of light coming through a gap in the heavy curtains. However, Feddy realised this couldn't be. The rest of the room was still too dark – the curtains so thick they excluded the presence of the bright April morning.

Miranda was perturbed. She had stood up, naked, trying to ascertain the star's cause. Feddy, more attuned to what was around him, had guessed that the light was coming from behind the wall, through some kind of a ventilation grille. Miranda would have none of this. She leapt off the bed and threw open the curtains, expecting the star to disappear. It didn't. It remained shining stubbornly, despite the sunlight now filling the room.

Those mornings, thought Feddy. Those mornings were beautiful. Just him and her. They made love in the mornings. He preferred the mornings to the nights. Naturally aroused it seemed the simplest thing in the world for him to slide into her and fuck them both awake. I miss doing it, thought Feddy, even after all this time; I miss her long, heavy, substantial body and her pungent femaleness next to me at night and upon waking. Her scent was always strong, but never unpleasant. Like him she enjoyed slipping into bed without preparation, no teeth cleaning or face washing. Sneaking up on sleep. Maybe that's why they slept together as well as they did. Some nights the sleep was so deep Feddy thought he could have been anaesthetised.

I miss her peculiarly bright diamond blue eyes. I miss the fullness of her mouth. It was rare that Feddy stared directly into her face. She was never comfortable under his gaze. But he knew her beauty well. He observed it in brief glances, or when she slept. I can stay here, he thought. I can settle here quite happily. He suspected they could have been something very good indeed. He didn't have time to find out. It hadn't surprised him to wake and see a star shining on her wall.

He sat outside his bar, gazing down the hill into the town. Mdina could still look quite lovely to him despite twenty years of mornings such as these with the sun rising slowly, turning the old white stone orange and then yellow. The rest of the island, or at least the rest of its major towns, was quite charmless and even unpleasant (Valletta aside – though that was far too busy for Feddy's tastes). But Mdina was Malta's concealed jewel, five kilometres inland, away from the cheaply built hotels and the English tourists. The tourists came, of course, but somehow they were absorbed by the antiquated buildings – their irritating presence neutralised. Besides, they rarely strayed up to this part of the town. Feddy's patrons were the locals, the native Maltese who ran the surrounding businesses – the barber shop, the tannery, the bakery. He'd never relied on the tourist trade to sustain his income. When he'd bought the place in the mid-seventies the vendor had encouraged him to rename it. You should call it Feddy's, sir, or Jason's if you don't mind me saying, he had suggested. But that was a time when Feddy had been reluctant to announce his presence to the world. Instead the bar remained Stetson's. It also retained its red leather sofa seats and malfunctioning juke-box along with its heavy aroma of cigar smoke and stale beer. Feddy had never seen any reason to renovate or refurbish. In fact sometimes he liked to sit at the back on quiet evenings and imagine it in earlier times, before he had arrived, forty, fifty, even a hundred years ago. He pictured the customers coming in and out. The details of their lives not so different from their descendants'. Their loves, their needs, their fears, their pleasures. The past was there in the scuffed wooden floor, in the depressions in the stone steps that led to the lavatories, in the tobacco-stained alcoves that filled the wall opposite the bar. And Feddy took comfort from its presence. Thinking of Miranda, as he did most days, he reminded himself that she would not have liked it here. But then he would never have found himself here had it not been for her.

"Mr Feddy. Mr Feddy." Here was the baseball-capped figure of Aldi hurrying up the hill. That in itself was an unusual sight. Not just the hurrying, but at this time of day. It was rare to see his barman lit by a sunrise.

"What on earth brings you out at this time?" Feddy looked at his watch theatrically. "Don't tell me. I leave you in charge for one night and you were robbed."

"Mr Feddy. We not take enough to be robbed." The little man wiped the sweat from his upper lip, blackened by a day's growth of beard. He must have been five years older than Feddy but he had all the authority of a paper boy. "I come with an important message."

Feddy laughed. "Now what could be so important to get you scurrying out here at this time?"

Aldi paused whilst he caught his breath.

"I just get some water, Mr Feddy. Would you like some?" Feddy shook his head. Aldi lifted the shutter so as not to have to bend to get under it. Feddy looked down the road then went inside after his assistant. He didn't like the fact he looked so scared.

"Who brought us a message? O'Donnelly hasn't been at you again with his gangland stories, has he?" Aldi, always the barman, was fussing with lemons and ice cubes. "They're all made up. The only criminals he knows are some dodgy builders in Buggeba." Feddy was aware he was babbling. He sensed something difficult was coming.

"Someone come for you. A man." Aldi sipped at his water.

"What man? Did you know him?"

Aldi shook his head. He was holding his glass with both hands like a child. "No. But he say you know him. He say he was your friend." Feddy tried not to let the expression on his face change. "He ask me to give you this." The little man put his glass down then reached inside the pocket of his suede jacket. He pulled out a small piece of white card.

Freddy turned it over. It was a photograph. An old one from about thirty years ago. About five inches square, glossy with a white border. It was of Miranda. Feddy felt his legs give way. He reached out for the edge of the bar to prevent himself falling. His heart was racing so he sat down.

"There was something funny about this man, Mr Feddy. I'm not sure he was your friend. I not like how he said I had to give this to you."

"What?" Feddy's throat was tight. He found it hard to get the word out.

"He did not shout at me. He said it soft and he smiled. But it made me feel bad inside. Like if I not get it to you something bad would happen to me." Feddy found a stool and sat down. "Are you all right, Mr Feddy?" He nodded. "Do you know this man?"

"What did he look like?"

Aldi looked down, his forehead furrowed. "He wore a white suit and a hat. A little straw hat." Feddy was surprised to find himself smiling. "He said he come back tonight. Or if you not here tonight he come back the night after." Feddy nodded again. "Is he trouble, Mr Feddy? Is it bad news?"

Feddy poured himself some water from the jug Aldi had prepared. "He's my executioner." He looked out at the oblong of light beneath the shutter. It was going to be a beautiful day.

Feddy sent Aldi back home and locked up the bar. He walked the half-mile to his apartment smoking a cigar all the way. He rarely smoked in the mornings. His head was crowded with even more memories. Naturally he thought of Miranda. Of the time that photograph had been taken. She had been in the second year of her degree. He had just started his third year teaching. Koran had been there only a year more than he, although his natural authority suggested otherwise. It was Koran who had introduced Feddy to Miranda. It was Koran who had first been her lover. Miranda had been a student in his department. He taught a course in Metaphor and Meaning, although his real interests were far more esoteric. But when Feddy had been introduced to her – at one of Koran's Friday night "services" – he had fallen instantly in love with her. She was truly beautiful. He was surprised to see her there; Koran had a strict rule about not allowing students to *sabbats*, even those who had expressed a genuine interest in matters of his "reputation". Miranda's pale skin shone, burnished by the candle flames, glowing with an inner light. When she turned and smiled at Feddy, she cast her long-lashed eyes down slightly. He knew at that moment that he had to have her. When he found out later that evening that she was Koran's, he trembled inside. Trembled because it made no difference. Something had happened and he had to have her, regardless of consequence.

Feddy kicked at the heavy oak door at the front of his apartment block. It always stuck at the bottom corner. The wood was scuffed and scarred from the ten thousand strikes it had received over the years. He ground the cigar butt against the side of the doorpost and entered, the clack of his feet hollow on the tiled floor of the entrance lobby. He wondered if Koran would be waiting for him here. Of course he would know where Feddy lived – the apartment was no harder to track down than the bar. The locks would hardly have kept him out. Feddy would talk to him, reason with him. They were nearly old men now. The past was gone. It was time to let go. As he walked up the banisterless steps, past the doorways lined with terracotta pots, Feddy even allowed himself the possibility that this was why Koran had finally come.

Surely time and age would have softened him. That possibility was not enough to prevent Feddy entering his flat with supreme caution. The thing was not to allow Koran to kiss him. That was the thing.

As far as he could tell, the apartment was empty. He scanned the three rooms, even the tiny bathroom – as if Koran would have allowed himself the indignity of hiding behind a shower-curtain. Eventually Feddy sat down on the edge of the bed, his heart pounding. There must be something he could do.

Feddy had never thought it serious. Feddy had considered it nonsense. Well, not nonsense exactly, but affectation; theatre. He'd liked the buzz and the thrill of the ceremonies. And the sex, of course. But it just went with the times. The age of Aquarius. Their Satanic Majesties Request and all that. Sure Koran was a charismatic man. A charmer. An entertainer. But when he spoke of magic and power and rivers of fate, Feddy had assumed they were just more metaphors. He hadn't thought … If he'd thought for a moment that any of it were true …

Miranda wasn't just another conquest. Miranda was unique. "Do whales have faces?" were the first words she'd ever spoken to him. She wasn't one of his students but she'd sat in on one of his Moby Dick classes after they'd met at Koran's. She'd invited him to her flat, which she shared with two other girls – one a music post-graduate and the other a mathematician. Even this, thought Feddy, had been charming. He remembered that first visit clearly. The imposing entrance hall of the old Victorian building. It was ochre yellow, with a mosaic floor. On one wall was a faded cut-out from the *Yorkshire Evening Post* telling you about the house. Some minor poet used to live there. Feddy couldn't remember which one. Novels were his thing. He avoided anything that wasn't prose. Miranda loved poetry though. She would send him poems, neatly typed on plain white paper. Jacques Prévert, Allen Ginsberg. It charmed him, impressed him even. One poem he'd assumed was by someone else, someone famous although there was no name at the end. It turned out to have been written by her. Feddy even admitted to himself that he was vaguely threatened by what she called her "attempts". Who knows how far she might have travelled in her life had Koran not cut it so short?

Feddy stared at his reflection and sighed. Not a day went by without him thinking of her. Of her beauty, of her talent, of the life that should have been theirs. After she had died and he had fled, first to California and then – when his attempts to legitimise his presence had failed – to Malta, Feddy had tried to involve himself with other women but with no success. Miranda's perfect memory always interrupted. Miranda had been the one he had waited for all his life. Then Koran had taken her. And now Koran was here to take him. Feddy thought of fleeing. Of packing his brown leather suitcase and leaving the island, maybe to Africa or the Middle East. But if he was honest he knew he didn't have the energy. In truth he had been waiting for this moment since he had arrived. He was too weary to wait any more. He went to the bathroom, turned on the shower and began to undress.

"Ah, Mr Feddy. A pleasant surprise." Shiloh the barber put down his broom and went to shake Feddy's hand. "A drink for you, sir." He reached behind a pile of pomade jars and brilliantine tins, producing a labelless bottle of what was presumably whisky.

"I won't if you don't mind."

"Oh yes you will." He was already filling a teacup. "I hear you have had a visitor." Feddy found himself tightening. He refrained from saying anything. "There are no secrets in this town, sir, you must know that." He handed the cup to Feddy. "But do not worry. I will not ask any unnecessary questions."

"I want to look neat, Shiloh. I want to look … together. In charge. You understand?"

"Of course I understand. I always understand. We will shave you. We will trim your hair and I will press your trousers. You will look a picture for your visitor." The barber's foot depressed the pedal at the base of the chair and Feddy lurched backwards. "Let us begin." He slapped a hot towel on Feddy's already sweat-sheened face.

The last days. Feddy still remembered the last days. It had begun with the inevitable visit from Koran. At the time neither of them had been that concerned. Miranda had a T-shirt which read "Love Conquers All" and that was very much their attitude. It had been a wonderful time. Feddy knew that Miranda was "the one". He had been waiting for her since the early days of his adolescence. This perfect creature whom he desired infinitely, who engaged him completely. Those days after they had decided they were going to be together were a joyful anticipation of their life to come. There was no need to talk of marriage, there was enough certainty in their togetherness to dispense with the artificial bonds of ceremony. Feddy imagined – for some reason – a small house by a river, autumn afternoons, a range in the kitchen, overhanging trees. He had never felt so complete. A visit from Val Koran was hardly going to disrupt things. Let him come. He would see the truth – maybe even give them his blessing once he apprehended the strength of their feelings for one another.

And so he did come. One Thursday afternoon as Miranda and Feddy were discussing their move to London. Feddy had made inquiries about a teaching post at London University and Miranda had made a decision to give up her studies completely. She was going to pursue her poetry (and work part-time for her friend Fiona who had a hat shop in Chelsea). The doorbell had rung and Madelaine the mathematician had run down to answer it. Feddy and Miranda were sitting in the kitchen. Feddy was both surprised and not surprised to see Koran standing in the doorway. He had heard they were leaving. He wanted to see them both before they went. There was a long silence. Feddy contemplated beginning an apology, or at least an explanation. This was the first time all three of them had been in a room together since he and Miranda had become lovers. He started to speak. Koran cut him off. He had only come to say goodbye. Feddy had stood up and put his coffee cup down. He extended his hand but the gesture was ignored. Instead Koran moved to Miranda and brushed back her thick black hair exposing the pale skin on the side of her face. Feddy wondered if he should defend her in some way: she suddenly seemed very vulnerable. But Koran was only going to kiss her. He leant forward and gently kissed her just below her ear where her jaw-bone began.

"Goodbye, my love," he said softly. Then he left without looking at Feddy.

Feddy would have been lying if he had said he wasn't unnerved by the visit. He and Koran had been good friends, at least on a professional level. Even given the circumstances of the visit he had hoped for a farewell of some kind. Something that might have hinted at some future reconciliation. The complete stonewalling he received he found considerably unsettling. Miranda was quiet too for a couple of days afterwards. Doubtless she felt guilty about the way things had happened. Feddy even put the rash that had begun to spread across her face down to being a psychosomatic expression of her feelings. Funny how its epicentre seemed to be the exact spot on her jaw-line that Koran had kissed her. On the third or fourth day the inflammation seemed to cover her whole body. She said it was painful to the touch. Madelaine was concerned about Miranda's rising temperature. By the weekend she had been admitted to hospital. The following week they had moved her to the infectious diseases unit at Seacroft. It was a virus of some kind. At least that's what the doctors kept repeating, though Feddy knew they had as much idea as he did about its actual nature. She passed into a coma after her fever had refused to respond to any of the steroids they gave her. Before the month ended she had died. Feddy had been so distraught he became ill himself, although he recovered. He thought about contacting Koran but all his instincts told him to run away, to get as far away as he could from the man and his power. Was it senseless to think he could escape? Whether it was or not he knew he could not remain.

Feddy sat himself outside the bar. It was approaching five o'clock and once again the white walls that stretched away from him were washed in orange. Perhaps finally it was time for courage. He'd always thought it an overrated and precocious virtue – almost a neurosis. At least cowardice was an honest state. But now, as he sat waiting for his nemesis, he thought there was some sincerity in stoicism – at least in these circumstances. He was too tired to run. Let it end now. Aldi brought him out another *citron pressé* – he wouldn't drink alcohol until his visitor arrived. He took small sips and watched the gentle incline of the road.

About seven o'clock, half an hour after it got truly dark, a shadow appeared at the foot of the hill about a quarter of a mile away. It walked slowly but lightly up the road, becoming more defined in shape as it approached. A Panama hat was clear in outline against the moonlit buildings. Eventually the figure reached the bar.

"Jason Feddy." The hair was grey, but the face was undoubtedly Koran's, the green eyes still bright, even in the flickering fairy lights and lanterns that illuminated the front of the bar. Feddy was taken by surprise for his first emotion was one of delight – the delight of seeing an old friend for the first time in many years. It seemed that Koran shared the emotion. He broke into a broad grin and held out his hand. "I always knew you'd end up in some disreputable establishment." He squeezed Feddy's hand with enthusiastic vigour. "May I join you?"

"Of course. Aldi!" Feddy called back to his barman. "What would you like to drink?"

"Some brandy would be nice."

Feddy looked at his old mentor. A mêlée of emotions filled his belly. He remembered being in awe of the man's intellect. Being honoured at being invited into his inner circle. The thrill whenever Koran spoke to him like a friend. How likeable he could be. How frightening too, particularly when he spoke so intensely about his esoteric studies.

"Would you like a cigar?"

Koran shook his head. He studied Feddy's face. "I was visiting Malta. I hope you'll forgive my calling."

Feddy searched his pockets for a match. He knew Koran was playing a game, but maybe everything was going to be all right. The wisest course of action was to co-operate. "Are you still teaching?"

Koran looked at him as if he were surprised that Feddy had spoken. "I'm no longer attached to any single institution. I have a number of students I've been instructing privately – though in subjects few universities would recognise."

"Have you been writing?"

"Indeed, but, again, no conventional publisher would have an interest in the texts." Aldi came out with a bottle of brandy, two large glasses and a small porcelain jug of water. He stole a quick glance at Koran before scurrying back inside. "And how do you find the victualler's trade?"

"I make a living."

"Do you still teach?" Koran poured himself a drink.

"God, no."

"A pity." He slooshed the liquid in the glass. "You were a good teacher." Feddy felt pride spreading in his belly that Koran held him in some esteem. It warmed him like the brandy. "Well, you have chosen a beautiful place to live. There are few of the inane distractions of the modern world here. Tell me, are we in Rabat or is this street still part of Mdina?"

"Technically it's in Rabat although I think of the whole place as being Mdina. Do you know Malta?"

"There are two sets of catacombs here, one of which has occult connections. It lies in the crypt of St Paul's church. I have often wished to visit. Have you been?" Feddy shook his head and sipped the brandy. Maybe that was the reason Koran was here. Maybe he was more interested in the arcane history of the area than Feddy's long-forgotten misdemeanours. "How do you fill your days, Jason?" Feddy instantly revised his opinion. There was ice in the question, although Koran was still smiling. Abruptly he changed tack. "Did you ever read Alisdair Macintyre?"

"Hmm?" Feddy was thrown. The charm had returned to Koran's voice.

"Alisdair Macintyre. 'After Virtue'. I used to teach it. 'In his thought and his actions, man is a narrative animal.' "

"I don't remember." It had been a long time since Feddy had talked philosophy to anybody.

"Come now. You must remember the concept. We used to speak of it."

Feddy reached for the matches. His cigar had gone out. "Remind me."

"Macintyre asserted that narrative lies at the heart of who we are. That stories are vital to us because that's how we understand the world and our place in it. Stories are a model of how our minds make sense of things. We like beginnings, middles and ends. A man comes home to his wife. She asks him how his day has been. He makes a story of the events. I did this, I did that, then he said this etc, etc."

"Seems like a reasonable idea."

"But the downside is the stories – their shape, their structure – can be more important than the truth. Because accuracy matters less than things making sense."

"You know I never went in for any of that stuff."

"What 'stuff' is that?"

"Things not being as they are. 'Rose is a rose is a rose is a rose' always made more sense to me."

"Even when things happen that don't make sense?"

" 'It is only a shallow person who doesn't judge by appearances', as Wilde said." Feddy was beginning to enjoy this parrying. It reminded him of better times.

"But appearances can be so treacherous. Particularly the appearances of things that are not here."

"But they're all we have."

"All some of us have," Koran corrected him and grinned. "Now does your establishment serve food?"

"It does, but I wouldn't eat it. There's a Moroccan restaurant two streets away that's very good."

"I shall try it." Koran drained his glass then stood. Feddy stood also.

"Let me pay. It will be my treat."

"No. Thank you. I shall eat alone." There was a firmness in Koran's voice that made it clear he wasn't open to persuasion. "Perhaps you would be good enough however to accompany me on a tour of the catacomb of St Paul's tomorrow morning. Shall we meet here? About ten thirty?"

"If you like."

Koran nodded and was off down the street into the darkness with a surprising speed. Feddy stared after him. He thought about running after Koran but he knew he didn't dare. He poured himself some more brandy. When he returned the bottle to the tray he noticed that his hand was shaking.

That night Koran came to him in his dreams. Things were as they were. As they had been thirty years earlier. Koran wore a suit of purple velvet and presided over one of the monthly ceremonies – the one that coincided with a new moon. The room was lit with candles whose reflections flickered in the silver cloths draped over the furniture. He turned his eyes on Feddy who felt himself disappear. He reappeared in Miranda's bedroom. She was in bed – naked, waiting for him, but Feddy was unaroused, not wanting to sleep with her. Then they were lying on silver sheets. Koran and the rest of the coven surrounded them – fully clothed, scrutinising them with their gaze. Feddy tried to cover himself but he now had the body of a child. He looked down at his hairless penis and was ashamed. He awoke sweating and nauseous. He went into the bathroom. There he perched on the toilet, the seat cold on the back of his thighs, waiting for it to get light.

Feddy made sure he arrived promptly for his meeting. It was warm for late September. He didn't bother to open the bar. A light wind gathered leaves half-way down the hill and rattled the shutters behind him. Once again Koran appeared – hat first – marching with purpose up the road. He carried a small canvas bag over his shoulder. Feddy felt none of the unexpected delight of the previous day. There was now merely a sense of foreboding – like a long-postponed dental appointment.

"Good morning, Feddy."

"Morning."

"Have you taken breakfast?"

"I wasn't hungry."

"A pity."

"Why a pity?"

"No matter. Do you have anything planned for this afternoon?" Koran was at his side now. He wore a large pair of sunglasses with tortoiseshell frames. They gave him a faintly comic, matronly air.

"Nothing in particular."

"That's a good thing." He removed his sunglasses and polished them with a silk handkerchief. "You may want to lie down after our business is completed this morning. You may feel a little ill."

"What business?" Feddy's legs went weak again. His heart was racing. Koran regarded him with his unearthly eyes before covering them once more with the opaque lenses.

"Come. Let's see what lies under that church."

It was about fifteen minutes on foot to St Paul's. The shops, bars and houses gave way to large scrubby patches of empty ground. The wind picked up in the exposed areas, lifting small clouds of dust from the dry earth. Koran paused occasionally and looked back down over the town. There was no small talk. After a journey that felt as if it had taken hours rather than minutes they arrived at the small whitewashed church. A faded, crudely painted sign directed them to the catacomb, which had a separate entrance about ten metres from the chapel. A shrunken white box of a building stood at the side of the road like a bus shelter. There was an iron gate across its entrance.

"It looks like it's closed," said Feddy hopefully.

"Surely not. We've come all this way." Koran smiled. He approached the gate and it seemed to swing open. "It's merely pulled to." He beckoned for Feddy to follow him and dropped some coins into the honesty box at his side.

A very steep staircase led down into the dark. Koran gestured for Feddy to go first. As they descended the gate clanged firmly shut. Feddy was certain he heard a bolt being drawn and a lock click although there was no one there to have performed such an action.

The steps went down much further than it felt they should. The air became chilly as they reached the bottom and rounded a corner into the catacomb. The flickering light – an unsettling combination of electric bulb and wax candle – revealed an architecture that was anything but church-like. The place seemed to have been carved out of the rock although no geometry governed its shape. It was more a random collection of alcoves and recesses with oblong holes hewn out of their dividing walls. Hidden in these spaces were black letterboxes full of bones. Feddy was shocked that these remains had been strewn in such a casual manner.

"It is ironic that this catacomb is connected to the church above," said Koran in tutorial manner. "It is far older and has little to do with Christianity. Come. Let's see a little more." Feddy was uncomfortable walking away from the stairs but Koran was keen to walk among the narrow walls. They turned a corner, then another, before walking down a long, narrow passage. There were more stone bays at regular intervals, each one piled high with random bones. "The Knights Templar are responsible for some sections – others were established by older, even more secret societies."

"I never even knew it was here."

"And it's so close to you." Koran had removed his sunglasses and placed them in his pocket. "It's funny. When we were talking about Macintyre last night – I never mentioned his key insight: Only in fantasy do we live what story we please. In life, as both Aristotle and Engels noted, we are always under certain constraints. Yet fantasy can be so tempting, can't it." Koran had opened his canvas bag and removed a small bottle of mineral water. He placed this on the brown stone at his side and produced a small bag of dark powder from one of the bag's pockets. Feddy was thrown by his action and the sudden change of subject. He watched as Koran twisted open the bottle of water and tipped the black powder into it. The water fizzed and sparkled slightly in the iridescent light. "I thought long and hard about what to do, Jason. I wasn't going to kill you. I knew when I took her I wasn't going to kill you. I wanted something that would satisfy more completely. So I waited. And waited." Koran shook the bottle. The black powder which had appeared as heavy as iron filings had now dissolved completely. The water was clear.

"Val, I –"

"Shut up, Feddy." Koran's eyes flashed. "You desired her certainly. And you could have her. So you took her." For a moment the natural authority seemed to vanish from Koran's voice. He sounded like a lovelorn teenager. "We each have our areas of weakness," he continued. "No man can perfect himself entirely. I never seemed able to penetrate or work with a particular area of my self-esteem relating to women. That is why Miranda was a gift to me. Until you came with your charm and your looks and enchanted her. You took her from me. But you never really wanted her."

"Now that simply isn't true. I loved her. She was the woman I'd waited all my life to meet," said Feddy.

Koran started laughing. "Oh Feddy. If you could hear yourself."

"Damn it, Val, it's the truth. Not a day goes by without me thinking about her."

"I know. I know." He ceased laughing but he grinned broadly. His teeth were white in the candlelight. "But you mistake your thoughts for the truth. I know you so well, Feddy. Far better than you know yourself. Even though we haven't seen each other for thirty years. You don't know how pleased I am to find you unchanged." He unscrewed the top of the Evian bottle. "Now I want you to drink all this down for me."

Feddy looked at him helplessly. He felt sick and small. "I don't know if I can do that."

"Oh you can. It's a very simple thing." Koran handed him the plastic bottle. "Surely you don't want me to *make* you drink it. I can do that, you know."

Feddy took it. He couldn't help but sniff the contents. "What ... what will happen?" he asked fearfully.

"Just gulp it down." Very slowly Feddy raised the bottle to his lips. "That's it – swallow." The water hardly tasted of anything. There was a slightly bitter feeling at the back of Feddy's throat. That was all. The smile had dropped from Koran's face. "Really it's a good old-fashioned curse. Administered orally – like medicine."

"What do you mean, a curse?" Feddy felt himself tensing up.

"Were you a younger man you might consider it a gift. There are people who meditate for years in order to attain the insight I have just bestowed upon you. However you can be sure you will not thank me when I am gone. You will find something has happened to your mind."

"What has happened? What have you done to me, Val?"

"From now on – whenever you turn to your memory – you will find it has been replaced with the truth. Not a past that you have constructed for your pleasure out of the dots and lines of what occurred – but a cold and actual record of things as they happened. You will never again have the experience that is labelled 'nostalgia'. For you, Feddy – dreamer that you always were and still are, I have no doubt – this will be a forbidding place. I am afraid this state will continue until you die." Koran took the now empty plastic bottle from him and placed it back in his canvas bag. He then took Feddy's arm and led him back towards the daylight.

"I suggest that you spend the afternoon at home. I think you are liable to feel a little ill." Koran had returned him to the shuttered bar. "You will not see me again. Goodbye, Jason Feddy." He walked back down the dusty slope. Eventually his distinctive hat disappeared beneath the brow of the hill. Feddy stood there for some time watching the empty road. Eventually a car went past, disturbing his reverie.

By the time Feddy got home he was beginning to wonder if he'd dreamed the whole morning. There was something insubstantial about his recollection of the events, something feverish. He was about to dismiss the whole thing as a fantasy when he was gripped by the most intense stomach pain. He went into a sudden spasm – as if all his limbs were joined by strings like a wooden puppet's that emerged from a hole in the base of his spine and someone had abruptly pulled those strings taut. He fell to the floor with his knees drawn to his chest and his elbows tight against his belly. The pain hit his head like a rockdrill. Somehow he managed to manoeuvre himself on to the bed. Then the nausea began – a terrible sensation – an imperative to empty out everything from within. He tried to fight it but was unable to. He opened his mouth and vomited.

Time disappeared. All there was for Feddy was the desire for the pain and sickness to stop. It went dark outside. Someone knocked on the door but he couldn't speak. It became light again.

He must have slept although he couldn't remember closing his eyes. There was puke and fluid around him on the bed. When he tried to move he felt raw and brittle – as if he had been remade, or had shed a skin like an old spider. Somehow he managed to swivel his legs off the bed. They trembled beneath him as he found his way to the shower.

At first Feddy thought Koran's curse an elaborate joke, but he didn't dare call on any memory to test it. The first inkling he had that something might have happened was on the Saturday night. He was in bed trying to sleep but the events of the day before were far too vivid in his mind. He remembered how much change he had given for every transaction. He did drop off but woke again about a quarter to four in the morning. A look at the clock brought to mind a limerick he once uttered trying to make his class laugh at the start of a new academic year in 1967. A girl had asked the time. It was three forty-five and he had told her so before quoting:

> "My back aches, my penis is sore,
> I simply can't fuck any more,
> I'm covered in sweat,
> You haven't come yet,
> Christ! It's a quarter to four."

But he had misjudged their mood and temperament. There were a few nervous giggles but mainly embarrassment and disapproval. He felt, once again, the agony of his own shame at trying to be amusing and failing in such a crass and coarse way. Then another memory came to his mind. It was about the poem that Miranda had sent him – the one he had thought had been authored by someone famous, which in fact she had written. Except the memory was different now. It had all the unwelcome brightness of camcorder footage. It was the other way around. It *had* been authored by someone famous. It was by Thom Gunn. Feddy had mistakenly assumed it was hers. He had been ashamed at his own lack of knowledge in front of Miranda. But worse were his memories of a poem she sent him after that. A poem about their relationship. She had once again left a name off the bottom – although he knew it was hers. It was childish and adolescent. It had made him wince. He could even remember that at one point she had spelt "their" as "there". That led to another memory of lying in bed one night and not wanting her because she felt young and foolish. He recalled the excruciating feeling of her touching his flaccid cock trying to arouse it. He remembered driving down Otley Road one day and seeing her walking into college. She didn't see him. She had her hair tied back. Her face looked odd and unattractive. He didn't want to be with her.

The following day Feddy sat outside the bar, cradling a glass of brandy. He stared down the dusty hill at the distant white roofs shimmering in the noon haze. Many other memories were coming unwelcome into his mind. Most upsetting, of course, was the revised version of their first week together – formerly the most precious recollection of all. It was no longer the soaring peak experience he had savoured all these years. He now saw the fantasy in it. Miranda was just a girl. He was just a young man. There was little more to it. Then there was the morning with the star on the wall. The star was still there. But it was joined by his disinterest in it, by the fact that he was more concerned with being late for a lecture, by the smell of Miranda's fart in the bed. He remembered walking to work that day, wondering if he should end it with her and if Koran would have her back. It had been sunny yes, but he was not particularly happy. Things had been OK but that was all.

He knew these memories were the truth. He knew he had constructed something else around them, a structure he had built and built over many years. That structure had now had its foundations removed. It had collapsed silently around Feddy leaving him exposed and cold. He drained the glass and called for Aldi to fill it once more. Perhaps later he would go for a walk. Perhaps he would visit the catacombs and stare at the bones. It was going to be a long afternoon and an even longer night.

The cash-point oracle

There was a girl. Simon Sacker thought she was absolutely beautiful. Her face wasn't obviously pretty, but once he was familiar with it, it was the only face he wanted to see. Her voice was low and deep and sexy. Every time he heard it he imagined chocolate mousse running slowly down the front of his body. She had this very distinctive shape, seemingly comprised of interlocking 'S's and 'C's, that made her look like she would fit exactly against him if he were to embrace her. He'd even discovered that she was single. Simon's only problem was that he would find it easier to cut off one of his fingers than tell the girl how he felt.

Simon was a DJ. He had his own night called Skylab – which had been running for nine months every Friday at Café Mex ("superb rabble-rousing antics" – NME, "rampant eclecticism on the loose" – ID), and anybody looking at him would probably have thought, I bet he doesn't have to worry about the ladies, but the truth was Simon hadn't so much as kissed anyone for over a year. It wasn't that he didn't meet people – he'd met more this past six months than in the previous eighteen – or that nobody fancied him. There was a bargirl at the Mex – a Cultural Studies student called Elsa – who'd packed in her job there and gone to work in a horrible pub called the Swan because she'd fallen for him so badly. Simon's lack of action was sponsored by a crippling fear. In simple terms he was – and always had been – terrified of making a move. If there was the tiniest sliver of doubt about the other's intentions it would spread through Simon like a computer virus, unravelling whatever program ran his faculties of

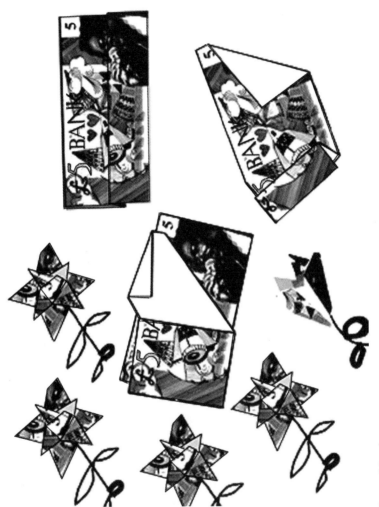

seduction, leaving him helpless and inactive, a trembling mass of uncertainty and unimplemented actions.

The girl's name was Allison Costello. She was assistant editor of *01132* – Leeds' very own listings magazine, which had only been going since March but was already succeeding in a way that previous ventures of a similar nature had made seem impossible. The history of these enterprises was characterised by failure and tragedy, from the underfunded seventies idealism of *Leeds Other Paper*, to the misplaced mid-nineties cockiness of *Brag*. But *01132* was redefining the zeitgeist of provincial what's-on guides. It was sassy, stylish and vivacious, displaying a curious mixture of self-deprecation and fuck-you insouciance. This struck a chord with everyone in the West Yorkshire area who knew what it was about being there that was better than living in London, but had, up until then, been unable to articulate their conviction. *01132* had given them a voice, and whereas its predecessors saw most of their print-run bound up and returned at the end of each fortnight, this latest incarnation was sold out from the city centre vending sites two days after it arrived. The early issues were now prized possessions, their stylish and imaginative front covers hanging clip-framed in more than one front room in Headingley and Chapel Allerton. (The editor and creator of *01132* was an ex-friend of Simon Sacker's called Roman Suzman. They'd drifted apart for reasons neither was sure about, although they both had a clue it was something to do with jealousy and the fact Roman was gay.) Much of the magazine's success was down to the verve of the editorial team and Allison in particular, who had an uncanny knack of knowing what people wanted to read about a month before they did, which translated into the "must have" factor each edition seemed to possess.

It was this uncanny knack that brought Allison into Simon's life on the first Friday in September. She turned up at Skylab with Rebecca from the advertising sales department, who'd been going on about the place since the start of the summer. Allison knew something about clubs, and certainly liked her dance music, but had become a little out of touch with what was happening. This was partly because she'd been working insanely hard since the magazine's launch, but mainly because she'd been living for the past five months with Mark, an Art History lecturer from the university who pretended he was into such things because he'd read that Techno was a natural extension of *musique concrète*. Really his favourite band were The Police, and everything he knew about current music he gleaned from the arts pages of *The Sunday Times*. Allison found this out about the same time she discovered his cache of pornographic videos at the back of the airing cupboard. She didn't object to pornography as such, but she did oppose hypocrisy. Since Mark – in a much trumpeted professional coup – had persuaded Andrea Dworkin to lecture on the subject, had nodded intensely at everything she'd had to say, and joined her in fiery vehemence during the meal afterwards, Allison felt she had no choice but to move out, which she did very quickly. She left nothing but a terse post-it on the subject fixed to the TV screen, and a tape in the video recorder, stopped at a scene that Ms Dworkin would consider particularly supportive of her views.

And so at the end of this particular Skylab, as the cello reprise from 'In the Trees' by Faze Action charmed the packed throng on the dance floor to disperse, Allison squeezed her way against the flow towards the turntables and into Simon's fantasies.

"That was so good," she grinned as she offered him a cigarette. Simon took one, although technically he'd given up, but he was so captivated by her sweat-sheened face (and crop-topped upper half) it would have been unthinkable not to. He tried not to stare at the orange star stretched arousingly across her chest. Before his mind had a chance to spiral into the enchanting possibilities – and subsequent anxieties – suggested by her approach, she established the professional basis of her presence.

The following Monday afternoon they sat together, cosy in a booth in Indie Joze, Simon trying to work out how best to get the little mound of brown sugar he had thoughtlessly piled upon the whipped cream of his hot chocolate to submerge, Allison removing the cellophane from a new D90 with a practised skill that both impressed and intimidated him.

She placed the scuffed black box of her tape recorder next to the ashtray and pressed the record button. Simon noticed that her nail-varnish had sparkly bits in it.

"Simon Sacker – Skylab, Monday the 10th," she announced to the air in front of her and he tried to adopt a casual expression as if this was the fifth interview he'd done this year. It was in fact the first he'd done in his life. "Tell me how you got here."

"On the 36," he replied without thinking.

"No, I mean Skylab, DJing. The whole story." She didn't react to his stupid answer so he dropped his hastily drawn plan to pretend it was a joke and gladly unrolled his recent biography. He was only too pleased to do so, since he was rather proud of the club and its growing reputation and it allowed him to recast what had come before as if it was all part of an elaborate plan, when in fact it was actually a series of mistakes and misjudgements that happened to have come right due to a series of fortunate events beyond his control. The truth was whenever he tried to plan anything it ended in disaster, mainly because he didn't trust his own judgement (although he liked to pretend that he did) and that always undermined the results. So he told her about the fine art degree, and the shop called FAB 305 that sold seventies kitsch, and Twenty-Four Hours, the sub-My Bloody Valentine band he'd played in back in '91, leaving out the two and a half years' worth of weddings and bar-mitzvahs with Night Owls Mobile Discos and The Cinnamon Sticks – the appalling sub-Northside baggy band from whose ashes Twenty-Four Hours had sprung. And he played up the best bits, like Jools who booked for Café Mex offering him a night after hearing him DJ at Carla Fowler's Christmas party, and a shared session with Justin Robertson. He didn't however tell Allison that she had the nicest pair of lips he'd ever seen or that he wanted to kiss her neck, despite the fact that these two thoughts occupied his mind for most of the thirty-five minutes they sat together.

"Listen, thanks for that. I'm going to send Danny down to do some photos on Friday. And I want to run this on the 21st in the Student Special." Simon was barely listening. He was delving inside himself to see if he had the courage to ask her out for a drink. All he found was a burning fear that incinerated his wish and planted a mask-like grin on his face which made him say:

"Excellent. Cheers for that." For a moment or two he pretended to himself that this was a good thing, as if he didn't really fancy her anyway, but as she put on her denim jacket, he held his breath and thrust his hand into the flame: "Here. Give me your number. If there's anything else I remember I wanted to say." Realising that qualification still amounted to a cop-out he braved the furnace one more time as they passed the framed Rolling Stone covers on the stairs. "Or if you want to come again. I'll get you on the guest list." That over-familiar phrase suddenly made him feel completely naked now he'd actually uttered it with the ulterior motive it was usually attended by. He wouldn't have felt any different had he actually said, "I want to pull down your knickers and fuck you" and he expected an outraged and angry reaction from Allison. Instead she just said:

"Thank you. I'll see you soon. Take care." Her smile suggested she was neither offended nor impressed as she handed him her card. He noted there were three numbers on it. Home, work and mobile. Three different options to chicken out on, he reflected as he pushed it in his back pocket.

At first he thought: She's all right but I'm not that bothered, and he pretended that this was the truth. Then he thought: OK, OK, I do fancy her a bit, but she's not perfect, she seems far too serious for me and I wouldn't enjoy being with her that much because she's not really my type. When he found himself buying a pack of cigarettes he was dismayed, not because he was smoking again but because he asked for Marlboro Lights – a brand he abhorred because they were the new Silk Cut and everybody smoked them nowadays. It took him several hours before he admitted to himself that he'd bought them because Allison smoked Marlboro Lights. He then winced with shame at the thought, put them in a drawer and went out and bought some Dunhills.

Two days later he sat by the phone with his heart dithering in his chest, not because he was waiting for it to ring, but because he was trying to decide whether he should call Allison at work. He knew he wanted to, although he was still only prepared to squint at the fact from the side, rather than face its full-on glare. Eventually he decided he was going to phone on the pretext of placing an advert in the edition he was appearing in. After one hundred and seventy minutes, he picked up the phone and dialled the number printed on the inside cover of the magazine spread across his lap.

"Hello. *01132* ..." He slammed the phone down.

Twenty-five minutes later he picked it up and tried again. This time he spoke:

"Can I speak to Allison Costello, please?" He was convinced that somehow his nervous warble contradicted the anodyne nature of his request so obviously that it actually sounded like "Can I ask Allison Costello out, I really fancy her" to whoever was on the other end.

"She's not in this afternoon. Can I help?" Wasn't that a hint of weary anger, as if the voice was forever fielding importuning calls on Allison's behalf?

"No thank you. I'll call back." (Although it sounded like "No thank you. My name's Simon Sacker and I really fancy Allison Costello.") He put the phone down again.

He was certain she'd come on Friday and so he took extra care to dress as if he wasn't really bothered about how he looked. He craned his neck every time a figure came downstairs, dropping records, miscueing tracks and generally fucking-up. Eventually Danny the photographer arrived, who seemed to be perpetually laughing, accompanied by a stunning black girl whose name Simon misheard as Dabs (it was in fact Debbie). Her presence immediately frustrated Simon a) because she wasn't Allison and b) because he entertained the illusion that if she wasn't there he would have been able to share a conspiratorial and laddish conversation with Danny which he could gradually steer on to the subject of his employer. Aware that she would be viewing the photos he smoked three cigarettes in a row while Danny clicked away. As the camera was unscrewed and packed up, Simon cursed his aching throat and wondered why, at the age of twenty-eight, he still thought a woman might be impressed to see a fag hanging out of his mouth.

He lay awake that night, the room lit only by the distant orange and green fluorescence of his amplifier and CD player from which *UFOrb* lapped somewhat inappropriately. He didn't know what to do. He sprawled on his bed thinking about all the girls in his past that he had wanted but who had never wanted him. Joanne Armstrong who was thirteen when he was fifteen, who used to come over to his house all the time, her face always glowing from the bike ride. She never actually got off with him and he never really tried because he was sure she didn't feel the same. And Barbara McNicholl whom he met at Glastonbury in 1986, whose name should have put him off because it sounded like one of his mum's friends. She was taller than him and thin, but with pouty lips and intimidating cheekbones. She lived in Leicester and became the one and only pen pal he ever had. But he could still remember the exciting anticipation of waiting for the fortnightly arrival of one of her bizarrely decorated envelopes. She came to stay three or four times and he had wanted to kiss her so much but he had never said anything. He had a vague idea that she might make a move but she never did. And Dwarfy Karen who worked in FAB 305 whom he was obsessed with but never did anything about because he told himself she was just a little bit too small. But it now occurred to him that if he fancied her that much (and he did – he used to go home and wank about her – which was unusual for him) her height – or lack of it – obviously didn't matter.

"I don't know what to do," he announced to the ceiling. He hadn't prayed since he was eleven years old and asked for Mr Wightman to be off school the next day because he hadn't finished his project about pampas grass. The reason he hadn't prayed since then was because Mr Wightman was indeed off school the next day and, terrified that he might have such a direct line to God and all that it implied, Simon felt it best to curtail the relationship. But his desire for Allison had now become so powerful that he pressed his palms together beneath his chin and spoke aloud: "Tell me what to do. I don't know what to do." He heard nothing but the gentle throb of "The Blue Room". He went to sleep hoping he might dream an answer but he didn't (he dreamt about doing a set at the Big Kahuna Burger but only having two records with him: *Club Tropicana* and *Geoff Love's Big War Movie Themes*).

On Saturday he decided that he had to see Allison although he had no idea where she was. He went to town in the afternoon and sat in Indie Joze, in the same booth he'd sat with her the previous Monday. It wasn't very likely but he thought she might be there. She wasn't. He ordered a second hot chocolate and hoped she might come in. She didn't. His friend Matt entered instead.

"My man. Where you been?"

"Here."

"What's with the horse face?" Matt released Simon's hand, removed his hat, placed his bag on the table and introduced him to his girl. "Pavla. Simon. Simon. Pavla." Pavla was beautiful but probably only sixteen. Matt seemed to have a different partner every week, each one more youthful than the last. Simon wasn't going to say anything about Allison because it seemed wrong to talk about it in front of a girl he didn't know, particularly one with a child's bus pass, but then he thought, Fuck it, because talking about her was a step closer to being with her than just thinking about her. He gave the pair an edited account of his week. "Sweet man," said Matt. Pavla giggled and sucked on her straw. Neither of them had anything more constructive to add. Simon felt dismayed. "You Favvin' it tonight?"

"Yeah, yeah."

"Catch you later."

Simon hadn't intended to go to the Faversham, since he was supposed to have given it up, like the cigarettes, but of course he thought Allison might be there. He didn't know whether or not this was a likelihood but the thought was comforting because it fuelled the engine of possibility and he was desperate to keep it running. Having made that decision he thought he'd better get some money out because there were drinks and taxis and cigarettes to be bought and so he headed for the cash-point.

The one by the market had the little red bit down that meant it wasn't working so he had to walk up to the NatWest. The queue was so long he almost didn't bother but then he thought, No, stick it out, because you'll only have to stop off in the taxi later if you don't. His turn came. Impatiently he held his card against the slot until the machine flashed:

PLEASE INSERT YOUR CARD

He did. The options appeared. Better get a balance, Simon, he said to himself. Of the services offered there were two arrows to press. One read:

ADVICE

and the other read:

BALANCE ADVICE

Without thinking he pressed the former. The screen flickered.

THINK OF YOUR PROBLEM

it suggested, somewhat obscurely. Without pause Allison came to mind, although Simon assumed that he'd misread the text.

PLEASE WAIT A MOMENT. WE ARE DEALING WITH YOUR REQUEST.

The machine chugged and ground to itself. Eventually the slip appeared. Simon sensed the queue behind him shuffling impatiently as he pulled the paper out and read it. It didn't say what he expected it to say. He read it again. There was no reference to his current balance. Instead it stated, in fuzzy dot matrix purple:

VICAR LANE 2

DATE	TIME	CARD REF NO
15/09	16.09	6759 16712

ADVICE

NURTURE RELIANCE SHINING

LISTEN AND DISCUSS

mutual support   raising cattle is good   fire within fire

0409 THANK YOU

He looked up. He looked down at the puzzling square of paper. Intimidated by those behind him he reinserted his card in the machine and withdrew £30.

Bemused, Simon wandered down the road and made his way into the Victoria Quarter. He sat on a hexagonal bench and lit a cigarette. Shoppers thronged around him, their chat and hum echoing in the cathedral-like space. It seemed preposterous that NatWest was now offering such a service. Surely it was just a promotion of some sort. But the epigrams seemed very specific to Simon. He was quite happy to connect them with Allison because he found their positive tone very encouraging. He just wished they were a little clearer.

In the Fav – heaving as usual – Simon pressed his way through the assorted thoroughfares towards the conservatory where he knew Matt and Co would be. Of course he was more preoccupied with seeing if he could find Allison's face somewhere in the blue-red murk as he pushed through the crowd. There were several other faces he didn't want to see but there was no sign of hers.

"Sack-man. How you doing?"

"Hey. Sack-man."

"The Sack-man's here."

Simon acknowledged the overlapping greetings from Matt and his mates and took up the offer of a drink. He was soon cornered by Olly Turner – who always displayed an unexpectedly feminine interest in other people's love affairs and who knew all about Allison through Rebecca from the advertising sales department, of whom he had once taken a set of nude photographs, supposedly for a club-flyer, although the flyer never actually appeared.

"She's single but hurting. She's pretending she didn't care about her ex but she does. She don't want no reconciliation, but she needs a period of mourning. Trouble is she's too proud to admit it. She thinks she can just hop from one thing to the other and you just can't do that man," said Olly. Simon thought: What do you know? Since Olly Turner's assessment didn't benefit him he changed the subject and they talked about the fortunes of Bradford City; if there was one thing that Olly Turner liked talking about more than other people's relationships it was Bradford City.

After another two pints of Kronenburg Simon could not put off a toilet visit any longer, so reluctantly he forced his way towards the Gents which was on the exact opposite side of the Fav from where he had been standing. He thought, as he always thought whenever he made this maddening journey through a sea of pissed-up or some-thing-upped Saturday-nighters, that surely, with all these punters, they could afford to install another set of toilets, but oh no, they had to retain as much space as possible for drinking in and it was funny how they managed to find money to double the length of the bar but that they couldn't find any for …

Oh fuck.

Fuck fuck fuck.

Fuck fuck fuck indeed, for what else could have stopped his rant in mid-flow but the presence of Allison and there she was, standing with a group of other girls, looking more beautiful than he'd ever seen her because he had his beer-goggles on – and even better, he'd had three pints so he could easily imagine bringing himself to speak to her, but he so needed to piss and he didn't want her to see him until he came out of the toilet.

And then when he was in there facing the urinal – leaning just a little too much – it suddenly occurred to him that she might leave while he was in there, and his piss became the longest piss that he'd ever done in his life and it wouldn't stop and he tried talking to it to make it hurry up – oh please stop wee, please be quick and finish because Allison's out there and she might leave and I so so so want to speak to her because I think she's got the best face of any girl I've ever seen and I want to smell her hair so finish now please. He started forcing out what was left but he knew he was being premature because there was still a considerable amount. Finally it finished. He buttoned his fly as he sped to the first of the doors, only just completing the action as the second swung open.

She was still there, and as he moved towards her Simon's mind went momentarily clear, as if someone had tinged a small bell and everything had gone quiet. In that moment the three fuzzy purple words of advice appeared clearly in his head:

NURTURE RELIANCE SHINING

LISTEN AND DISCUSS

They seemed to blend with Olly Turner's earlier information until the two things combined, producing a rare new sense for Simon of knowing exactly what to do.

"Good evening, Allison Costello." He knew it sounded drunk, but not in a bad way. There was no question of a lecherous tone however. His advice had put that from his mind. He was now taking a longer view.

"Hello, Si." He liked that. He didn't normally approve of his name being abbreviated, but in her case it was fine. "Are you not working tonight?"

"Uh uh. Saturday night is lads' night." This was intended ironically but it may not have come across as such. Realising this he added, "Out on the sniff, looking for a bit of lady action." Then because he thought that qualification was seriously ill advised he tried to negate both statements with a third, more prosaic one. "No, it's just I don't like to do every weekend right through, I mean Skylab's only Fridays anyway and I don't always have Saturdays booked so you know –" Fortunately she interrupted him.

"The piece is great ... you come out of it really well, like you know exactly what you're doing when it's obvious you haven't got a clue."

Simon nodded and laughed without really understanding what Allison had just said. His mind was still on what he had to do.

"So how are things in your life?" he asked, trying to sound concerned and supportive.

"Oh not so bad, up and down, you know."

Emboldened by Kronenburg Simon continued: "Olly was telling me you've just split up with your boyfriend."

"Was he?"

"I'm not being nosy or anything ... well I am, but ..."

"No. It's OK. I left him. It's no secret."

"It's always a big thing ... ending a relationship ... don't you think?"

"It doesn't have to be ... no. Not if you discover you didn't want to be in it after all."

"Even then ... especially then."

"Why especially then?"

"Because you have to deal with disappointment and that can be the hardest thing." Simon was puzzled by his sudden attack of wisdom but he was quite happy with it. It sounded very convincing.

"You sound like you're talking from personal experience." Allison's face had taken on a different expression. She now looked as if she was paying more attention. Simon glanced down at the floor, amazed at how sober he suddenly felt.

"Maybe ...."

The conversation continued and deepened and both of them looked at their watches in surprise when last orders was rung. But once again Simon felt the ting in his mind when it came to leaving. Rather than feeling pressured into making a clumsy pass he remembered the purple print and thanked her for listening to him.

"No. Thank you for listening to me," she countered.

"Well, I like listening, so, any time ..." He smiled and climbed into his taxi. It didn't hit him until the following morning that there hadn't been a minute when he had not known what to do.

The unexpected calmness of Saturday night quickly wore off and by Tuesday Simon felt the knot of uncertainty tying itself in his stomach again. He wanted to see Allison more than ever but found the double fear of not knowing how to behave and getting it wrong kept him from doing anything at all. Although he had no shopping to do and he wasn't meeting anybody, Simon found himself on the 36 bus that afternoon heading for town.

It had occurred to him that it should work at any cash-point but a few experiments had proved otherwise. Terrified that what he had encountered would prove to be a one-off occurrence, Simon wasn't surprised to see his hands were shaking as he stood before the screen. When he could bear it no longer he pushed the card into the slot, his heart thumping a little harder as he felt it snatched away from his fingers. The relief he felt when he was offered the same set of options as before was akin to a terrible headache suddenly fading. He prodded the arrow next to ADVICE. The procedure was identical. He filled his mind with Allison and held his breath as the print-head buzzed and the advice-slip made its appearance. It said:

VICAR LANE 2

DATE	TIME	CARD REF NO
18/09	10.13	6759 16712

ADVICE

COURAGE DAREDEVIL TAKING RISKS
treading on the tiger's tail but the
tiger does not bite
0409 THANK YOU

Simon was pleased. It was the kind of advice he was hoping for.

That afternoon he found himself phoning Roman Suzman to float the possibility of a combined *01132*/Skylab promotional event. Roman, having read Allison's piece, was only too happy to talk about things, as well as being pleased to hear from Simon after such a long time. He invited Simon to the office that afternoon.

"Hello, my friend. I was very glad you rang. And I'm so pleased that things are going well for you. As you know, I despise dance music but I'm not fool enough to allow my own bigotry to infect our editorial policy." Simon remembered why he'd allowed his friendship with Roman to drift. "I took the liberty of inviting Allison to join us. I'm sure she'll have plenty to contribute." She was wearing pin-striped trousers that made her legs look incredibly long. Her panty-line was the sexiest he'd ever seen. Her tight black jumper made him want to put his hands on her breasts.

"Hello, Simon." She smiled.

The trio thrashed out an intriguing idea for a pre-Christmas promotional night to be held in the grounds of Kirkstall Abbey. ("The oldest example of Leeds' culture brought face to face with the newest," said Roman. Simon winced inwardly but said nothing. Allison lit a cigarette.) Allison agreed to investigate the costs. As he stood up to leave Simon heard the little bell ting in his head. He prepared himself to jump on the tiger's tail.

"Do you fancy seeing Lionrock this Saturday? They're playing in Sheffield."

"I thought Saturday was lads' night."

"Well, it is, but Justin's a mate and all that so I thought I'd give it a miss this week." He smiled.

"That sounds good."

"I'll give you a call."

For a time Simon's heart was arpeggiating with pleasure. He felt like he was in a film but somebody else was playing his part. He was just saying this stuff without worrying about how it would be received. All he had to do was keep the advice clear in his mind and everything else took care of itself. At one point he even noticed he was enjoying the anticipation of spending a whole evening with Allison without any of the attendant anxiety about how he would have to be, or what he would have to do in that time.

But this didn't last. The following afternoon he caught the bus into town and found himself walking towards Vicar Lane.

It was OK. No, really it was. What could be dangerous about asking for help? And that was all he was doing – asking for a little help. They were offering the service after all. They didn't care how many times you used it. He reached the paired machines, one of which had a short queue of people at it; the other – his machine – was clear. Pulling his wallet from his pocket he walked up to the cash-point.

His belly filled with ice.

The little red flag was down.

BECAUSE OF A FAULT WE ARE UNABLE TO SERVE YOU

apologised the screen in fluorescent green. Its partner chugged away quite happily, spitting out tenners. Why, why, why? Why wasn't it working when the other one was? You'll just have to wait. Just wait. Go and have a coffee and a wander. Then come back. It'll be working then.

Ignoring his thudding heart Simon crossed the road and slipped into the Victoria Quarter. A flick through the records in Way Ahead would calm him down. But he couldn't even keep his mind together enough to read the names on the covers. He kept trying to crane his neck in order to see the cash-point and see whether it was back in use. He gave up after a few minutes and walked back outside. There was still only one queue but maybe the machine had just come back on and they didn't know yet. He quickly ran over to check, but before he'd even reached the pavement he could see the green line wasn't flashing.

OK. Relax. It won't stay like that all day. It'll have just run out of money or something. They have to fill it up sooner or later. He thought about going into Indie Joze but somehow he didn't think that time would pass quickly there. Instead he forced himself to tramp up to the Merrion Centre and the greasy comfort of the Merrion Coffee House where they still served treacly cappuccinos in dark brown glass cups.

The sugary froth didn't bring much comfort at all. All he could see was a night in Sheffield, an extended agony of indecision. Not knowing what to talk about, not knowing whether he was allowed to make a move, not knowing whether he should be assertive or attentive or friendly or mildly aloof. Without advice every decision he took might be the wrong one. About fifty minutes later he trudged back, the hot panic still breathing in his stomach. He didn't even bother to pause when he saw a single queue still in place.

Simon tried pretending he was waiting for a bus near the bank but was unable to keep sufficiently still to do it comfortably. He then walked up and down Vicar Lane so many times that two girls at another bus stop started giggling on one of his approaches because they thought he fancied them. He didn't care however since that misapprehension coincided with the cash-point coming back into service. He wanted to throw his arms around the people who had formed a queue in his most recent absence, he felt such spontaneous joy. As he pushed his greeny-blue plastic into the slit, delighting in the initial resistance followed by the mechanical snatch, Simon caught sight of his watch. He'd been in town for nearly four and three-quarter hours.

His joy at the service's resumption was short-lived.

VICAR LANE 2

DATE	TIME	CARD REF NO
19/09	15.37	6759 16712

ADVICE

ABYSS CRISIS PITFALL

THE EARTH RUNS OUT BEFORE THE PIT FILLS IN

trust your heart and you will get through

0409 THANK YOU

read the slip. He went cold inside again. Not now. It couldn't go wrong now. Not yet. Nothing had happened. It wasn't fair. Why should she go off him now? He really, really wanted to weep. He didn't. He went home.

It was only as he was getting off the bus that it occurred to Simon he didn't have enough information. He needed to know more about what the crisis was going to be if he was to be able to deal with it successfully. Without thinking about it too much he crossed the road and stood at the bus stop on the other side. It was much colder now, and he had to wait twenty minutes for a 36, but at least he would soon be clearer about what to do. The sense of panic seemed to be lodged firmly inside him now. It made him feel a bit sick.

He got back to the machine and took his place in the queue.

VICAR LANE 2

DATE	TIME	CARD REF NO
19/09	16.52	6759 16712

ADVICE

PRESSURE TENSION TRANSCENDENCE

the roof beam sags

0409 THANK YOU

He read the words so quickly they barely made sense. He scanned them again, more deliberately, and they made even less. He kept doing so, trying to force meaning into them, but he could find none nor make any. He pushed his card into the machine a second time. Someone coughed behind him.

VICAR LANE 2

DATE	TIME	CARD REF NO
19/09	16.53	6759 16712

ADVICE

SOURCE THE WELL RESOURCES

be

0409 THANK YOU

These were just nonsensical. There was no use in them. He rammed his card in again.

"Excuse me," said the indignant voice behind. Simon ignored it as provocatively as he could. The machine whirred and grumbled. No paper was forthcoming. Instead the screen read:

WE HAVE BEEN INSTRUCTED TO RETAIN YOUR CARD.
PLEASE REFER TO YOUR BRANCH.

"No!" Simon shouted. "No. Shit. *No.*"

"Is there a problem? Oh dear. If you wouldn't mind I'd like to get some money out," said the horrible-suited man behind, forcing his way in front of Simon.

Simon was cold and shivering now. And frightened. And despairing. And worst of all he didn't have any money. It was too late to cash a cheque. He walked home.

He should have rung Allison that night to make arrangements but why bother, he thought, what was the point. He'd rather avoid the humiliation and rejection that were surely waiting for him. And worse was the sense of shame that he felt. Shame about fancying her in the first place. Shame that she might know of his desire.

It was all so typical. When did he ever get what he wanted? Things just never worked out his way. He lay on his bed staring at the ceiling, thinking about his unlived past.

All right, all right, there were girls. It wasn't as if he'd never been out with anybody, but they always, without exception, approached him first. He never chose them, or so it felt. And the ones he really, really wanted – wanted the most – he'd never said anything. Somehow, suddenly it seemed to make a difference. That he'd never allowed his lust expression. He'd always relied on the actions and lusts of others. But that was how things were, that was how he was, and if Allison didn't fancy him then she didn't fancy him, so he would leave it and let go, which he always seemed able to do, and that would be the end of it, and everything would be all right in the long term.

Simon went to Lionrock on his own and had a shit time. He'd told Allison that Justin Robertson was a mate, when in fact he was a mate of a mate, and although there was supposed to be a ticket on the door, there wasn't. He almost had an argument with the security man, and ended up having to go to the back of the queue and paying. About an hour later he drove back up the M1 miserable, sober and alone.

Gradually he thought less about Allison Costello and more about Skylab. He went down to London for a day, buying records in Soho, and got stuck in a boring conversation on the way back with an eighteen-year-old girl who presented a children's programme on Cable TV. He didn't fancy her. He had a meeting about some new flyers with a designer called Tom Morris who looked remarkably like a white Jimi Hendrix. He even went to visit his parents in Morecombe, where his mother sat him down at the breakfast bar and told him that Phillipa Land was getting married as if it was a matter of great importance. He had to struggle to remember who she was and then his mother helpfully reminded him that Phillipa was the girl whose heart he'd broken when he was fourteen years old and she was twelve, because he'd rung her up to ask for her friend Caroline's number rather than ask *her* out. His mum had told him off at the time for being insensitive and pointed out that the poor girl must have been so upset. Simon remembered that he never even rang Caroline because his mum had made him feel so guilty.

"Well, I'm glad she's obviously put it behind her now," he said, to which his mother responded by asking him when he was getting married.

Matt rang him on the Wednesday to ask him if he'd like to go for a drink. They met at the Pack Horse and then crossed the road to the Feast and Firkin to meet Pavla and her friend Kate – who was apparently a fashion student but didn't look old enough to get served at the bar. Simon suspected he was being fixed up and spent most of the time silent, staring at the three fly buttons on Kate's black trousers.

"Sack-man, are you all right?"

"I'm just really tired that's all. I think I'll make a move."

The next morning his replacement cash card arrived in the post which was just as well as he was sick of going to the bank to cash cheques. It made him think of the advice slips, all of which he'd kept. He retrieved them from the various pockets he'd left them in and sat cross-legged on the living-room floor smoking a cigarette, reading them. The last one worried him. It hadn't meant anything at the time and even now it remained obscure but he stared at it anyway.

VICAR LANE 2

DATE	TIME	CARD REF NO
19/09	16.53	6759 16712

ADVICE

SOURCE THE WELL RESOURCES

be

0409 THANK YOU

There was something about it that made him feel … he searched inside for what it was. After a few moments he settled on guilty. Guilty because it suddenly felt like he was wasting something.

That night he got an unexpected call from Pavla's friend Kate, asking him if he'd like to meet her for a drink. Why not, he thought, expecting to feel cheered by the fact that somebody obviously fancied him, but he found that he didn't because he hadn't fancied her.

"You aren't listening to me," Kate complained, but Simon had been. It just looked like he hadn't because he was so distracted. I don't want to be here, he thought.

"You were talking about how you wanted to set up your own

designer label," replied Simon. Kate smiled back at him and carried on outlining her plans of empire and he carried on feeling sorry for himself. Kate was good-looking and well turned out but he might as well have been with his little sister.

'be', the advice slip had said. 'be'.

"Kate, I'm really sorry. I'm not feeling that good. Do you mind if I just go home?" Kate had suggested they go out dancing. Simon knew he couldn't.

She looked confused and then cross. "Simon? Can I ask you something?" She turned towards him looking very serious. "Are you gay?"

When he got home Simon had to search through three pairs of trousers until he found what he was looking for. He sat cross-legged on the floor for a few minutes. Then he went over to the telephone.

The front door had a panel of rippled glass in it. Simon rang the bell and then pressed his face against the rippled window. A distorted shape appeared much sooner than he had expected and he moved his head away sharply, not wanting to look stupid. He wondered how fast it was possible for the human heart to beat.

"Do you want a cup of tea?" Allison asked him. Her hair was wet. She must have just had a shower.

"Are you sure this is all right?"

"No, I want you to leave now," she said. Involuntarily Simon moved to get up. "Of course it's all right." He sat back down again and hoped she hadn't noticed. "I'll make some tea." She smiled and left the room.

Simon looked around. The front room was still in the process of being made Allison's. There was a flyer for Skylab propped next to the mirror, which had yet to be hung. Simon caught a glimpse of his own eyes reflected back at him. His heart was still beating far too fast. Or maybe it wasn't, it occurred to him. Of course it wasn't. It was right it was beating that fast. It meant something that it was beating that fast. It was a language that up until now he had been refusing to understand, but now he was aware of it, it was suddenly plain enough; he just hadn't been listening.

Allison came back in holding two white tin mugs. Simon looked at her face and his heart speeded up again but that was all right. Just do it, he thought.

"Allison. The thing is ... look ... I'm not sure how ... I need to ... I'm in love with you." The words came out. Articulating them had felt like pushing a big ball over the top of an incline. It was done now and there was nothing to stop the ball rolling all the way down to the bottom – except he didn't know where the bottom was.

He waited. The world didn't end. He didn't die, consumed by the expected violence of her anger. He breathed in. "I'm very much in love with you." The words came out again, less tentatively. He felt proud of them now. He was willing to own up to the fact that they were his. Another pause, less agonising, more contemplative. And then: "I fancy you more than I've ever fancied anyone in my life. In twenty-eight years. I want you so much I've cried at the thought of not having you. Oh God ..." He started laughing and he felt tears wetting the corners of his eyes. "It's so simple. I want you. I mean I want to be with you. Well, both things. Do you know, this is the first time I've ever thought you're allowed to say something like this. Allison, I want you more than anyone else I've ever wanted in my life *and it's all right to say it. It's allowed.*"

There was a moment of silence. Allison looked at him. She put the mugs of tea on the floor. Then she looked at Simon again.

Then she turned towards him and slowly brought her lips against the side of his neck. She kissed him very lightly at first. The weirdest thing was that though he thought he should be surprised he wasn't in the least. Each of her tiny movements became magnified through a series of pleasure-lenses until Simon experienced the final sensation as one of almost unendurable delight somewhere in between his stomach and his heart. His cock pointed towards the heavens in praise. Allison rolled herself around him and brought her lips on to his and Simon thought, This is worth everything. This is worth my panic attacks in '87, and appendicitis and every previous rejection and Dad thumping me for breaking his record player when I was eleven and every other shit thing. Just this. Just being alive now, for this. And then he stopped being aware of thinking and got on with the moment because Allison was simultaneously pulling his clothes off and licking his ear.

"You fool," she laughed as they rolled to the floor. And sometime around dawn they fucked each other with big smiles on their faces and then they fell asleep holding each other and the curtains glowed blue in the morning sun.

£250,000 electrical clearance

I needed an iron. That's how I ended up there. I don't think I'd have been enticed in without a good solid reason.

Anyway, as I say, I needed an iron. Ellie had just left and she'd taken all that stuff with her. Iron, tea-towels, cleaning stuff, bathmat. All the little knick-knacks from the bathroom. Wind-up penguin. The jar of foam rubber letters that you could stick to the tiles and spell words with. The iron was the thing I required. Shirts needed doing, trousers too. So I'm there walking down Oxford Street and this young foreign guy comes running up to me.

"Sir, sir!" he's calling out, as if he knows me or something. Well, naturally I stop, anybody would. He's wearing a big grey coat, and carrying a sheaf of creamy yellow papers. He didn't look in any way dodgy. His coat looked quite expensive and designery. He was good-looking with dark hair and Italian features. I thought at first he was with one of those language schools – the ones that hang out around the entrance to Tottenham Court Road Tube giving out leaflets. "Sir, sir," he repeats as he gets close. He hands me one of the leaflets:

Sony Kenwood Sega Nintendo Phillips Alba

£250,000
ELECTRICAL CLEARANCE

Sony	Laptop	JVC
Handycam	Computer	Camcorders
£~~599~~ £100	£~~699~~ £100	£~~599~~ £100

James Hood

Sony	Sony	Sony
Playstation	Discman	Walkman
~~£299~~ £50	~~£99.99~~ £20	~~£39.99~~ £8

Casio	Nintendo	Super
Pocket TV	Game Boy	Nintendo
~~£89.99~~ £20	~~£34.99~~ £5	~~£89.99~~ £20

All Goods Subject to Availability   All Major Credit Cards Accepted

SALE NOW ON

100 Dean Street

Remington   Sharp   Bosch   Pioneer   Sony

I looked down the list of brand names he'd placed in my hand. I didn't necessarily think it was bogus or anything, I just didn't consider it had anything to do with me. Before I could say anything he was pulling at my jacket.

"Come on, come on." He was actually taking me across the road. Instinctively I resisted. He was on the other side of the road now. I was still outside the B2. He looked at me. "Come on," he repeated. I shrugged my shoulders and smiled, although I don't know what I was smiling about. I was about to walk back to Virgin, when he dashed back to my side of the road again, narrowly avoiding a cab. He reached me panting. "It start very soon. Come on. Come now." He had his arm on my shoulder. There was a bus coming but he pushed me across the road nevertheless. We both had to run to reach the other side safely. "Yeah, that's it. This way." We were walking down Dean Street now. I was making excuses in my head about why I would actually want to go to this thing. "Come on, that's right." It was all he kept saying, along with "This way, this way."

We arrived at an anonymous-looking shop front. On one side there was the entrance to a jazz club, on the other some kind of film editing place. The shop had windows but they were tinted dark brown, and there were drawn venetian blinds so it was difficult to see what was going on inside. There was a bigger version of the leaflet I had been handed sellotaped inside the glass. The place had a temporary look about it – it would probably be a porn emporium in three weeks' time.

I went inside. Almost immediately I sensed my Italian friend had disappeared. I looked round but the door had shut behind me and you couldn't see through the glass back into the street.

The shop itself was pretty empty. There were brand logos painted on the artex wall – Sony, Panasonic, JVC – in big red and blue letters. In the centre of the room there was a metal trolley of the kind you might see food served from in a hospital. There were a few people standing over it, eyeing its contents. I was reluctant to move towards it – embarrassed about my presence there. I think I was still entertaining the idea that I could leave. Also I didn't want anyone else to think I was weak enough to have been so easily coerced into being there. But they were all there too. They were hardly in a position to sit in judgement over me. I found I'd taken a couple of steps forward anyway, fired by my curiosity about what was on the trolley. There were a number of small boxes with their contents removed and laid next to them: a pocket TV; a gameboy; an electronic organiser. There was a sense of awe around the people who were examining them, as if they had never seen such things before. I found myself amongst them. It was the low prices that inspired awe. Items that normally retailed for over a hundred pounds were all marked under ten. I looked up. Ahead of me there was a high wooden counter. Much higher than you would usually find in a shop. It made you feel like a child. Behind it there was a young man in a blue sweatshirt. He had blond hair, closely cropped – almost a flat top. He was fiddling with a laptop computer, ignoring our presence. Behind him, stacked in temporary-looking piles, were more electrical goods. Panasonic CD players. Toshiba televisions. Kenwood kitchen stuff. And, as if to confirm I was in the right place, right at the top of one pile, a Russell Hobbs iron. Well, that was it. It was well worth staying now. I'd probably never get round to buying an iron otherwise – and while I was here why not get some other things for the flat, particularly because it was feeling so sparse at the moment. It would be nice to have a CD player in the kitchen, and what about a separate telly in the bedroom?

I could just imagine what Ellie would say about my presence here. Or would have said. She wasn't going to say anything now that she'd gone. I didn't anticipate seeing her again, at least not to have a conversation with.

Ellie. What can I tell you about Ellie? I was glad she'd gone. Glad I'd been able to keep it so surgical.

So the fellah starts talking. The man behind the counter. He'd got something round his neck. It was a kind of harness thing with a microphone in it, so he could move around and gesticulate while he was speaking. He began talking as if he was picking up a thread of an earlier address, except he had been silent all the time I'd been in the shop. He had a cheery, likeable cockney accent.

"So basically ladies and gentlemen what we got here is something so good you will not believe it." All the time he spoke he fiddled with his laptop, glancing at the screen every so often. "You will not believe it. I tell you. I'm telling you. Like that joke about the blue comedian in the Jewish old age home – you know, the little old lady pipes up from the back –" he adopted a surprisingly good Jewish accent – " 'He keeps telling us but when's he going to show us,' well I'm going to show you now." He produced from under his counter a top-of-the-range Sony camcorder. "Put your hands up who'd want this for a hundred pound. Come on. Someone must." Two or three hands went up. "Woman earlier put both her legs up and I gave it to her for free. Come on. It's Sony, not phony, not macaroni." He shouted the last six words like a football chant. He looked at his computer screen again. A few more hands went up uncertainly. "Well you can put your hands down now my darlings, because I ain't gonna give it to you for a hundred pound." I looked at the bearded man next to me. He smiled to himself as if he'd had something confirmed. "No I ain't, not ninety either. Or eighty or seventy. Or even sixty. You can have it for fifty, five zero, that's five oh as in Hawaii." The bearded man raised his eyebrows. "Thought you'd like that one. Where you from sir?" There was no response. He was looking at the bearded man. "Yeah you sir – I ain't asking you to get your doodle out. Do you know what a doodle is madam?" He turned to the young woman closest to the front. "Do you know the difference between a doodle and a chicken leg?" She shook her head coyly. "Remind me to ask you on a picnic. So where are you from sir?"

"Poland," the man answered. He had a thick accent.

"Ahh Poland. *Wiecej madrosci nauczy cie jedna zona niz tysiac kochanek.*"

The Polish man raised his eyebrows again and muttered: "*Prawdziwy, prawdziwy.*" He was clearly impressed.

The salesman's patter continued in this vein for some time. As he hustled and jived there seemed to be many new customers filling the room. I hadn't noticed them arriving but there were more and more hands going up in response to his cod questions. They were a real mix too: mainly tourists, I suppose; some single men. Everybody looked a bit lost. It seemed most of us had been asked a question about where we were from. The salesman seemed to know something about every place, saying something in the appropriate language or if you were from England something specific about where you lived. To me he said, as he waved an electric carving knife:

"The wife'd love one of these. I've been married six years. You get less for murder don't you. Are you married sir?" I shook my head. "Do you have a girlfriend?" Reluctant to speak I shook my head again. "That only leaves one option. I wish I hadn't asked now." Other people laughed. "Where you from?"

"Leeds," I told him, without thinking.

"I know a club there. Back to Basics. Had some friends from Chapeltown. I went home in stitches."

I suppose I still could have left at that point but I was convinced I would be going home with a range of top quality electrical goods. I had it all worked out in my head. How good the flat was going to be. A portable CD player in the kitchen. Good for entertaining new lady friends with whilst cooking dinner. After all I was a single man again now. I could have someone new by the weekend if I wanted. Just for the weekend. A video and telly for the bedroom. Good for watching the following morning, in between bouts of hot sex.

"Now I know none of you trust me. So just to prove I'm trustworthy I'm gonna give you all a free gift before we carry on. A free bag. How'd'ya like a free bag?" There was a low farmyard murmur. He pulled up a wad of black plastic bin-liners. "How d'ya like Gucci?" He held one of the bin-liners up. "No?" He tore a hole in it. "How about Versace?"

See the thing with Ellie was – well, she was a pain. We'd been seeing each other a year or so. She moved in about three months ago. I didn't want her to move in but somehow she did. It was all right at first. Well, for the first couple of weeks anyway. Except even then I was scared. I remember going into the bedroom on the first night and thinking, This is how it's going to be for ever now – someone else in the bed for ever.

"Right! Like Buddy Holly, I'm gonna tell you how it's gonna be. What we're gonna do here is we're going to have a bit of an auction. You know what an auction is don't you. Like an anorexic on a hunger strike. Going, going, gone." Some of the crowd shuffled uneasily. I was sure there were some who didn't understand a word he was saying. "Now we can't not let you take advantage of what we got here, so we're not going to let you just buy *one* of these bargains. We're going to sell them in batches. You want this telly, and this CD player and this video. Then you going to bid for the lot. Come on.

Who wants to start?" Nobody said anything. "Have you all died or something?"

A voice piped up from somewhere: "Fiver." I looked round but I couldn't see who spoke. Nobody had their arm up.

"A fiver? For this lot? You're joking aren't you? Nobody else? All right ..." Is this serious? I thought. Should I put my hand up? I could have all that stuff. It would be all right, that stuff. In my flat. Just as I was about to put my hand up someone else pre-empted me.

"Ten pound." It was a youngish man, German I think. His girlfriend stood next to him, grinning.

"That's better. Ten pounds now. It's still a pisstake though innit."

"Twenty," someone else called.

"Twenty-five," shouted the German.

"Twenty-five." The salesman seemed pleased. "I'll pack this up. You pay at the end. This lot's yours to take back to Deutschland. *Wie sagt man – das ist nicht tern.*" Well, that was that, I thought. Twenty-five quid was more than I was planning to spend but why shouldn't I have what I wanted when it was so easy? I kept thinking about a lovely portable TV sitting in the corner of the bedroom.

Ellie and the bedroom. Ellie in the bedroom. Before she moved in we'd had sex quite a lot. Fun sex too. I remember flat-sitting for some friends once – we only stayed one night to look after the cats. We were messing about with food and stuff. I was licking things off her. This is quite unlike her, I remember thinking at the time. There was another time, just after we'd first moved in, on the first day in fact. There were unopened boxes everywhere. There was hardly any space. We were in the living room not the bedroom. We were kissing then we fell to the floor. We pulled off each other's clothes.

"What if somebody sees?" She motioned with her head to the open curtains. It didn't matter.

But then after we'd moved in, there was this gradual decline. Actually if I'm being honest it was me not her. There were other people I fancied more. In the way I used to fancy her. "Talk about it," she'd say. "At least try and talk about." She was always on at me, often when we were lying in bed. It was easier not to.

"Now I'm gonna be leaving you," said the salesman. "I'm gonna be handing you over to my colleague. He's the auctioneer."

We did have a laugh together, but I was bored, you know. What else are you supposed to do? I mean I liked her and everything but I didn't want to be stuck being miserable. And there was this girl who'd started work in the credit control department who was much sexier. If I finished it with Ellie things would be much better. It was going to be awkward of course, but I knew I could do it cleanly. A clean break. It would be like having a filling done. You have to gird yourself when you go in but when it's finished you're really happy. It wouldn't be a nice thing to do but it wasn't going to bother me for long.

So I sat her down one night. I said: "We've got to finish."

"Why?" she said. Her face was white. It's just how it is, I explained. It's just how it goes. She cried for ages, but I knew I had to stick it out. I was really firm. I'd made this plan about going to stay at Nick's for a week and she could move out while I was there. When I came back it would all be done with and she'd be gone. I knew she'd be all right. She could go back to her dad's until she was sorted. Eventually she quietened down and accepted it. I had to go out though that night. It wasn't nice listening to her cry.

But in the end it had been simple and, to be honest, pretty easy.

What was amazing was how quickly the atmosphere changed when the salesman left. He'd gone through into the back taking his laptop with him. For a moment we were all just left staring at the piles of boxes behind the high counter. Suddenly they all seemed tatty and battered.

Then there was a commotion. All these men piled out from the dark door that the salesman had disappeared into. They looked like they'd come off a building site, wearing paint-spattered sweatshirts or dirty tracksuit bottoms. They were heavy set, most of them, with pale, blotchy faces, like they were all fresh from prison. They filed around the side of the room, and the back. There was a smell of cheap after-shave. Everyone looked around at them. It wasn't what anyone had been expecting. There was an extremely loud crack. We all faced the front.

Standing behind the counter was this huge fellah. He wore a pink satin shirt with a Ralph Lauren insignia. The two top buttons were undone, revealing masses of thick black hair amongst which, half-hidden, was a little gold crucifix. His hands were covered in rings. He held what looked like a heavy old hammer, the metal part of which had been removed. He cracked it again on the surface of the counter. It made a terrible noise.

"*Affederziniz bakar misiniz*!" His accent was thick – Cypriot or Turkish. "Can I have your attention please?" he growled. "Thank you. Right. The party is over my friends, the party is over. We are here to do business." He cracked the handle once again. "To do business. You understand?" I looked over my shoulder to see if I could get to the door. It was now blocked by two of the rough-looking men. The young German man said something to his girlfriend. "You, Germany! Be quiet." The Turk pointed with his hammer handle to a sign behind his head, written in blocky, felt-tip letters. "Please Keep Quiet During Sale." One of his eyes was funny, pointing in the wrong direction. "Now I want you all up here, up by the line." There was a line of white tape on the floor near the counter. "I want you to move now." The rough men mobilised, one showing us where to stand, three others pushing from the back. The Turk raised his eyes to the ceiling as if we were idiots he was already tired of dealing with. We shuffled together, uncomfortably close to one another.

"Now who wants Toshiba?" Nobody said anything. "*Cahil budala.* Who wants Toshiba?" he shouted. "Put your hands up." He looked straight at me with his good eye. "You, Leeds. Stand up straight. Are you homosexual?" I felt nine years old, back at school. Felt it in my stomach. "Are you homosexual?"

"No," I heard myself saying.

"Then answer me. Do you want Toshiba?"

"Yes." I could see that a middle-aged couple had detached themselves from the side of the crush next to me. They were trying to reach the door. "Two dwellers," muttered the Turk into his mike. "Stop the dwellers by the door." There was a commotion but I didn't look round. "*O kapayi kapalin*," he shouted before turning his attention back to us. "You want Toshiba, we gonna have to bid. I'm gonna tell you how it works." Two of the rough men had gone to stand next to him. "Now we got so many bargains here, we have to know you're serious before we let you bid. Your eyes should be on me Poland, nowhere else. So you want to be in, you put your money where your mouth is. I want to see five pounds. Take five pounds from your pocket. I want every hand in the air with a five pound note." I found my hand in my pocket. I wasn't going to get the money out. Someone came up behind me. I could smell coffee-breath and unwashed clothes.

"Come on Leeds," a voice muttered in my ear. "Get your fucking money out. That's it. In the air." Everyone had their hands up clutching a banknote. The men came round and took the banknotes, replacing them with battered little bits of yellow plastic. They had "£5" written on them in marker pen.

"These are like vouchers now. You claim them back yeah, against anything you buy." There was a sudden emptiness in my stomach accompanied by a rising gloom. "OK. First thing up. This is a bargain ladies and gents. An absolute bargain." Another crack of the hammer handle. "A marvellous tool set. Every tool you'd ever want in there. Screwdriver. Spanner. It's all in there." He pulled up a grey plastic box shaped like a briefcase with a black plastic handle. It looked like a child's version of a toolkit. He opened it and briefly flashed it around. It was not something you would ever want. It was cheap and dull and ugly. "This gonna cost you a hundred, hundred and fifty in the shops." It wasn't. You wouldn't find it in the shops. You'd be hard pushed to find it on a street market. It looked like ex-catalogue stuff that they couldn't shift. "I got ten of these here. We start the bid at twenty-five pound, yeah." There was a muttering at the back and someone put their hand up.

Unbelievably people started bidding. The price went up from twenty-five to thirty to thirty-five and stopped at forty. Money was taken off people together with their yellow "vouchers". Someone asked if they could pay by card. "The machine's broke. But it's all right. You know your pin-number yeah. You come out with them to the cash machine and pay us that way." I looked around at the variety of faces – the tourists, the single men, the young couple. No one reacted, no one seemed outraged. A couple more lots went by – a cheap-looking camera, a set of cutlery. I made a personal resolution that I wasn't going to buy anything and that I would just keep my head down until it was time to leave.

"Now. We come to our last item. This one's for anyone who's missed a bargain so far. Hands up who's still got a voucher left. That's it hold it high in the air." A few arms went up around me. I still had mine but I gripped it tightly and put my hand in my pocket. "Come on now … we don't want anyone leaving thinking they missed out, yeah." The Turk scanned the room with his funny eye. It had gone very quiet. Oxford Street's just round the corner, I thought to myself. I'll be out of here soon. "There's a lady there. Miss, you got your voucher?" Her hand joined the small crop of plastic cards. I made the mistake of looking down at my shoes. "What about you Leeds? You not looking for a bargain today? Get it up."

I don't know why, or where I found the courage, but I said: "I haven't got one." I immediately regretted it. I felt raw and vulnerable under his scrutiny.

"You haven't got one. What d'you mean? You haven't got a penis. Is that what you mean? Or maybe it's two you haven't got. You haven't got balls." A thump on the desk from the hammer. Then he shouted, painfully loud: "Get your fucking voucher in the air!"

"Come on Leeds, do as he says." Another of the men had come behind me now. "Hold that arm high." He pulled my hand from the pocket with force.

"That's right Leeds. I want you reaching for the skies. On your tiptoes. You can't miss this bargain. *Haberzis sicma.* Now we got one each for you here, one each."

He pulled up a load of white boxes, each one about the size of three cigarette cartons. He moved them around and arranged them into a stack. As he continued talking he kept rearranging them into stacks of different sizes. "Now this is what we call a mystery lot. You going to have to bid blind for this one. All I'm saying is it's something valuable. Of real value."

"Keep that arm up."

"Leeds. You want to start the bidding?" I didn't say anything. "I can't hear you Leeds. You have to shout louder."

"Five pounds."

"Say it louder."

"Five pounds."

"How much?"

"Five pounds," I shouted.

He cracked his hammer firmly, three times, as he said: "Going, going, gone." The men came between us snatching our yellow vouchers from us. They threw the boxes towards us. Each one found a hand with alarming accuracy. There was a box for every one of us that had not bought anything else.

"Thank you, thank you. Feel free to come back again any time. *Gule gule. Shalom.*" With that the Turk disappeared through the beaded curtain. The rough men too, having unlocked the door, faded back into the darkness at the back of the shop apart from one who herded everyone out with great speed.

I didn't look at my box as I made my way back to Oxford Street. It was now dark, past six o'clock, and I was grateful for the cold November night. It brought me back to somewhere I knew. I hurried off in search of a Number 19 bus.

When I got home I turned on all the lights and locked the door. As I walked round the flat I noticed there were big gaps everywhere, things I'd got used to seeing were now missing. A line of books on the windowsill in the hall. The curtainy things she'd put up in the bathroom that were really just a bit of muslin. The toy theatre she'd kept on top of the television. I sat down in the kitchen. I was going to throw the box away – leave it on the greengrocer's rubbish by the front door for the bin men to take away. I didn't. I brought it back. I sat with it in front of me on the kitchen table. I slid my thumb in the gap between the side of the box and the lid and pulled back the white card. Inside was a piece of unpolished wood. I pulled it out. It was the base of an alarm clock. The clock was unusual. The wood was rough but it was laquered dark brown. The clock within it was metal, its face covered with a dome of glass. I placed it on the shelf above the table. Its tick was loud. I sat there for some time listening to it.

Then I thought about Ellie. About her face. About watching her have a bath once. About not having dinner with her again. About being alone.

I started to cry.

The maze

When Carver thought about the maze he could picture it very clearly. The thick green walls of leaves, the scuffed brown pathway that may once have been lawn, the iron trellis that was pulled across the entrance at six o'clock each evening. But apart from the fact that it had been somewhere in Roundhay Park, he could never recall its exact location. He wasn't one for remembering anyway. The past is a closed book, he'd thought to himself, as if it were something that he'd decided. The truth was, the more he tried to open the pages the tighter they clung together.

"Do you remember going to the park on Sundays – when we were kids?" he asked his sister one evening. He was baby-sitting, yet again, but had arrived earlier than usual. He leaned against the doorpost of her immaculate bedroom, watching her reflection applying lipstick.

"Once or twice. I don't think they were Sundays. You make it sound like a regular thing."

"Maybe it was before you were born." There were five years between them but increasingly Carver caught himself thinking he was the younger of the two. It dated back to Cathy's marriage. She had developed an independent life and grown in stature. It wasn't just the acquisition of a husband and children. Having them had brought it about. "What was your favourite thing? What did you like the most?" he persisted.

"I don't remember liking it very much at all. I think I fell in the boating lake once and it put me off going – Caroline Foody pushed me in."

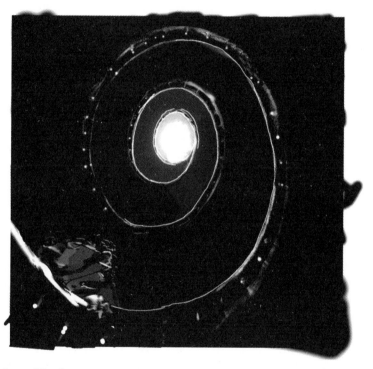

James Hood

"What about the children's fair?" For some reason Carver didn't want to prompt a recollection. He wanted to hear his sister recall the maze spontaneously. He was pleased to see her smiling as she spoke.

"The helter-skelter. Now I did like that. The scary thrill when you got to the top and you had to force yourself to slide down."

"Anything else?" he inquired, a little too eagerly.

"No ... What's the sudden interest anyway?" She broke off suspiciously.

"Nothing. No reason." Carver found himself feeling stupid and childish, as if there were something to be ashamed of in his questions.

"I've got to finish getting ready. Go speak to Alistair."

He sloped from the room sheepishly. Watching Cathy from behind, hunched over her dressing table surface, covered with its confusion of tubes, brushes and pots, he realised how much she looked like Mum – and how similar she sounded. He could have been nine years old again, the way he felt dismissed.

"Aye, we used to go quite a lot. It was either there or once round Eccup Reservoir." Alistair dribbled the last of the foam out of the Guinness can before passing it to Carver. "I loved the outdoor swimming pool. It's closed now though. Do you remember it? Right down the bottom end."

"Yes. With the artificial waterfall in the woods behind." Carver sat down with his drink and watched Alistair polish his shoes.

"We'd sneak behind the cubicles and peek at the girls. There were loads of holes and gaps in the wood. The lasses would plug 'em up with toilet paper but it was easy enough to poke out. That was only in summer though." He smiled as he spat at the leather.

"What about the rest of the year?" Carver continued trying to make his interest sound as natural as possible.

"We used to hang around the bandstand – smoking, drinking cider ..."

Carver felt deflated. Alistair's reminiscences were dismayingly adolescent, and worse, they reminded him of an adolescence he never had. He wanted to encourage earlier memories.

"What about the children's fair? Did you ever spend time there?"

"Och, yes. Too much time." Carver smiled. This was more encouraging. "Richard Frost had a weekend job running the mini-octopus. We thought that if we sat with him showing off, the girls would come flocking." Carver sighed inwardly. Alistair wouldn't stray further back than fourteen. "They did of course, but only the wee ones. Nine and ten." He winked at Carver. "And that's no good to man nor beast."

Perhaps the best thing was to be open. It might be the only way he'd hear what he wanted.

"Do you remember the hedge maze?" Carver asked.

"Hedge maze?"

"Yes. Before they got rid of it?"

There was a pause before Alistair's face shifted into a smile of understanding. "That'll have been before my time. We only moved down from Dumfries in '79."

"Come on, Mr Chatterbox. Get those shoes on. We won't be able to park." Cathy had appeared, fussing around the kitchen door. She turned to Carver. "And make sure Anne stays in bed tonight. I'd rather not come back to find her watching videos at half-past eleven, thank you." He winced a little at her rebuke and tried to smile as Alistair squeezed past him, winking again.

That night, at home in bed, the duvet rolled tightly around him, Carver closed his eyes and attempted to place himself back in the park. Not as it was now – faded, smaller in size – but as he remembered it: huge, ever-changing, packed with surprise, with key points of delight whose presence guaranteed pleasure every time. He could see the black-watered boating lake with its moss-legged pavilion hovering above one end. The water lapped gently in his head and he found himself in the little train carriage that circled perpetually in the children's fair. He could see Mum through the cut-out window, waving each time he passed her, Dad at her side with his hands in his pockets, rocking on his heels. Now he was at the cream and green bandstand that smelt of wee and wet tobacco, and then he was running through the maze, trailing his hand against the spiky twigged hedge to his left. Try as he might, he could not connect these locations together. He would flip from one to the other with no journey in between. The hedge maze could have been anywhere and that was what infuriated him most. If it was anywhere, as opposed to somewhere, then it could also be nowhere. A fragment of an imagined past as opposed to a remnant of a real one. Tomorrow he'd work a little harder at finding his way back.

The home wasn't that bad. The nurses cared. The floors were clean. There was a bright sun lounge they'd opened last year where everyone could sit and sip watery tea from the vending machine. Carver always thought Dad was too young to be here and really he was, but two strokes had left him needing constant nursing. Mum had managed with the first one but the second came with her death and the home had been the only real option. Some of the fees were covered by an insurance policy Dad had taken out through the company he'd worked for most of his life and Cathy and Alistair made up the rest. Carver would have liked to contribute but he was in no position to do so.

Dad, slumped to the left, made for one of the biscuits on the tray in front of him.

"I was remembering the park, Dad. When we used to go on Sundays." Dad nodded, munching his digestive. Carver waited anxiously for a smile. It didn't come. "I was talking to Cathy. She doesn't really recall it, but it was before she was born, I suppose." He felt a little embarrassed at this naked reminiscing. He'd never talked to his father this directly about anything. But he needed to know.

"It was always cold. That place. The wind whipping around the trees." He remembered it. That was a start.

"I was thinking about where we used to go. The boating lake. The children's fair. The helter-skelter ..."

"Aye ..." His father nodded again, releasing a few crumbs down his sweater.

"I wondered what you could recall." There was a pause and some more munching.

"Cold. It was always cold."

Carver sat back in his seat and reached for the thin plastic cup of tea which was also cold. Dad slumped a little more and released a roaring yawn. For a moment Carver contemplated reaching for his hand but he suppressed the urge. It would be an impossible thing to actually do. Instead he spoke again.

"The maze, Dad. Do you remember the maze?"

"The maze ..." His father looked at the floor and the edges of his mouth twitched. Was he smiling? Carver, his teeth tightly clenched, willed him to speak some more. Very slowly Dad's eyes closed. His breathing increased in depth as he drifted into sleep. Carver waited for a moment.

"Dad?" The only response came in drowsy respiration.

On an impulse walking to the bus stop, Carver crossed the road. He'd decided to take the bus into town instead of back home. Then he could get another up to Roundhay. It seemed the obvious thing to do. A walk round the park might jog his own memory. Why seek the help of others when surely somewhere inside he had an answer himself?

He took the Number 10 from outside Lewis's that ran all the way to the park gates. It was funny to be on a bus journey that he hadn't travelled for nearly twenty years. He had been to the park since, but usually by car. To do it this way was like riding back to his childhood. Much had changed but the topography remained the same. The Clock

Cinema was now an electrical showroom, Texas Homecare had sprouted from what he remembered as open ground but then, as Carver approached the park, things became increasingly familiar. High metal railings flicked past on the right, first black, then bright green. Huge Victorian homes, veiled by poplars and oaks, lay to his left, although many of them were now announced as hotels or nursing homes by conspicuous signs.

The terminus came at one of the park's entrances. With a faint feeling of excitement Carver dismounted and made his way in. It was a fine autumn afternoon. It was strange to be so cold under a bright blue sky but very pleasant all the same. The frosty air was sharp with the dull tang of mud. The cries of children mingled with the calls of birds over the lake. The occasional skateboard roared across the car-park. Carver trod discarded lollipop sticks underfoot, the remnants of a summer now distant.

It wasn't just that the place looked different, it also felt different. This was partly because he now knew its geography – how one entrance linked with another, how the park fitted into the rest of the city. It was still huge, but in adulthood, Carver could conceive its size. When he was a child it had been boundless.

He passed the crumpled metal nets of bins and wandered off the concrete into the park, to begin his search for clues. Sure enough, there was the children's fair up ahead. He paused at the miniature dodgems cowled for the winter and the little merry-go-round, its chair-swings trussed up like game in a butcher's shop. The train wasn't here but there was a line of slot machine rides: two faded clowns on a see-saw; an angular Bambi with an extended neck, staring ahead with an expression of permanent surprise; a little Noah's Ark sporting, absurdly, a racing car's steering wheel.

Carver closed his eyes and tried to imagine walking from here to the maze. He saw nothing. Then he wondered if he might look suspicious, skulking around the children's rides in his overcoat with his eyes pressed closed. Frustrated and embarrassed he opened them and moved on.

There was another car-park, visible behind the fair. It must serve as an overflow during the summer. Perhaps the maze had been there, its roots buried for ever beneath heavy grey concrete. If this were the case there was nothing to mark it. It was just an empty guess – Carver felt no confirmation within.

Although there were other people about, the scale of the park made it feel quite empty. People stood out as spikes on distant hills ... or moved quickly past, trailing dogs and children. Carver wondered about a woman he saw bending down in the middle of a patch of grass until he drew closer and saw it was in fact a long-haired man, searching for magic mushrooms.

The lake lay up ahead, preceded by a rolling incline. There was the pavilion, which had recently been converted into a waterside café. The new wood around the walls smelled like freshly sharpened pencils. As he moved round the side, Carver tried to force another memory. Could the maze have been up here, an added attraction after taking a boat? Ducks pulled rippling Vs across the brackish water. He knew it wasn't at this end. He felt like stamping his feet. How could he be so sure about where it wasn't and not know where it was?

On his way back to the bus stop, Carver fought off despair. The maze had been here. He knew it had been here. Perhaps what dismayed him was the fact that he had so few people to ask if they too remembered. He shook off the feeling and tried to focus his mind. There must be other options. Official channels. Public records. He looked at his watch. He had time to get to the library before it closed.

The bus ride back to town touched Carver with sadness. He had travelled here in expectation of reaching something, only to discover that there was no entrance available. The late afternoon gloom and the percussive rain didn't help. He thought of the present and shivered a little. The world outside slipped past, wet and unreal. He remembered the front of the maze the last time he had seen it, the dark iron padlocked gate, strange against the rich green of the leaves which encircled it. He'd asked Mum why it was closed in the middle of the day. She'd mumbled something about a boy being hurt. How could you be hurt in the maze? He'd wanted her to take him round, lead him to the park bench in the middle, lift him up to drink from the water-fountain that stood at its side. But she didn't. Not ever again. He couldn't remember when they went to the park after that.

There were other mazes. Hampton Court on a school trip. Its seedy replica in the Blackpool Pleasure Beach. A mirror maze at a visiting fair. But although they all promised it, none of them actually delivered the same feeling. They were available to too many people. Just another attraction. The maze in Roundhay Park had been made for Carver.

Hurrying down the Headrow, his collar up to keep off the rain, Carver glanced at his watch. It was almost five twenty-five. He wasn't sure what time it closed. Passing the squat blocks of the Art Gallery, he ran towards the ornate shelter of the library buildings.

Not unlike the park, the library offered a sense of Victorian comfort – a suggestion of a simpler, more ordered past. Perhaps there was something sterner here, a building of learning, not pleasure, but the general air was the same – a steady municipal calm. Breathless from his sprint through the rain, Carver had to take the steps slowly. They doubled back on themselves making little landings as they rose and at each corner was carved a chunky stone griffin, clinging fiercely to the banister. They looked strangely out of place against the mosaic tiling and polished brass rails.

The reference library was right at the top, softly lit behind heavy swinging doors. Carver passed inside and made his way to the inquiries desk. His heart was still thumping at speed, no longer from exertion, but rather fuelled by nervousness and a touch of excitement. The roomy silence only added to the difficulty of speaking to the untidy young librarian intent on his computer screen. Forcing himself, Carver managed to form his question.

"I'm trying to find out about Roundhay Park, about its history …?" Without looking up the man directed him through a passage that ran behind his desk and told him to walk right to its end.

It felt like he was doing something he shouldn't be allowed to do. The narrow corridor seemed out of the public domain. But then, unexpectedly, it opened out into shelves and shelves of books, an extension of the library that Carver never knew existed. Someone old looked up as he passed, before coughing and returning their gaze to the page.

The passage continued amongst the bookcases ending at another room without a door. "Local History", read the sign over the entrance. It was brighter inside than the main library. The shelves stretched higher, holding a greater variety of books. A large woman in a pink cardigan smiled at him as he entered. He wandered towards her desk.

"I'm trying to find out about the history of Roundhay Park, particularly the maze?" The woman smiled and gestured to him to sit down. As she did so, Carver noticed, with an unpleasant little jolt, that three fingers were missing from her left hand.

He found himself terribly excited. The prospect that he might have his memories confirmed so directly promised a feeling of great satisfaction, as if the hole he had observed growing within him might be about to be filled. The woman returned with a small number of items. She looked at her watch as she spread them out before him. Carver tried to avoid glancing at the shiny, pinkish stumps between her index and little finger.

"If there's anything more you want just come and ask."

The first book he picked up was a tatty pamphlet, produced in the 1980s. It looked older than the others even though it was the most recent thing there. Carver flicked through its thin pages, eagerly scanning the pale grey photographs and text for a hint of the maze. There was none. He ran backward through the leaves just to be sure. Nothing. A little desperately he picked up another book. This one was mustier, bound in heavy green leather. *Roundhay Park: a complete record*. It was dated 1897 in faded gold type on its spine. There was a set of engravings, clustered in the centre. The waterfall, the folly, the old mansion house. No maze.

Carver felt panic tugging at his stomach. He reached for a larger book, an A3 size laminated folder containing a pull-out supplement from the *Evening Post* dated 1981. *Roundhay Park Centenary*. Pictures of the Canal Gardens in faded colour, a panoramic photograph of the lake. He scoured each page for the merest hint of hedge and trellis, but found none.

Fighting tears, he pulled across the last item – a cardboard-mounted section of an Ordnance Survey map. Resigned to finding nothing, Carver still traced his finger carefully across its dirty white surface. He could make out various landmarks from their shapes: the bandstand; the cricket pitch; the old refreshment rooms … His eyes jerked back to the edge of the cricket pitch. There was an oblong shape at its edge that he didn't recognise. It had a little block protruding from one corner. Could that be it? Frantically he examined it more closely. It was terribly nondescript. There was nothing around it or in it to indicate its nature. This was maddening. What he really needed was an aerial photograph – or any collection of photographs. He was sure they kept them somewhere in the library – maybe away from the public section.

The large woman was tidying things on her desk. Carver hoped that he wasn't too late.

"I was really hoping to find out what the maze looked like, and where it was located. Would there be any photographs, anything that might show that?" He was aware of the tremor in his voice. She picked up her glasses with her crippled hand and went round a corner. After a moment she returned with a card.

"We haven't much time. Come on," she said a little conspiratorially.

Carver had difficulty keeping pace as the woman walked ahead, briskly taking a twisting path through the warren of book-lined shelves that made up the local history department. He hadn't realised it extended this far back, or that Leeds' history was so thoroughly archived.

They passed down a small flight of steps into a lower-ceilinged room. The light was dimmer here, the air stale. The woman paused by some shelves. As she reached down, Carver realised they disguised a door. The bookcase swung inwards and they walked through.

They were in a small, stone-floored corridor with a spiral staircase just visible at the end. The woman handed Carver the yellowed card reference. "Down the stairs, love, but you haven't got long." She turned and walked back through the door.

Carver gripped the elaborate iron banister tightly as he descended. He'd never liked stairs you could see through as you walked down them. The clang of his feet on the metal echoed softly off the stone. He looked at the reference on the card: 720.6.2.

The staircase was surprisingly long, so Carver was relieved when he reached the dim and musty-smelling corridor that lay at its bottom. The corridor curved round slightly as it progressed, so he was unable to see where it ended. Iron doors were visible on both sides. He hoped they had a photocopier down here. The doors had white numbers painted on them, in a rather fussy italic script: 720.5.9, read the first; 720.6.0, the next; then 720.6.1, 720.6.2 ... Carver realised with a little shock that this was his card reference. Tentatively, he pushed open the door.

It was dark inside, but not dark enough to prevent him from seeing. His legs went suddenly weak and he almost slipped down the three small steps that led into the chamber. It wasn't the smell that so disturbed him, unusual and specific though it was – dry yet earthy, like a pile of autumn leaves brushed into a garage and left to moulder until spring. No, it was the thing that faced him, so impossibly, that sent his heart thumping and brought a jagged taste of metal into his mouth. He leaned against the wall staring and breathing heavily, feeling the fusty air in his nostrils.

It was brown now – a light, almost sepia shade – not a hint of green anywhere. The leaves had thinned out revealing a skeleton of iron railings beneath. There was no doubt this was the maze – imperfectly preserved but here all the same. Carver must be facing the back, or one of the sides, since there was no sign of the entrance. For a terrible moment he worried that it might have been sealed up, that he would have no access to the interior, because he knew, even now as he gazed, that he must walk within.

Very slowly, he stood upright and edged towards the desiccated hedge. The fence rails that were visible were brown too, rusted darker than the leaves. The hedge still had its height – it nearly reached the low ceiling – and its shape. In fact the corners were sharper now, where the foliage had thinned and stubbly little twigs poked out like knuckles. He wanted to touch the branches but restrained himself. He would wait a little longer.

There was a gap between the hedge and the room's wall, just wide enough to walk down. As Carver did, he thought how peculiar it was to see the shrubbery, even in its dried-out state, against the shiny tiles. He held his breath when he saw the entrance; the trellis less rusty than the railings, folded open around the darkness within. The hedge formed a little arch over it which Carver found himself remembering perfectly. As he came level with the opening he couldn't help but wonder whether the bench would be there, still the goal to aim for at the maze's heart. Breathing again, he passed inside.

Almost without thinking, Carver found his hand reaching out to touch the hedge to his left. The leaves felt surprisingly resilient. He had thought they might crumple if he pressed too hard but they were stiff and tough, making a noise like riffling a pack of cards as his fingers ran along. He turned the first corner not caring if his route were correct; he was just happy to be back there. In fact it was hard to remember when he had last felt joy like this.

Another junction came, the hedge opposite him almost naked, the rails clear with branches twined around them. He looked down for the first time and noticed the thick tarpaulin on the floor, in place of the scuffed pathway that he remembered. Of course not everything could be perfect, he thought as he turned another corner, and passed through a further gap. He was almost enjoying the idea of getting lost when he was startled by a noise some distance away.

Someone else was there.

Carver stopped moving and listened anxiously. The footsteps made it clear they were outside the maze. That was a relief. He wanted to be alone in it. In fact, when the trellis hinges groaned and squeaked as they were closed behind him, Carver felt himself moving deeper inside once again. Somewhere, far, far above, the Town Hall clock struck six while nearer, much nearer, a key twisted solidly in its lock.

The engine of desire

Aspici quo vos ducit Desiderii Instrumentum

i

The palace of Bandar bin Turki bin Abd al-Rahman was truly something to behold. The Prince was frowned upon by other members of his family for his extravagance, which was saying something, thought Jack Sleighmaker. He had a taste for excess which was fuelled by his love of Hollywood movies. His fondness for different periods – from the silk-curtained opulence of 1940s MGM musicals through to the shiny-floored futurism of the seventies sci-fi boom – led to a collision of styles within the palace that was almost frightening.

Sleighmaker had to keep biting the inside of his cheek to counteract the feeling of woozy unreality inspired by his current location – a perfect reproduction of the Warner Brothers backlot version of *Hell's Kitchen*. It wasn't the fact that the cobbles beneath his feet were turned from fine, white marble that so perturbed him, rather it was the way it felt one was walking outside until one looked up, and saw the softly lit domed ceiling curving high above – complete with scudding clouds projected from some unseen source. As the facsimile New York street gave way to the more traditional mock renaissance styling of the Prince's private apartment, Sleighmaker remembered what the ceiling reminded him of: the entrance to the Pirates of the Caribbean ride at Disneyland.

The silent attendant led Sleighmaker into a small office – small by

James Hood

the Brobdingnagian standards of its surroundings – and placed him in a white leather armchair. He sat alone for a moment listening to the hum of the air conditioning, admiring the flock of the gilded wallpaper, a roll of which probably cost more than the entire contents of an average Homestyle store. The door opposite him opened and a tall man in an immaculate suit entered. As Sleighmaker had feared, it was Maksoud.

Maksoud was the only route by which the Prince could have come to Sleighmaker. The man's attitude was a strange mix of admiration for the impeccability with which Sleighmaker carried out his job and a contradictory loathing for the actual text of his work. Sleighmaker himself thought this was unfair; his own position was entirely neutral. The strength of his service (and what his considerable reputation rested upon) was that he was a guaranteed provider. What was guaranteed – for the happy few who could afford Sleighmaker's fee – was the absolute fulfilment of their request, regardless of what that request was. The only way Sleighmaker would fail was if he died attempting to obtain whatever it was his clients desired – and then they wouldn't have to pay anything at all, which was why they were always so happy to sign the contract. As far as the client was concerned once Sleighmaker was employed they themselves were in a no lose situation.

Maksoud's antipathy dated back to a prior assignment – not for Prince Bandar but for the Prince's younger brother Khalid. It had involved the removal of a young woman from the United Kingdom and her transportation to Khalid's palace. It seemed that Maksoud found the whole charge distasteful in the extreme, but since he was bound by an oath of loyalty to the Royal Family he could not direct his aversion at Prince Khalid. Therefore Sleighmaker himself became the object of loathing. Maksoud never conducted himself in anything other than a professional manner but Sleighmaker knew people well enough to sense the distaste beneath. Still the man admired Sleighmaker's own professionalism enough to hire him again so Sleighmaker could hold no real quarrel with him.

"Mr Sleighmaker. How pleasant to see you." Maksoud shook Sleighmaker's hand lightly, almost caressing it.

"Maksoud." Sleighmaker stood up. He couldn't help but admire the man's beautiful suit.

"I trust we have been looking after you since your arrival."

"I've been shown the palace. It's quite amazing. Almost unreal." He smiled, wanting it known there was no insult intended in this remark.

Maksoud inclined his head slightly. "What is it the *Bhagavad Gita* tells us? 'The unreal never is; the real never is not.'" Still holding Sleighmaker's hand lightly he led him towards the leather-panelled door in the far side of the room. "The Prince is keen to meet you."

Unlike the flowing robes favoured by his brother Prince Bandar sported Western clothes, although it was clear he didn't share the taste of his retainer. When he turned to reveal his double-breasted pin-stripe suit Sleighmaker was reminded of Peter Sellers in *The Return of the Pink Panther*. Perhaps the thought was assisted by the thick moustache and slightly bewildered expression.

"Mr Sleighmaker?"

Sleighmaker adopted the prostration protocol demanded. "Your Highness." The Prince nodded and he stood upright again.

"You come highly recommended. Maksoud tells me you are the perfect man for this assignment." As always Sleighmaker had to restrain himself from asking what the assignment was. His wasn't purely a mercenary spirit. Part of what appealed about the job was the nature of the tasks he was asked to carry out. More often than not they involved women and more often than not those women were very beautiful. Left to his own devices he would never pursue what he was asked to pursue but in the service of someone else he could allow himself to enjoy his clients' pleasures peripherally.

The Prince seated himself behind his oak desk. Its huge surface was clear apart from a small item covered by a white silk cloth.

"What do you know of automata, Mr Sleighmaker?"

"Very little. I'm aware that certain items are considered very valuable. Fabergé in particular." The Prince raised his eyebrows slightly, impressed perhaps that Sleighmaker's knowledge stretched that far. Sleighmaker was used to that. Since his background was in Close Protection Services many of his clients assumed he was little more than a trained ape. In fact he had studied Classical History at Durham University and completed an MA in Economics. He read widely and there was little point in acquiring the wealth that his trade brought if one couldn't enjoy the things that it could buy.

"Fabergé made some interesting pieces, it is true," the Prince continued, "but essentially he was a jeweller with a dilettante's interest in the subject. Automata were highly fashionable items in the late nineteenth century. Fashion dictated Fabergé's pieces rather than vocation." The Prince raised his hand and flicked his forefinger. Maksoud disappeared to the back of the room. "There were others – predecessors of Fabergé – for whom the creation of automata was something closer to a religion." He smiled curiously and his finger twitched around the edge of the white silk trailing over the object in front of him. Then he leaned forward as if what he were about to say were in some way conspiratorial. "You know, Mr Sleighmaker, the idea that automata are toys – or at best exercises in mechanical ingenuity – is totally unrealistic. There is much evidence to suggest that a substantial portion of our technology evolved from the minds of the makers of these pieces." Maksoud returned with two cut glass tumblers containing a dark red drink. The Prince nodded at him and drank. "Developments in the field undoubtedly contributed to the Industrial Revolution."

"Is it one of these seminal items that you want me to obtain?" asked Sleighmaker. He was eager to find out what was concealed beneath the white silk.

The Prince waved his finger. "Patience, Mr Sleighmaker." He smiled like someone telling a good story who looks forward to observing the impact the end will make on the listener. He gestured for Sleighmaker to drink before continuing. "There are four individuals whose achievements tower over any similar work done before or since they practised their art. They were all children of the eighteenth century." Sleighmaker sipped cautiously at the cinnamon-coloured liquid. It took him a moment to realise what it was. Dr Pepper. "Jacques Vaucanson, Friedrich Von Knauss, Henri Jacquet-Droz. Those with an interest in this area are familiar with their names. Vaucanson in particular created some extraordinary items. The word 'android' was coined to descibe them."

Sleighmaker raised an eyebrow. "I thought that was a modern term – from science fiction."

The Prince smiled triumphantly. He became even more animated. "Again we see the hidden influence of the engineer of automata on our culture. Vaucanson's greatest accomplishment was the figure of a full-sized duck. It floundered in water, drank, ate, then digested and excreted the material." Sleighmaker obviously looked sceptical. The Prince's tone became more emphatic. "The actions of this duck were so lifelike that many believed it real. They were only convinced of its artifice when mid-demonstration parts of the body were opened to reveal the digestive process occurring. Did you know, Mr Sleighmaker, that we owe the development of the india-rubber tube to Monsieur Vaucanson? He himself designed and produced the thing in order to simulate the duck's intestine." The Prince leant back in his chair as if a point had been won.

"Von Knauss and Jacquet-Droz also produced seminal figures. Lifelike human beings who played musical instruments, drew pictures and wrote poems. Again, Mr Sleighmaker, you will be sceptical but Jacquet-Droz's organ-player reproduces physical movements which a contemporary computer would find difficult, while Von Knauss's scribe utilised a keyboard-based input device which set tabs on what was effectively a short-term programmable memory. Imagine that! Fifty years before Babbage."

"You said there were four such geniuses, but you've only spoken of three."

The Prince smiled at him. "Very good, Mr Sleighmaker. Very good. The fourth name is unfamiliar even to students of the field. This is not because his work was any less extraordinary than his peers'. Quite the reverse."

"Why then?"

"His pieces were so craved by collectors that they became jealously guarded. Each owner sought to protect what he had acquired by erasing records that they had ever existed. Soon their creator's name passed into legend. Many assumed his reputation was fictional. Then as the whereabouts of the pieces themselves became uncertain, and interest in such things waned, the creator's name moved beyond legend into total obscurity."

"What was it about his work that was so special, to bring about such a fate?"

The Prince smiled again and looked up at Maksoud for the first time. His eyes seemed to flash with excitement.

"I want you to see something, Mr Sleighmaker. But before I show her to you I want you to know you are one of less than a dozen men to have gazed upon her in the two centuries since her creation." Sleighmaker nodded but his expression must have lacked the reverence the Prince required for his hand snaked out and grabbed Sleighmaker's wrist in an excruciating grip. "You will tell no one of what you are about to see. Even today there are men who would kill to obtain her." Sleighmaker pressed his mouth closed in order to avoid laughing. He felt sure that if he let one escape the Prince would probably have him whipped.

The Prince loosened his grip on Sleighmaker's arm and took a moment to relax. Then with a conjurer's flourish he pulled the silk away from the object. Sleighmaker forgot about keeping his mouth closed.

It was a small square cage turned from brass, not ornate in any way. The word that came to Sleighmaker's mind was practical. It looked most like a cage you would keep something living in, to prevent it escaping rather than display as an ornament. Considering that you were presumably supposed to be gazing at whatever was inside, the bars were surprisingly thick. Sleighmaker leaned forward to ascertain what was within. At first he thought it was a fish. Indeed there was an amount of water around the cage's base. A carved piece of rock protruded from the centre and resting upon it was what looked like a small salmon. Its silver scales glistened and its tail fanned out into the water. However upon closer examination the scales faded out half-way up the body to be replaced with fine pink skin. The skin was partially concealed by straight black hair that flowed down from the creature's head, as was its face. It held something in its miniature hands. Sleighmaker bent his head to look around the bars. A perfect silver mirror and a miniature comb.

"She is beautiful – yes? Perhaps you would like to see her face." The Prince pulled at a sliding catch on the side of the cage's base. The fishtail began to twitch. It rose off the rock and down again. Then one of the tiny arms – no thicker than a pipecleaner – moved up to the little head and began combing hair away from the face. Sleighmaker's eyes were level with the cage now. The creature had the face of a beautiful girl – but it wasn't just her features that now transfixed him. The slow, studied nature of her movements, the coquettish expression as she raised the petite mirror to her face, the way she had been made to brush the black tresses away from her perfect breasts.

"The nipples, Mr Sleighmaker," exclaimed the now giggling Prince, "observe the nipples." Unbelievably the perfectly rendered pink areolae seemed to contract on exposure to air and the nipples themselves became pert and erect. This action was accompanied by an unearthly sound – subtle at first, above the faint whirr of the mermaid's mechanism, but increasingly more defined as she began to sway and undulate her upper body. It was only when Sleighmaker noticed her mouth had opened that he realised she was singing. There was no conventional melody to her song – it was more oceanic in its character, like the call of a whale. As she raised and lowered her head her song became more complex, more hypnotic, before it finally slowed, bringing her other movements to a halt. Soon she was as she first had been, her face concealed, her arms at her side – inanimate, no longer alive. Sleighmaker found himself sad. He had wanted more of her.

"She's remarkable." He looked up at the Prince. His awed tone was sincere.

"The Mermaid of Thomas Narcejac. Thought missing for nearly a hundred and fifty years. And suddenly she appears on the market in the brochure of a small auction house in Cairo. Thank the heavens they were totally unaware of what they were selling."

"This is the fourth man? Thomas Narcejac?"

The Prince nodded. "It is important to understand that Narcejac was different to his peers. They were clockmakers and jewellers by trade – not educated men. Thomas Narcejac had been schooled in Geneva and studied Philosophy at the University of Ingolstadt under Monsieur Krempe. His family were very wealthy. The construction of automata was not a commercial matter for him, but rather a …" The Prince spent a moment searching for the correct word. "… a fascination."

The Prince stood up and replaced the silk cover over the mermaid's cage. Sleighmaker experienced another pang of disappointment; he had wanted to see her perform once again. The Prince gestured to Maksoud who at once approached carrying a small leather-bound book.

"The mermaid was merely an apprentice piece, Mr Sleighmaker, a trifle when compared to Narcejac's later work. His obsessions took a very particular turn. But we will have to talk further tomorrow. I have duties this afternoon. In the meantime I would like you to study this." He nodded to Maksoud who handed the book to Sleighmaker. "It is a handwritten monologue by Professor Alfred Chapuis – co-author of *Le Monde Des Automates*. It was privately produced for the emperor of

Japan – hence it is written in English. It details everything that was known about Narcejac's creations." The Prince exited the room leaving Sleighmaker alone with Maksoud.

"I will show you to your apartment, Mr Sleighmaker. The Prince welcomes you to avail yourself of all his hospitality." Maksoud smiled again.

Prince Bandar's tastes were very different to those of his brother Khalid. His hospitality had a very different character. But then his assignment also had a very different character. There had been no lecture from Khalid, no history lesson was required, at least not of the kind Sleighmaker was in the process of currently receiving. The facts required for the execution of that particular assignment were very straightforward: who the girl was, where she lived and why the Prince wanted her transported to his palace. Strictly, the last piece of information wasn't required but Sleighmaker's curiosity had got the better of him, particularly when he saw the girl's photograph. He was always free not to take any particular job that came his way – and sometimes he did turn work down, particularly if kidnap or worse was involved. He certainly considered saying no to Prince Khalid on this occasion. The girl was a young solicitor who worked for a large firm in Central London. She had been responsible for the conveyancing on a large riverside property the Prince was buying in Chelsea. It seemed the Prince was very taken with her and asked if she would join him for dinner one evening. The nature of her rebuttal he had found as insulting as the rebuttal itself. She had laughed at him "as if I were a child, Mr Sleighmaker." Apparently Khalid had made several extravagant attempts at wooing her. He bought her a small apartment in Pimlico. He opened a credit account for her with British Airways to fly Club Class anywhere she pleased. But she refused all his gifts with the same slightly indulgent laugh. "Now, Mr Sleighmaker, I *require* her. You understand." He pushed the ten by eight photograph across the marble table-top. Jack looked down at it. He was touched by the breath of wanting too. She stared out from the fuzz of the grain. Her impertinence was part of her exquisiteness. She was bending down slightly. Blurry though the picture was, the allure of her cleavage was captured. Imagine having the power and resources to have anyone you wanted. Imagine having her because you could.

Later that night Sleighmaker found himself flicking through the book Prince Bandar had given him. Professor Chapuis' dense prose did not encourage him but the detailed pen and ink illustrations were more engaging. It seemed Monsieur Narcejac's work had taken off in a particular direction. He became fascinated with all aspects of sex and sexuality. In 1772 he had completed a detailed male genital cluster fashioned from brass, the penis of which became erect while the scrotum tightened. The motion climaxed with the penis ejaculating whatever fluid the device had been filled with prior to the demonstration. Apparently the item served as a cruet on Napoleon's table dispensing vinaigrette. More intriguing still was the model of Evadne – a courtesan that Narcejac had had knowledge of. The figure – a good deal larger than the mermaid, about a third life-size – reclined on a chaise longue and masturbated to orgasm. The mechanism reproduced faithfully all of Evadne's movements and those who knew her testified to its authenticity. Interestingly, as Narcejac became more and more reclusive and protective of his creations, he turned his energies to fashioning ingenious devices to protect them and his property. Upon hearing of these creations several royal families inquired about purchasing the machines in order to protect their property but upon discovering their lethal nature all changed their minds.

Thomas Narcejac had continued his studies after he had left university. It seemed his tutor had given him a taste for the more esoteric philosophies of the East, as well as the secrets of the Kabbalah. According to Professor Chapuis increasingly elements of this arcanum found their way into Narcejac's figures. There were gaps in the Professor's research inevitably, given the lack of documentation about his subject, but it seemed Narcejac died before he completed his *coup de maître* – a piece that was conceived on an almost operatic scale. Sleighmaker fell asleep before finishing the book, most of which was devoted to diagrams and descriptions of working mechanisms. He dreamt of England and the toys of his childhood.

"Ah, Mr Sleighmaker, good morning. I trust you slept well." Prince Bandar was in his games room – a perfect reproduction of the bridge of the Nautilus from *20,000 Leagues Under the Sea*. The Prince was sitting at a felt-covered card table; opposite him was a surly-looking adolescent. "May I introduce my nephew, Saurabh." The youth looked up momentarily then returned his gaze to the board game spread beneath them. "Saurabh does not like losing. But lost he has." The Prince clapped his hands lightly and clicked his fingers. His nephew stood up, bowed his head – somewhat grudgingly, it appeared to Sleighmaker – then sloped off. "Have you ever played 221b Baker Street?" He gestured to the board on the table.

"I don't believe so."

"It is based on the Sherlock Holmes stories. I must admit to having the advantage over my nephew. He has never heard of Conan Doyl, let alone read any." The Prince gestured for the book Sleighmaker was carrying. "And how did you find Professor Chapuis' treatise?"

"It is fascinating, Your Highness – although it takes me no closer to what you require of me."

Prince Bandar looked him squarely in the eye. "Come. Let us walk."

They left the Nautilus and made their way along the corridor to the terrace that stretched along the length of the entire east wing. Sleighmaker reached for the Aviators in his top pocket. The sun was painfully bright even though it was not yet ten o'clock. The terrace overlooked the desert. Sand undulated against the wall to Sleighmaker's left – the dunes broken abruptly by the marble. The great yellow nothing extended into apparent infinity. It made one want to turn the other way and face the architecture. The Prince however moved to face the open space as he began to speak again.

"Chapuis' book talks of many things but its major omission is that which interests me most."

"Is this the masterpiece that Narcejac died before completing?"

The Prince did not answer him directly. "She is called Aveline. And she exists. The appearance of the mermaid on the open market confirms this."

"She?"

"There is another manuscript that I haven't shown you for reasons of my own. A monograph by Gregory Chisholm – a private collector of some repute. Aveline's existence was considered little more than a legend. But Chisholm had unearthed detailed construction drawings for several pieces – one of which was the mermaid you have seen. Another was Aveline."

"What … who is Aveline?"

"Aveline was Narcejac's finest creation. A life-size figure – modelled after the thirteen-year-old daughter of his cousin. Narcejac had fallen in love with her."

"Sounds a little indecent," Sleighmaker said, immediately wishing he hadn't, remembering the tastes of some of the Prince's family.

"It was not her age that was an inconvenience, but rather her father – a cleric who had his daughter reserved for admission to the Convent of St Thérèse in Lyons. Her purity and inaccessibility only served to heighten Narcejac's need for her. Inflamed with desire he began to build her in simulacrum." A small wind had picked up and blew towards them off the desert. The Prince brushed a particle of sand from his eye. He turned to face Sleighmaker. "It is rumoured that Narcejac put everything he knew into this android and more. Every piece of knowledge that had been garnered over twenty years was employed to create a finished item that might satisfy his yearning. By the time she was complete her living counterpart had abandoned the

Church and was married to a composer in Vienna. Narcejac cared not. The focus of his passion was now with his creation."

"How can one love a machine?" asked Sleighmaker, fascinated, but more by the absurdity of the tale than its drama.

The Prince gripped his arm. "This machine was built *to* love. She was designed to satisfy her creator's craving – physically. Do you understand, Mr Sleighmaker?"

"You mean ..."

The Prince pulled Sleighmaker towards him as he lowered his voice. "First she danced. She removed her clothes. Her vagina moistened and opened. Then, if the viewer were positioned correctly, she lowered herself on to him. Her genitalia gripped his. She rode him to completion, throwing her head back and giving every impression of being carried to paradise herself."

"Surely such a thing isn't possible."

"Legend suggests there was something in Aveline's construction that was closer to alchemy than engineering. She was greater than the sum of her parts. The experience of lying with her was calculated to take the user to a state of ecstasy he had never experienced before."

Sleighmaker was naturally dubious. He thought of some of the states of ecstasy he had experienced with partners both willing and unwilling. It was hard to imagine how a construction of cogs, springs and whatever else was employed could equal what he had known. He thought it wise to keep his doubts private.

"And you want me to locate ..." He hesitated momentarily. "... Aveline and deliver her to you?"

"Mr Sleighmaker. You understand everything." The Prince bowed his head slightly.

Sleighmaker was packing his small Cerruti suitcase when Maksoud appeared in his room. He hadn't knocked.

"I have a cheque for you, Mr Sleighmaker. Made out in US dollars as you requested. This will cover your initial expenses. If you require more you are to contact me directly."

"Payment in full must be made in advance of delivery – once I have secured that which the Prince desires." Sleighmaker had turned his back on Maksoud and returned his attention to his luggage.

"You know we pay promptly, Mr Sleighmaker. Even when you have not adhered to the letter of your covenant." Maksoud smiled his infuriating smile.

"I believe I'm correct in assuming that Prince Khalid was satisfied with the service I provided."

"As satisfied as you were by that which you secured for him." Sleighmaker heard him turn to go. His heels clicked on the polished floor. "A man should master himself. And that means mastering his desires. Otherwise they make a monkey of him, do you not think, Mr Sleighmaker?" He could hear the smile without having to look at Maksoud's face.

"Would you arrange for someone to collect my case? I feel like a final swim before my flight." Sleighmaker placed the case on the floor and made to exit the room. As he passed through the door Maksoud laid a hand gently on his shoulder.

"Many, many men have gone before you, trying to obtain what you seek. They thought they had her in their grasp only to be taken themselves. I doubt the Prince told you that."

"With the fee I charge I don't expect a shopping trip to Knightsbridge, Maksoud."

The grip became momentarily firmer. "I would be very wary if I were you. And remember – there is *always* opportunity to turn from a treacherous path no matter how far down it you have travelled – whatever you might have told yourself in the past, Mr Sleighmaker."

As the Prince's Lear tore through the skies Sleighmaker pondered on the task ahead. He would begin in Cairo at the auction house. Bribery and a little intimidation should be enough to ascertain where the mermaid came from. And from what he had understood the route from there to Aveline – if she existed – would not be too circuitous. He considered the idea of her. Who would actually want to have sex with such a thing? Surely that was not why the Prince wanted her so. Unless it was true – all that he had been told. That the magical qualities made the experience almost transcendental. He preferred flesh and blood. Warmth. Another person and what was in their head. Now that was what inflamed him. That was real spice. He thought of the solicitor again. Of how the awareness of her predicament had made him want her more – the fact that she was aware of it. A young woman who was sure of her place in the world – who thought herself powerful, both financially and occupationally – in charge of her own destiny. Able to choose who she had, if she had them at all. And then that authority was removed in one swipe, because a man wanted her. She was shown that she never had any real power after all. That her certainty about her position was a complete illusion. She was made prostrate. And he was the instrument that had brought about this revelation. He'd wanted her when he'd seen her photograph – more when he'd seen her in life – but when he'd reached the above conclusion he knew then that to actually have her was imperative. He had no choice.

ii

The owner of the Matruh Auction House had required very little persuasion to disclose his source. The mermaid had originated from the estate of Mrs Lorelei MacBride. A little research revealed that she had run a private English school in El Faiyum but had died intestate. What little she owned was sold off to cover accumulated debts. There was only one surviving relative he could trace – a sister, Wendy, who lived in Ripon in North Yorkshire, in the shadow of the great cathedral.

*

"And did you say you were a journalist, Mr ...?"

"Baldwin. David Baldwin." Sleighmaker could see into the house behind her. It seemed there were four rooms' worth of furniture crammed against one wall. "I'm a researcher with the BBC." The old woman looked at him suspiciously with keen eyes.

"You're a little well-dressed for their wages."

"I'm a freelance writer as well. You're correct in thinking I could not survive on radio money alone, not with my tastes." He inclined his head slightly and grinned his sincerest grin. She continued her scrutiny for a moment. Then her features softened into a smile, which made her look quite different. She gestured for Sleighmaker to enter.

"Would you care for some tea?"

"Tea would be fine."

"I shall have bourbon." She disappeared into the kitchen. Sleighmaker looked around at the photographs which crowded the walls. Some recent, some black and white, some faded sepia. There was no logic to their arrangement but they advertised a full and happy life. Smiling children from many generations held hands with laughing adults. There were animals too: dogs, horses, even a pig, being cuddled by a small girl dressed in a tutu. "You'll find none of my sister there, Mr Chamberlain – at least not as an adult."

"It's Baldwin. Why is that, Mrs Cox?"

She settled back into her chair and began playing with the glasses that hung round her neck. "Lorrie – God rest her – was always adamant she wanted no one discussing her life. There were no photographs. At least none were distributed to us."

"She was a teacher. Why the secrecy?"

She looked at him sharply over her tumbler. "Tell me – what is the programme you are working on again?"

There was a brief moment of internal panic when Sleighmaker forgot his fabrication. He calmed himself and it came to him.

"Radio 4. The History Programme. A special about colonial educationalists."

Mrs Cox laughed. "It's him you should be asking about, not her."

"Him?"

"The Loony. Her late husband. He was the colonialist on a mission."

Sleighmaker reached for the button on the DAT recorder in his pocket. "But your sister had the school."

"She had no vocation. She hated that place. It was an excuse to get away from him and his music boxes. And it earned her a living. She had to take what she could. Life was difficult for women on their own earlier this century. Or has your study of modern history circumnavigated that subject?"

"Forgive my journalistic instincts, Mrs Cox, but what did you mean about her late husband being the colonialist on a mission?"

The old woman sighed. There was a pause. Sleighmaker could smell the whisky in her glass. She spoke again.

"I always respected my sister's wishes when she was alive, Mr Baldwin. She requested that I told no one of the events of her life – maybe she anticipated a day like today. But she is dead now, and to tell you the truth I found her hush-hush behaviour a little neurotic and a little prissy." The old woman suddenly looked guilty. Then she put down her glass and seemed to gather herself. "We were very different, Lorrie and I. She always seemed to want so much. You know, Mr Baldwin, I've only left Yorkshire three times. There seems to be quite enough beauty here to satisfy me for one lifetime." She smiled sadly. "But Lorrie – she wanted to travel, to see the world. She wanted to be famous. She wanted beautiful things. It was the only reason she married him."

"Why did you call him the Loony?"

"The late lamented Lieutenant Colonel Samuel Maxwell MacBride," she saluted theatrically as she said his name, "was the oddest man I ever met. And I only met him once, but that was enough. He was much older than her, you see. They met when she was at Oxford. She reminded him of someone. Someone he once loved. She was nineteen, he was forty-six. He was over from Africa for a brief visit. He followed her in the street apparently, having passed her. Asked her to marry him three days later and join him on his estate in Rhodesia. And she went. She gave up her studies and went. We found out a month later. They had the ceremony out there."

"Doesn't sound like the done thing."

"Mr Maxwell was not concerned about the done thing. He was emperor of his own realm. Have you never heard of Polporrah, Mr Baldwin?"

"Polporrah? Isn't that in Cornwall?"

"Some researcher you are. Do you mind if I smoke?" Sleighmaker was taken aback. Mrs Cox must have been in her late eighties. "Polporrah was Maxwell's estate built on the edge of Lake Bangweulu, five hundred miles from nowhere. Like somebody had taken a piece of Kent and dropped it into the bush. This massive, mad bloody mansion. I never visited it. But Lorrie wrote to me, describing it in all its absurd detail. She liked it at first. But pretty quickly she grew to hate it. It went on for ever and ever, stretching back into the marshland. Nothing there. No village even. Nothing but him and his clocks and his waistcoated servants done up like golliwogs."

Sleighmaker, who had been lost for a moment in this romantic melodrama, found himself jarred back to his purpose. "His clocks?"

"He collected clocks. Musical boxes. Anything you could wind up. Kept it all there on display like a museum. By the time she left him for the second time – just after the war – that was all he cared about. Didn't even try to get her back, not like he had before."

"I know your sister went to Egypt, Mrs Cox, but what happened to him, to MacBride?"

"As far as I know he stayed there, going slowly mad with the loneliness. He certainly didn't bother her. Nor did he give her any money, not a penny. She never pursued him. She stubbornly made a go of the school, just to show him." She paused before adding: "And us."

"It's a sad story."

"Maybe. Maybe not. I think she finally found something. Something that satisfied her. But it wasn't what she expected. She found it in that archaic English school, teaching little Egyptian orphans to read Beatrix Potter." Sensing that some kind of conclusion had been reached Sleighmaker reached in his pocket to switch off the DAT.

"I don't know how any of this fits into your programme," she said as she got up out of her chair. "But then I don't suppose you do either." She went into the kitchen.

"What do you mean?" Sleighmaker called after her.

"I don't think there is a programme, Mr Baldwin. Any more than there was going to be a biography called *Lorelei and The Little Ones* when I was visited by a 'writer' called Mr Tarrant six weeks ago. I checked in Waterstones in York. There was no such author. Funny how he asked all the same questions as you." He heard her stirring the tea. "Do you take sugar?"

As he drove back to London Sleighmaker cursed his own stupidity. It was as if he hadn't absorbed anything the Prince had said. Of course there would have been others looking for Aveline. His only consolation was the knowledge that he could still prepare himself better than any collector of antiquities.

iii

A visit to the Harrap Library in Pimlico proved fruitful. A privately owned collection which specialised in Military History and Personnel, it seemed to Sleighmaker the best place to start. It didn't take long to find a record of MacBride's biography. He'd been a lieutenant in the British Army with a post on the Border Commision. He heard that the British South Africa Company were making land available cheaply to white settlers in Northern Rhodesia so he applied and then set off in search of his desired property.

MacBride's uncle Gregory Chisholm – an exceptionally wealthy man who had made his fortune through mining copper – had died recently and bequeathed the greater part of his fortune to MacBride It seems that for some time the young man had shared his uncle's passion for all things mechanical. Hence the inheritance included his uncle's remarkable private collection. Now all he needed was some-where to house it – away from his disapproving family who thought his obsession childish and unhealthy. What could be better than a private estate surrounded by five hundred miles of harsh terrain? He was a man of private means now and the isolation rather appealed to him. He could indulge himself in his interest completely undisturbed.

The house was built to his own design. MacBride was no architect but he improvised a blueprint for an elaborate structure based on sketches of his favourite buildings from around the world. He was adamant however that Polporrah, as he had christened his kingdom-to-be, should have as English an air as possible. To that end he had his native workforce make red bricks from clay taken from the vast cone-shaped anthills that surrounded the lake, together with roof tiles fashioned from the white clay in the mud of the Mansa river.

And there MacBride stayed, building his unique, purposeless museum – intended for no one's edification, not even his own. Not surprisingly the details of his collection in the Harrap biography were sketchy to say the least. Describing it as a singular collection of clocks, watches and musical items, the respectful tones contained no note of any of the more extraordinary items Sleighmaker was now convinced rested at Polporrah. There was however an allusion to MacBride's obsession with completing some large antique device together with a reference to some private material also held in the library.

This turned out to be the diary of MacBride's old army friend and companion Charlie Royce. It was relatively easy to locate. The short-sighted librarian even let Sleighmaker take photocopies of the relevant pages when he flashed him an out-of-date press card identifying him as a defence correspondent for the *Daily Mail*. He would read them on the plane to Lusaka. He could not afford to waste any more time. It was highly likely that he had competition. If Aveline was gone already it didn't mean the game was over. But it would be better to acquire her directly from Polporrah rather than having to get her through, or from, a third party. It was always worse when other people were involved.

He had no problem with the fact he was aroused when stalking the girl. It was a new experience for him to be sure but he had never been so attracted to any quarry before. It was true that the assignment for Prince Khalid was unusual in that it was so driven by the Prince's lust and pride. Previous kidnappings had involved errant wives or children caught in custody battles. Was there a moment when Sleighmaker had thought of refusing the assignment? Maybe before the photograph had been slid across the table. But her face – with its surly beauty – together with the figure suggested beneath the immaculate clothes, had ignited something in his belly that would have required far more energy to extinguish than Sleighmaker could be bothered to expend. It was the possibility – the licence – that was given by the Prince's own yearning that enabled Sleighmaker to permit himself the possibility of fulfilling his own.

He took to the life of a voyeur with an enthusiasm that surprised him. Maybe because it was a kind of mental foreplay, because he knew he would get to have her and he could enjoy the delicious accrual of information about every aspect of her life – from the time she moved her bowels in the morning to the brand of tampon she favoured. It was as if he'd climbed aboard a rollercoaster and there was no way he could climb off it now the flame of wanting her had been ignited in his belly. Better to give in without apology and enjoy the ride.

Charlie Royce's diaries were interesting for the story they told about MacBride, a single-minded man who once set upon a course would not deviate from it. Royce was quite happy to go along for the ride at first.

July 25th, 1927
What a splendid venture this will be. I'm very happy to join Mac but one thing concerns me. I know that my father's business is farming, but I hope that Mac does not think I share the family facility for "tilling the earth". But we will see what we can make of this estate.

Sleighmaker scanned the neatly written script for references to anything that might resemble Aveline.

Nov 4th, 1927
The lake is very beautiful. I fancied a swim but Chakwanda – who it seems has attached himself to me as a retainer – warned me off. Crocodiles!! Mac has ordered the servants to wear little waistcoats and gloves. They look for all the world like some of his mechanical people.

Christmas Eve, 1927
Never have I been so hot at Christmas time! Mac – heathen that he is – would not join us for Carols. He is locked away, as always, in his workshop/museum. Chakwanda and his son sang "We three kings " quite beautifully.

Mentions of the actual details of anything mechanical were relatively scarce. Another story began to emerge however of Royce's inability to make anything grow in the dusty soil.

March 11th, 1928
This place seems cursed. I fear nothing will ever be harvested. We will have to survive on dry goods. There is no market for 400 miles. MacBride cares not. He seems as dry and lifeless as the earth these days. I fear this venture was a mistake.

Charlie Royce's involvement in the story came – not unpredictably – to a less than happy end.

May 17th, 1930
Lost my temper with MacBride today. A rare appearance from him at the dinner table. Chakwanda was struggling with the serving spoons. They kept slipping through his stupid white gloves. MacBride babbling on about completing some masterpiece. That he'd had news of some plans turning up in Oxford. All the time the cutlery was clanging against the tureen as Chakwanda was dropping it and picking it up again. Unable to help myself, I turned on MacBride. "You know how ridiculous you look? Trying to build your bloody empire in the middle of nowhere?" He became calm. I wanted him to be angry. "I'm not building an empire, Charlie, I'm building a Pantheon. A place of pilgrimage." "Pilgrimage?" I shouted back. "Who'd want to come here, across 5000 miles, to this hell-hole?" He smiled again, in that sick way he's developed. "That's the point, Charlie. It's got to be a struggle. To get here you'd have to really want to get here. And that's the point. You've to be a slave to want to take your seat." He suddenly went very serious and sincere. "I'm making it, Charlie. I'm going to build what he couldn't complete. I don't care what you think. I don't care what anyone thinks. I am

unhooked from your opinions." I looked into his eyes and didn't know what to make of him. He was babbling now. I lost my rag completely. "It's not natural to live like this. Dressing up sambos in shoes and gloves to wait on you. You might enjoy playing the great white chief, but it's not for me. I'm leaving." I stormed off but he reached out with his hand and gripped me hard. "I'm not the great white chief. I'm the great white medicine man." He cackled horribly. I left him vowing to leave.

June 1st, 1930
I am leaving. I have resolved. He'll be alone. I think it's what he wants. He does not protest.

Sleighmaker stretched out in his seat. Perhaps his abandonment by Royce explained why MacBride sought a wife. Perhaps he became too lonely, even with his machines and work. He imagined him there in his absurd domain, no one to talk to but his servants and his automata. Mind you, however bad it was for MacBride, it would have been worse for Lorelei when she got there. He turned his head and faced out of the window. There was nothing visible in the blackness beyond, neither light nor land. For a moment Sleighmaker thought about where he was going, the drive across the savannah, the empty crumbling manor. He felt suddenly alone. Then he thought of Aveline, of what he would be paid when he had retrieved her. He even toyed with the possibility of experiencing her pleasures: the absurdity of the idea had not left him but something had snagged in his loins, the Prince's suggestion that she could transport a man to paradise. He could surely allow himself the satisfaction of his curiosity. He smiled a little and slid down the white plastic blind obscuring the night beyond. He closed his eyes.

The girl was called Elizabeth. Her friends called her Liz. At the practice she was Ms Westerley. She lived in Shepherd's Bush with her boyfriend. Sleighmaker could have taken her there, as she left for work in the morning. He preferred a less turbulent abduction. She would have struggled at first. He could have silenced her quickly but it was an unnecessary risk. Instead he rented an office on Wimpole Street – using a reliable middleman with a false identity to make the arrangements – paying cash for a four-week let. When the police investigated they would discover – after several fruitless days consulting with their German counterparts – that the softly spoken Herr Siodmak did not exist. By that time Ms Westerley and he would be lost to them.

The capture itself had been straightforward. He asked her to his office to discuss whether he had a case or not in a copyright dispute on a computer program he had written – their practice specialised in such matters. Once there he simply gave her some coffee liberally laced with Rohypnol. He had to admit he had become aroused as she sipped the coffee, knowing what was to come. Observing the look on her face as the drug began its work was a delicious moment. She began to scowl as if she was cross with the fact that she couldn't understand what was happening to her. She tried to stand up but slumped back in her chair, her skirt riding up. He'd asked her if she was all right. She could barely get her response out. Then she blacked out.

It wasn't difficult getting her into the car. He'd chosen the building because it had a basement car-park. The office he had taken was opposite the lift. It was a simple matter to carry her down unseen. He laid her on the back seat, enjoying the scent of her Gucci perfume as he covered her with a dark cloth. He put her handbag and briefcase in the boot, returned to the office and quickly dusted the few surfaces he had allowed himself to touch. He put a note on the door asking the office manager to clean the room that afternoon. That way there would be some prints to be taken – the identification of which would waste more of the police's time.

She was still quiet when he returned to the car. He had calculated that she'd had enough of the drug to subdue her for two to three hours.

This was the crucial time. The private jet he had chartered had to be in the air and well on its way before any alarm had been raised. There was certainly no more than four hours available. The covering papers with matching false passport explained that his companion was visiting a doctor in St Petersburg for a revolutionary heart operation. She was sedated already because of her condition. In reality the plane was stopping in Kharkov to refuel before flying on to Prince Khalid's palace.

Before arriving at the airport Sleighmaker had adminstered a cocktail of barbiturate and morphine intravenously. Ms Westerley would be unconscious for some time to come. Getting her on the plane in fact proved to be the least difficult part of the operation. Once in the air he removed the make-up he'd applied to her sleeping face to give her the pallor of illness. She was beautiful indeed. Her hair was dark brown, almost black, cut into a loose bob. Her lips were full and well defined. Her face had a strong structure, enhanced by the distinct apostrophes of her eyebrows. Sleighmaker thought about undressing her there and then but he decided to wait.

As he'd hoped she began to come round about six o'clock. Her legs and arms were fastened firmly with nylon straps to her chair.

"I feel sick," was the first thing she said. He fetched her a bowl and wiped her mouth. Then he gave her some water. She looked around. He could see the muscles working beneath her brow as she attempted to cognise her situation. She remained calm and silent for quite some time. "Am I dreaming?" she asked. He shook his head. "Am I dead?"

"No," he said. There was another long pause filled with the droning song of the jet. He saw one of her hands straining against its restraint. Then she started crying, quietly. Then she stopped crying and looked right at him. It wasn't fear that he saw in her eye, Sleighmaker knew that look only too well. It was something else. Something deep he didn't recognise.

"You can't do this," she said, quite plainly. "Don't you see?" He didn't respond. "I'm not talking about me. I'm not bothered about me.

It's Paul. You can't do this to Paul." Paul was her boyfriend. He was a veterinary surgeon. "He won't … he can't … he won't be able to survive it." Sleighmaker shrugged. "I think it might kill him. You must take me back." There was another long pause. She looked at him quizzically. "Is there something wrong with you? Don't you feel anything?" He did feel something, but not in the realm she was referring to. He felt arousal. Desire. Wanting. Need. That was what concerned him. That was what occupied his head. The need to see her naked. The need to see her humiliated, because that was something that excited him. That was the only voice he was listening to.

He'd had this plan that he suggest a deal. That he would ask her to perform a series of acts – each one more demeaning than the last, culminating in him having her completely. In return he would think about faking an emergency landing – during which she could escape. When he put this deal to her she just laughed at him. She saw straight through him. For some reason he hadn't expected that. In the end he just dosed her with more morphine, unstrapped her and had her anyway. It was hardly the experience he'd anticipated. After that they didn't talk again.

iv

Sleighmaker favoured the Mitsubishi 4x4 over a Range Rover. Somehow it handled better, and felt more robust even though it was lighter. Every so often however he had to stop along the dusty track to remove some log or rock that was impossible to drive over. He had planned the route on the plane. By rail from Lusaka to Kasama, then driving the three hundred or so kilometres to the tip of Lake Bangweulu. There were roads for some of the way, and then dirt track. Although he anticipated the whole operation taking no more than five days he had brought enough supplies to cover two weeks. Experience had taught him to expect the worst and double it.

He approached the south of the lake late on the second afternoon.

He really had no idea what to expect from Polporrah. Whatever he had imagined was cancelled out by the reality of what he found as he neared the estate.

There was a light mist in the air. Although the Zambian climate was fairly temperate at this time of year there was an unpleasant humidity that he felt in every breath. The first thing he saw was a high brick wall. It loomed out of the hazy air – a visual absurdity surrounded as it was by scrubby vegetation and sparse, crooked *bubu* trees. Some of the wall was cracked, its top crenellated unintentionally where bricks had fallen and smashed on the hard earth. It reminded Sleighmaker of the garden wall in *The Herbs*.

He had to drive for a hundred metres or so before locating an entrance. A huge, wrought-iron edifice, it comprised two enormous gates of the kind one might see flanking the front of a municipal park. He pulled up the jeep as close as he could, reached for his rifle and leapt out of the cabin. He wasn't expecting to encounter anything difficult, but lions were indigenous here and it was better to play safe. The gates were seized shut. The first thing he checked for were any visible signs of entry but he was pleased to find there was nothing to suggest any recent visitor. The gates were bound together with a huge chain, which had rusted to the ironwork it surrounded.

A few minutes' work with some bolt cutters released the chain but he was unable to open the gates themselves wide enough to allow the Mitsubishi through. He gathered the rest of his gear, including the supplies and his 'tool kit' – a CIA-approved collection of all-purpose equipment – and squeezed through the gap into Polporrah.

He had only walked for thirty metres or so when he made an unwelcome discovery. A small portion of the wall had been destroyed – by explosives from the look of it. The debris had been flattened and there were footprints – what appeared to be two pairs in the dust. He bent down to examine them. It was hard to be sure given the climate but they were probably no more than three weeks old. They disappeared into the dry brown grass of the old lawn. Cautiously he poked his head through the gap in the wall. There were vehicle tracks which receded into the hazy distance but nothing else visible. Whoever it was may have been and gone. But it was also possible they were still there. He checked his rifle, then removed the handgun from his tool kit and placed it in the holster beneath his jacket. Maybe it wasn't going to be as straightforward as he thought.

The mist had cleared slightly. Sleighmaker followed the gentle curve of the long driveway. Some of the conifers that lined its edge were now dead and brown. Silence hung between them broken occasionally by a distant cry – probably a buzzard or a flamingo. Through the gaps in the trees he could just make out an overgrown tennis court. Wiry vegetation poked through cracks in the asphalt. He was surprised to find when he looked up again that Polporrah had appeared.

It was larger than he had thought. It must have been magnificent in its time. Now it had taken on another air. It looked ill-humoured, as if it were offended that it had been abandoned to slow consumption by the bush. Sleighmaker shook his head. It was just a building. It was three storeys high, a strange collision of styles and periods that somehow made sense combined. The basic shape was that of an English manor house, but there was European detailing built around it – such as a large first-floor terrace with a cloistered garden beneath that he could make out to the left of the front porch.

Above the door the tatty remains of a Union Jack hung flaccidly in the still air. The distant bird cry – if that was what he had heard – was slightly less distant now. Looking over his shoulder Sleighmaker climbed the steps to the entrance.

Two carved gorillas held up the porch-roof that jutted out over the huge oak door. The door itself was slightly ajar. Sleighmaker had now entered the automatic mode so ingrained in him – first by the army and then by years of private security work. Exercising extreme caution he passed within.

Although Sleighmaker now stood in the entrance hall it smelt like the cellar. The air was thick with damp and earth, as if he were still outside. The walls on either side of him were hung with the remains of two huge Shiraz carpets. In front of him was an enormous wooden staircase, guarded by two huge, fierce-looking porcelain dogs. As he moved towards them he realised they were wolves. It seemed sensible to recce one room at a time, as thoroughly as possible, then strike it from his mental register and move on to the next. The only problem was the scale of Polporrah and his lack of any floor-plan or map.

He'd just begun to move off to the room on his left when he froze involuntarily. He'd heard a noise. Listening intently he found his finger was on the trigger of the rifle. He breathed out and relaxed, halting respiration so he could listen as clearly as possible. It came again. Seven knocks or steps, of regular tempo. They came from somewhere above him. They could have been human. He breathed in again, then out. He listened. There were no more sounds. Sleighmaker, with great effort, reached a decision to continue his recce rather than rush off to investigate what might prove to be nothing at all. If he wanted to be out of this desolate folly as fast as possible it was best to be methodical. It was certainly the only way to be sure of finding Aveline. If he had just heard another person, best also to conceal his own presence. Treading carefully and lightly he passed into the first room – which appeared to be the library.

There was certainly nothing modest about MacBride's taste. A huge motto was carved into the stone over the door – "*Spero Meliora*". As Sleighmaker surveyed the walls of cracked and rotten spines he struggled to remember the Latin he once knew. Stepping over the remains of books, fallen to the floor, the translation came to him – "I hope for better things". He moved on. There was nothing here but damp ruined pages.

Other, subsequent rooms yielded only decay and dust. Sleighmaker had completed most of the ground floor – a dining room the size of a church, a sitting room dominated by an absurdly proportioned chandelier, a music room large enough to take a modest chamber orchestra. He'd established – as he'd assumed – that there was no electricity or water supply and was just about to climb the stairs when the knocking came again. There were nine steps now – again evenly paced. Then, almost without warning, it got very, very dark. Sleighmaker cursed himself. He had lost track of the time – and night fell like a stage curtain in this part of the continent. If he was to conceal his presence he could hardly continue his wandering announced by a beam of torch light. And his tool kit didn't stretch to night vision gear. Carefully retracing his steps he made his way back to the sitting room. There was nothing to do but wait for the light to return.

He settled himself against the remains of a chaise longue that lay beneath an enormous portrait of Lorelei MacBride, visible in the moonlight. She stared down on the room with a discernible expression of misery that the painter had obviously been unable to erase from her face, despite his efforts. Chewing quietly on his sesame seed bar, Sleighmaker wandered how she had been able to stick it out as long as she had. He closed his eyes, not really expecting to sleep, but at least he could rest. He kept his finger on the trigger of the rifle. Strangely there was more noise outside now that it was dark. At one point there had been a roar, followed by a cry. Sleighmaker forced himself to relax. There had been no evidence of any animals inhabiting the house. Surprisingly he found that he felt quite sleepy. As he drifted off there was another noise. He held off sleep in an attempt to discern what it was. It came again. Only a slight creaking and groaning. The house settling as the air temperature dropped. Unconsciousness rose and took him. He woke some time later – or perhaps it was a dream, because the house was still creaking and clicking, but in such a precise and regular way that it felt almost musical. There was a mechanical quality to the sound, a gentle clatter that reminded Sleighmaker of a fairground. The effect was almost soothing and he found he had dropped off again.

He woke with a start. The first hint of daylight had begun to creep into the room. Immediately Sleighmaker stood up and stretched. He coughed and cleared his throat with force. His lungs were full of dust and damp. He decided there and then that he would be out of this awful place before sundown at latest, and with any luck by noon. He took a swig of water then gathered his things ready for the final stage of his quest.

Light moved slowly through the house and the sun began to rise, pushing elongated shadows along the floor. Sleighmaker climbed the steps, avoiding the gaze of the porcelain wolves who were somehow more unnerving in this early morning glow, and tried to remember what he had gleaned from Charlie Royce's diary pages. He had referred to a "museum". MacBride had called it a "Pantheon". Somewhere there was going to be a room of considerable size that contained the collection. There had been no evidence of it on the ground floor. Its entrance was most likely to be on the first.

There were several doors that ran off a main corridor. Carefully opening them one by one, he found a series of bedrooms each slightly more decayed than the last, together with a bathroom whose walls were laid with copper tiles. Only a hint of the metal was visible beneath the green tarnish that had overrun them.

What had looked like the end of the corridor was in fact a right turn. It was very dark. There were no exterior windows here. Sleighmaker moved carefully as he rounded the corner. He wanted to risk the torch. It proved unnecessary. There was a soft glow up ahead – not from a window, but an open door.

His tread was as light as a ballerina when he arrived. The last thing he wanted to do was announce his presence. With caution he edged his head around the door.

At first he thought the room was empty. As he entered he could hear a low, soft buzzing. He was immediately hit by a stench far worse than he had encountered elsewhere in the house. The great bed that occupied two thirds of the area looked as if its putrid eiderdown had rotted and spread into the wall and ceiling. As he moved inwards Sleighmaker realised it was in fact covered with a gigantic spider's web. Involuntarily he jumped. At the end of the room, by a closed door, there was a body. It was definitely dead – the pool of dried blood that spread from it like a Venn diagram testified to that fact. It was a man, wearing a light safari jacket, now stained black with his viscera. Beneath the crawling flies what was left of his face was contorted by a bizarre expression – a mixture of surprise and agony. At his side was a small rucksack. Still exercising caution Sleighmaker approached him for a more thorough examination.

The man was European, in his mid- to late thirties. Judging by what was left of him Sleighmaker guessed he'd been there about a week. Gritting his teeth he rolled the body over in order to examine the wound. He was shocked at its viciousness. Something had sliced through the upper torso with great force. There was no sign of any weapon near the corpse, but a trail of bloody footprints led towards the closed door. Sleighmaker thought for a moment. From the position of the body it seemed likely the unfortunate man had been attacked from the front. Could he and his companion have argued and fought? It seemed an unlikely hypothesis given the extraordinary nature of the wound – which seemed to have been made by some kind of machine rather than a blade. He wiped his brow and realised he was sweating. His mind processed the possibilities. Was there someone else here still alive, hunting Aveline? Or just protecting her? Something clicked in his head, something he remembered. He skirted round the body and placed himself to the side of the door. Then, squatting down, he reached for the carved ivory handle and turned it. He began to pull the door open but suddenly it seemed imbued with a life and a force of its own. Sleighmaker rolled out of its way as it slammed back against the wall, just in time to see an elaborate, whirling disc of blades spiralling through the air from behind the door, then retracting at great speed.

He somersaulted back to prevent the door shutting, then he dragged the heavy oak night-table from the side of the bed and used it to secure the door open. As gently and carefully as possible he crawled inch by inch until he was able to see what was in the room beyond.

Affixed to a thick brass post in the centre of a small featureless chamber was a football-sized circle containing an arrangement of curved spikes and blades. Judging by its height it seemed designed solely for the purpose of tearing out a man's heart. Once he'd ascertained that its action was only triggered by opening the door, Sleighmaker gingerly entered the room and shone a Mag-lite on the disc. Embedded amongst the sharp edges were the blackened remains of what the device had taken from the man. The amount of ingrained matter at the root of each protuberance suggested there had been other deaths before. He took a deep breath and stood upright. He was going to have to remain mindful every moment.

The room was very plain, about eight foot by six foot – more like a cupboard. There was only the booby-trap and bare floorboards. Beneath the dust he was able to make out the bloody footprints that had begun in the bedroom. They seemed to vanish into the wall at the back. Only upon examination did Sleighmaker realise there was a frameless doorway concealed there, hidden by the stripe of the wallpaper. At first he was unable to see how it opened. Then, moving his hands apprehensively around the edge, he found an embedded mechanism, concealed in the wall. Standing to one side again he balled himself up against the floor. He knew Narcejac would not have made each of his protective devices differently. The only thing to do was reduce his surface area as much as he could and hope for the best.

He pressed the mechanism and the door swung slowly away from him. Nothing else happened. Gradually he stood up and turned round. He shrugged off his backpack and laid down the rifle. He removed the small handgun from its holster.

The room beyond was as plain as the one he was in. The only difference seemed to be that it was painted black. It was L-shaped and there was a small window high in one of the walls. Light spilled from it in a theatrical beam illuminating whatever was contained in the foot of the L. He would have to enter in order to see whatever that was.

He scanned the floor ahead of him as he walked. There was nothing that seemed threatening. As he reached the corner he moved his back against the wall to the right, again to reduce his vulnerability.

The shaft of light played across a diaphanous curtain. There seemed to be a shape sitting behind it, on a raised dais. Sleighmaker stepped forward a little and immediately regretted it. He felt one of the floorboards shift beneath his feet. This was followed by a profound click that resonated through the whole room. This began a whole sequence of gentle percussion that he felt in the floor beneath him, travelling towards the curtained stage.

He braced himself, but then relaxed as the curtains swished open. There sat an exquisite girl in a loose-fitting white gown. She stood up and bowed her head slightly towards Sleighmaker. Suddenly the air was filled with a chiming minuet. Then she began to dance.

At first her movements were delicate and balletic. She turned a pirouette on exquisitely defined bare feet. Sleighmaker studied her as she moved. Of course this was Aveline, but nothing he had read or been told had prepared him for her verisimilitude or her beauty. She looked young – a girl just on the cusp of adolescence but whose face carried behind its virginal innocence a hint of knowing carnality one might have shrunk from if she were real. But she was not real – or at least not flesh and blood. And Sleighmaker now understood her reputation, for despite her mechanical nature he found himself aroused at the idea of having her.

Gradually her dance lost its sweetness as her motions became slightly lewd. Her legs were placed further apart and her hips began to sway. The chiming music became more rhythmic. Sleighmaker had started trying to find out how her mechanism might be operating – she did not seem to be attached to the floor in any way – but as the seduction continued he decided he didn't care. The choreography had begun to cross over into something pornographic. The girl removed her gown revealing a luminous body which, though still childlike, carried the first hints of adulthood, making it seem to Sleighmaker tantalisingly desirable. Still standing, she spread her legs then gestured for Sleighmaker to take his place beneath her. Without thinking he stepped forward. At that precise moment an enormous shape loomed out of a shadow in the corner beyond. It moved at great speed with seven long regular strides directly towards Sleighmaker. It was a huge towering negro figure with fierce white eyes, dressed as an eighteenth-century French soldier. It raised its massive arms and grinned, revealing a mouth full of too many white teeth. In a state of absolute terror Sleighmaker fell backwards, not on to the floor, but on to a cold brass chair that had emerged from behind to receive him. As he hit the seat, a series of metal bands flicked out of the legs and arms, securing him by his ankles and his feet. Before he even knew what had happened he realised he had been completely immobilised. His handgun fell to the floor with a terrible clatter. He strained against the bands and was even more surprised when the chair moved to the left taking him at speed towards the wall, which a moment before he reached it swung aside allowing him to rattle along some unseen rail into the blackness beyond.

His heart thudded violently as he careered through the darkness. He felt the air whooshing past his face. At any moment I will die, he thought. But he didn't. The chair slowed, then tilted back almost forty-five degrees. There was a horrendous clanking as it was pulled up a slope by some kind of chain and ratchet system. After an interminable time it reached the top and straightened itself out. Another door swung open and Sleighmaker moved back into light.

Not much light, it had to be said, but the dim illumination that fell from the glass bricked ceiling above him was enough for him to make out his surroundings. A small cube of a room about nine feet by nine feet. The walls were lined with light brown sandstone. He tried to make sense of his journey, and his imprisonment. He had walked into a trap, as surely as if he were on the same rails as the chair that held him. But what happened now? As if in answer, almost simultaneous with the thought, the chair swivelled one hundred and eighty degrees. It then fell sharply, about three inches, and there was a heavy clunk as if it had engaged with another unseen mechanism. With a rapid round of clicks that descended in pitch like a scale on a deadened xylophone, more metal bands shot out of the arms and legs of the chair. They encircled Sleighmaker's arms and legs, like bangles, adjusting themselves until they encased him in his own private cage, fitted to his every inch. Instinctively he tried struggling, but that only seemed to make them tighten more. For the first time he noticed another phrase engraved in the arch that topped the wall in front of him. "*Aspici quo vos ducit Desiderii Instrumentum.*" The wall slid up and the chair rolled on.

Although the chamber beyond was mine-shaft black, Sleighmaker could sense its scale. He felt his head was close to the ceiling – a fact that was confirmed when he heard a rattling, inches above his scalp. Mechanised metal blinds rolled back and the light began to pour in. Had the view he looked down upon presented itself to him in a dream, Sleighmaker felt he would have woken from it in fear; unfortunately no such escape was available to him.

He was in an enormous chamber the size of half the house. The chair held him high in an upper corner – like being in the gods at the theatre. However the stage beneath filled the whole space. It was not built as an auditorium: the players here were their own audience. There were forty to fifty of them; each one looked as if they were made of metal, except, as he craned to look, Sleighmaker could see they were in fact made of bone, encased in metal bands, like the ones that held him. They seemed to be skeletons held in bespoke cages, the shape of each enclosure echoing the flesh they once held. They were paired up mostly, although some were grouped in threes or more – each set of figures contained within a little tableau, like the little replicas of Victorian rooms one might find in a museum. Many of these scenes contained beds, although there were others. One looked like a stable, another like a morgue. It was hard to tell from this height.

Just when it felt like nothing was going to happen, a noise began around him. Sleighmaker had heard it before, the previous night. It was as if the house was coming alive. Little flickers of gas-light burst into life around each scene, like flowers blooming in a time-lapse film. Shadows danced within the bones, filling them with an unholy glow. Somewhere deep in the walls around him the ticks of a thousand pendulums commenced and the skeletons began to move.

Slowly at first they rocked their hips and then the pairs began to grind against one another. Pelvis met pelvis, from the front, from behind. Jaw nuzzled sternum. Metacarpals tickled ribs. The figures had commenced an elaborate, mechanical ballet, like a giant antique slot machine. And as they moved they made their own music. The score had no melody; its rhythm was erratic; but the insane tarantella of rattling remains was its own perfect accompaniment.

So captivated was Sleighmaker by what lay below that he hadn't noticed the chair slide from under him. It didn't matter; the tight frame held him just as surely. It began to move along its established path – some kind of rail he couldn't see – standing upright; a decisive exoskeleton superseding the one within him that the cage would soon exhibit.

If there had been sufficient room he would have shaken his head when he saw what was heading towards him. The setting was a mock-up of a portion of a sailing ship's gun-deck. There was a rough wooden table over which was spread a corpse – a recently deceased corpse for it was still fleshy in parts. It could only have been the partner of the body Sleighmaker had encountered earlier – although already that "earlier" felt like another life. This was Sleighmaker's life now. However long was left – four, maybe five days – before he died of thirst and hunger. The corpse was bound in a metal frame identical to the one that contained Sleighmaker. Its posture was different however. It was face down with its backside in the air. All around the table looking on were other man-shaped cages – each containing human remains. They jostled one another and shook with silent, bony mirth.

Sleighmaker was trying to console himself with the fact he would be dead in a matter of days when he felt a mechanism stir in the cage round his head. A pipe had emerged, pressing itself into the edge of his mouth. It squirted a small amount of liquid. Sugared water. This machine was designed to keep him alive for a certain amount of time, long enough he was sure for Prince Bandar to get here – doubtless accompanied by Maksoud. Together they would triumphantly observe the completion of Thomas Narcejac's actual masterpiece – the culmination of his life's work. Not Aveline. She was merely bait. No, it was this demented tableau of which Sleighmaker realised he was the final component.

Assisted by the mechanism of its cage, the corpse ahead spread what remained of its legs and Sleighmaker felt an equivalent mechanism pushing at the back of his own hips, preparing him to make his first thrust of many.

Another machine that whirred regardless of what occurred around it was Sleighmaker's mind. It was struggling with the Latin he had observed earlier, carved into the stone arch. It didn't seem the most appropriate exercise given the circumstances but, once again, Sleighmaker was not giving himself a choice. He had a long time to ponder the accuracy of his translation as the skeletons danced around him: "See where it takes you, the Engine of Desire" was as close as he could get.

All in the telling

"Reelax, Meester Fletcher. Ees only a storm." For a moment the dank bar room had become electrically bright. Santini cracked his knuckles and smiled, revealing rotten keyboard teeth. He waved his right arm extravagantly in the air. "Another dreenk for me and my good friend." No one seemed to take much notice.

"Will she be here soon?" Fletcher asked. He didn't want to appear impatient even if he was, for his impatience was bred from fear, not boredom.

"Yes, yes, she weell be here, she weell be here. Dreenk, Meester Fletcher, dreenk." Santini placed his fat heavy hand over Fletcher's and moved it towards the tumbler that lay neglected on the table in front of him. The bourbon, if that was the true nature of the piss-coloured fluid in the glass, was almost undrinkable and yet Fletcher raised it to his lips at his companion's request. It seemed unwise not to. "Good, yes ..." Santini laughed. His laugh was worse than his smile.

Fletcher had doubted the wisdom of his visit to Mai Li's almost as soon as he had walked in. It was the first time he'd ventured into this part of the city although he had read much about it and heard even more. The laws of this country were strict, but perhaps the authorities were prepared to turn a blind eye to certain businesses. Of course, Fletcher had entertained the idea of visiting many times, but it was Santini's impromptu soliciting in the hotel lounge that had made it happen. That and a few too many Jack Daniels.

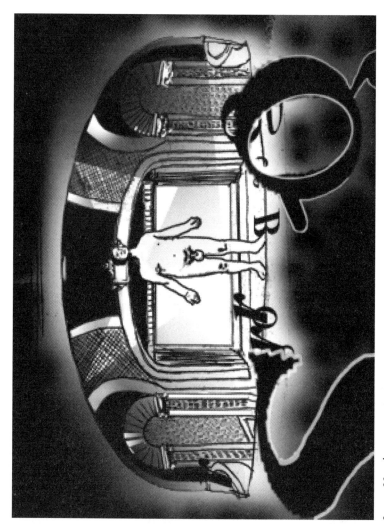

James Hood

He had never spoken to the fat Colombian before tonight, although he had seen him, lurking around various bars, telling extravagant tales in broken English to any foolish expatriates lonely or drunk enough to listen. Perhaps this evening, for the first time, Fletcher came into that category.

Santini had importuned and then seduced him as surely as any Latin lover, and the relief that he had promised made the trip across town seem worth a thousand dangers, imagined or real.

However, as the rickshaw rattled through the humid streets and the white faces thinned out to be replaced by their native counterparts, Fletcher's bravado began to evaporate along with the whiskey which transformed itself into a sheen of sweat over his burning face. The lack of street lighting did nothing to boost his confidence. The jolly yellow lanterns strung between poles that were so familiar were now nowhere to be seen; just an occasional bare bulb hanging over an intersection fizzing and buzzing in the soaking heat.

Fletcher was aware that there were those back home who might consider such a trip exciting – the boys in the Duchess, his bachelor colleagues – but he was not like them. Yet the memory of Santini's promises and the anticipation of their experience were just enough to keep him in his seat.

"When you see thees girl, Meester Fletcher, you weell fall een love. Een love. She ees called Tai De. She has a face like a china doll. She ees more beautiful than a rose. You will fall een love," Santini reiterated.

Mai Li's had appeared unheralded. In fact it was only the halting of the rickshaw that had indicated their arrival. For some reason, Fletcher had imagined a garish neon sign or a window full of naked flesh. As always, reality was more mundane. A black wooden door with no handle and a flickering white porch lamp marked the entrance. Santini gave a rattle of knocks – that may or may not have been coded – and the door opened.

Upon entering, Fletcher immediately found himself thinking of his one visit to a sex shop many years before. In London, on business. Drunk from a couple of afternoon pints. Stumbling down the stairs past the faded "Adults Only" sign. A library of multi-coloured "Continental!" magazines. A urinal's worth of men: young, old, faceless, colourless. Shaking hands, sightless eyes. Jostling a place amongst them. Reaching up for a pair of glossy breasts.

The men here were similar: all ages, mostly alone, clinging to anonymity as a shield against shame. They were dotted amongst the ill-lit tables, staring at their drinks.

However, it wasn't just the men. There was something in the décor that reminded him of that other "establishment", six thousand miles away on the Charing Cross Road. Perhaps it was the peeling veneer intended to suggest planks of stripped pine. Perhaps it was the burnt brown carpet or the empty booth next to the bar with its homely little Visa/Mastercard sign. Whatever it was, Fletcher tried to shake off the unwelcome association as their drinks were ordered and they took their seats. If what Santini had said was true, then it wasn't sex they were here for. Mai Li's offered a more exclusive service unavailable elsewhere.

"You have your story ready, Meester Fletcher?" Santini asked, returning from the bar. Fletcher merely nodded. The question seemed so unnecessary. How long had he been waiting? Too many years to count. With each passing season the pressure to narrate grew inside, and yet the opportunity for the tale's narration seemed to recede more and more. How he had come by this story he did not know, but it was there, inside him, like a child sewn into a womb.

"Have you told yours before?" Fletcher asked and Santini laughed his ugly laugh again.

"Oh yes, yes. But weeth each telling it becomes sweeter."

For the first time since entering the place, Fletcher found himself relaxing a little. Perhaps it was Mai Li's appalling bourbon, or perhaps it was the fact that he felt he was with his own kind: these lonely-looking, single men, all with untold tales which they could not release elsewhere. For years he had considered his affliction to be unique, a suffering particular to himself, but in this concealed and alien place it seemed he had found fellow victims, and with them a source of relief.

When Santini first spoke of his experience here, Fletcher was initially surprised but very quickly adjusted to the fact that there were others like him. And it also made sense that in this foreign land, with its ancient and wise culture, there would be those who would understand, those to whom he could unburden himself, those who would heal. That they chose to remain hidden and covert like the affliction itself seemed natural too.

Fletcher had attempted many times to convey his story: sometimes in speech, to lovers, to friends, sometimes in writing on paper, in pen. But the words never actually emerged. They remained both unseen and unheard, coiled together somewhere within. Tonight, however, things would be different, for beautiful Tai De, with her ancient Oriental skill, would charm them outside, persuade them to slither up through Fletcher's throat and slide over his tongue, until at last they would be revealed to the outside world and he would be free. The story would no longer be exclusively his. Someone else would have heard and understood.

A ripple of activity passed through the otherwise silent bar. Chairs scraped, glasses were put down, throats were cleared. Looking across the dimly lit room, Fletcher saw that a figure now occupied the wood booth.

"There. I told you she would come. Go to her, Meester Fletcher. Take your place."

Fletcher's heart began racing as he stood. His legs felt weak beneath him, his mouth dry. Like an inexperienced teenager about to ask the class beauty for a dance, he felt that now, when he most needed them, words might fail him.

Tai De was indeed sublime. For once Santini had not been exaggerating. Her skin seemed impossibly pure and white, her hair incalculably black. Her lips, blood red and wet, were ready to coax and instruct the reluctant fiction from Fletcher's open mouth. And her youth ... Although she possessed the body of a woman her face was that of a child.

Yes, thought Fletcher as he staggered toward her, adrenalin allowing his confidence to return, at last I will be able to tell.

Men clamoured around the open window. In the light cast from the adjacent bar, Fletcher was able to observe their faces for the first time. Expectant, eager, wide-eyed, they looked not unlike he imagined he did himself. A mixture of nationalities, although none of them native, they ranged in age from early twenties to late sixties. In fact, looking closer, the oldest of them could have been nearer seventy. Slack-jawed, slack-skinned, the old man waved a wad of paper money in Tai De's direction, a look of eager anticipation in his eyes. Fletcher wondered if the man had waited all his life for this opportunity.

"Please, please. Can only take one of you." Tai De's voice was as delicate as her face. But her tone was both confident and concerned. Fletcher experienced a flash of anxiety. What if he was to lose this one precious chance? As if in answer to this fear, the old man, utilising reserves of strength that seemed unfitting for someone of his age, thrust himself forward, forcing his money into Tai De's hand.

"*Madame. Moi. Moi.*" He was like a desperate child.

"OK. OK." The girl smiled as she tucked the notes into the silk purse that hung around her neck. Fletcher was enveloped immediately in black despair. He had to return to England in two days. What if he had just seen his only chance disappear, as suddenly as it had presented itself? No, he told himself, that cannot be. I will return.

The other men, presumably experiencing similar feelings, began dispersing gloomily to their tables. He was about to join them when he noticed the mien of horror that had settled over the nameless Frenchman, who stood gazing glassy-eyed at Tai De.

"*Non, non, j'oublie, j'oublie.*" There was a tone of such terror, such hopelessness in the aged voice that Fletcher's first response was one of pity. And then it occurred to him that this man's misfortune was his golden chance.

"Tai De ... I know my story ... I know it backward." She turned toward him, a faint smile playing across her incandescent face. She unbuttoned her purse and made to hand back the money to her former client. He did not take it; he had no interest. He stood rocking slightly from foot to foot, lost in misery. Observing how much money the Frenchman had given, Fletcher handed her the same as quickly as possible, which she took, her black eyes settling on his.

Stepping forward, Fletcher readied himself to tell his tale. He felt the words bubbling up from that hidden place, deep within, propelled by the accumulated pressure of enforced concealment. The back of his tongue began to press gently on the roof of his mouth, ready to receive the first phoneme cast its way. His lips parted ...

"No, silly. Not here." Tai De had stepped out from behind the booth, placing her tiny hand on Fletcher's forearm. He blushed and looked to the floor, embarrassed at his own naïvety. It hadn't occurred to him that the service would take place in private. "We go up here." She gestured toward a small wooden door behind the bar, decorated with miniature fans.

He followed her up the narrow staircase, lit by one dim bulb, its walls lined with the same familiar wood veneer wallpaper. Cheap perfume hung in the air masking another more unpleasant, unnamable smell.

They reached the cramped landing, which had three doors along each wall. Tai De turned to smile at Fletcher as she reached for the one in front of them. She had to force it open, as the wood didn't fit the frame, which seemed to have been knocked together at angles other than ninety degrees.

Fletcher felt his heart beginning to race again. A certain tension had settled at the base of his stomach, but the sensation was not unpleasant. He realised with a thrill that the telling had finally arrived; and not only that, but he would be able to enjoy it. He could relax and take his time. There was no need to hurry the narrative. He could savour the twists and turns of his elaborate little story line and relish its conclusion. And he would also be able to draw pleasure from Tai De's response: watch her react to the gentle subtleties of his plot, derive satisfaction from a smile that he, or rather his story, had placed upon her face.

The room was completely bare apart from a dirty-looking futon stretched across the floor. The fake veneer had spread from outside across the room's walls, its artificiality obvious even under the forty-watt bulb that flickered above them. Tai De reached down and removed her small shoes, before settling down on the unpleasant-looking sheets. She reached for Fletcher, pulling him toward her. She allowed her kimono to fall open a little as she arranged herself, revealing more of her beautiful skin. It made Fletcher forget his surroundings.

"So," she smiled, "you like it here?" Fletcher assumed she was trying to put him at his ease. Playing along he looked around the room. He was surprised and slightly unsettled to see a window behind Tai De. It seemed to look on to another room.

"It's ... not what I'd expected." Was that a figure in the room beyond? There wasn't enough light to be sure. "But then the whole place wasn't what I expected."

Tai De nodded, as if she had heard this before. She moved a little closer. Fletcher could smell the sweetness of her breath.

"Shall we lie down?" she asked, flattening herself against the sheets. Fletcher slipped off his espadrilles, quickly adopting Tai De's position. She smiled again as his head joined hers and a sudden wave of joy flooded over him. She looked so understanding, so sweet, so ready to hear him. But something was not right.

Fletcher was concerned about the lurking form behind the glass. He didn't like the feeling of being watched or the sense that his intimacy with Tai De was being compromised in some way.

"Is there ..." It was difficult to express his concern. "Is that a person ... in there?" He gestured towards the room beyond. Tai De looked over her shoulder. She turned back to Fletcher and smiled. She hadn't answered his question.

Fletcher tried to settle himself down once more. He wanted to recapture the feeling he had experienced, albeit momentarily, that everything was just right. Tai De looked at him, a hint of encouragement in her eyes. Perhaps things wouldn't get any more right than this. He closed his eyes. The feeling welled up once more. His heart began thumping ...

"Once there was –" A finger settled firmly against his lips. Fletcher opened his eyes. Tai De smiled like a mother having to deny an indulged, over-excited child. Her other hand fell to his belt buckle and began loosening it.

"There's no need to speak. Not here," she said softly. Fletcher felt his heartbeat quicken even more. Anticipation flipped over suddenly into anxiety.

"But ... my story ...?"

Tai De looked at him inquisitively for a moment. Then realisation settled over her face.

"Silly. That's just ..." She searched for the words. "... a cover." The room faded a little. For a moment Fletcher felt that he was no longer there. Suddenly he felt shame: shame at his presence there, shame at his misjudgement, shame at his lack of worldliness. He tried to disguise his humiliation with a little laugh.

"Oh. I am naïve," he stuttered. Tai De grinned at him although it was clear she did not understand his words. As she reached down and unbuttoned his fly, Fletcher felt his throat tightening and tears pressing their way into his eyes. He could just about make out a face pressed against the glass of the dark window. Although he was unable to discern its sex, he could see it was smiling.

Acknowledgements

I would like to thank: Sarah Such for suggesting it in the first place, and later, her keen eye; James Hood for his independence and vision; Simon Trewin for his perspicacity; and Mark, Steve and Reece for being a continuing source of encouragement and inspiration.